G-2

The Guardian of Earth Series

RIGEL CARSON

G-2

Contact information: maggietoussaint@darientel.net
Cover art by *Maggie Toussaint*

Muddle House Publishing
1146 Tolomato Drive SE
Darien, GA 31305
Visit us at www.muddlehousepublishing.com

Publishing History
First Digital Edition, Muddle House Publishing, 2015
Digital ISBN: 9780983361497
First Print Edition, Muddle House Publishing, 2015
Print ISBN: 9780996770606

Published in the United States of America

Shadows flickered in the darkness, black on black, Zeke's mental gaze keenly attuned to the dark nuances. Frissons of dread peppered his thoughts, rattling his senses. He floated in the timeless void of space. Cold. Alone. Afraid.

Without warning, a line drive of thought energy socked him. He struggled to hold the link. The vermillion-tinged darkness reminded him of primordial ooze from which there was no escape. Was his planet destined to go the way of the dinosaurs?

Several voices spoke in uneasy unison, adding to Zeke's disembodied sense. *We have not been successful in dealing with Maleem. They take. They do not negotiate. They do not compromise.*

His spirits plummeted. There had to be a way. He couldn't give up on his planet without a fight. Someone, somewhere must have beaten the Maleem before. Earth needed to build on that success. He fired a query across the vacuum of space. *Wait! What about those few stragglers on Drigil Eight? How did they survive?*

The link hummed with energy. It buzzed bright in his head as if hundreds spoke at once. Zeke allowed himself to hope. All wasn't lost. It couldn't be. More than seven billion people lived on Earth. So many innocent lives at stake.

We have sent a query, young Zeke. We will advise you in due time.

Praise for The Guardian of Earth Series

This was a thoroughly engaging and fast moving novel. I read it the span of twenty-four hours, finding it hard to put down. Carson has a flair for plotting and is particularly skilled at mixing in elements of science and technology. There's a dire warning in her message, both political and environmental, and that's what makes this novel so relevant to our times. I highly recommend this book!—Joseph Souza, author, 5 stars

G-1 is a page-turning ecological thriller that could become chillingly real.—Nancy Cohen, author of Bad Hair Day Mysteries, 5 stars

I found G-1 fascinating. There are quite a few interesting characters in this book, but my favorite was Forman, the brilliant robot.—Polly Iyer, author of Indiscretion, 5 stars

One of the best near-future books period. I'm a sucker for near-future books. I've read a lot of them, but I've never read one quite like this. It grabbed me from the beginning with an intriguing mystery and it was written perfectly to keep the pages turning. I was rushing to the ending because I couldn't put the book down. —Jake Lingwall, author of Freelancer, 5 stars

Challenges facing the earth in 2065 hit home in this tense ecological thriller, with water supply the primary currency in a power game that jeopardizes an already threatened planet. Maggie Toussaint's depth of knowledge shines through in astute and compelling science. Well placed humor flares throughout the narrative. G-1 marks the start of an intriguing and relevant sci fi series.—Jennifer Skutelsky, 5 stars

This story contains a little bit of everything, even humor and light-heartedness. If you've read any of her other books, you'll find the same kind of quick wit, scientific truth along with some new inventions, and enough dialogue to keep the story moving...fast. Trust me...even if you're not a science-fiction fan, you'll still enjoy this unique story.—Rising Star Reviews, 5 stars.

Dedication

This book is dedicated to dystopian fiction fans everywhere.
You rock!

Acknowledgements

Thanks to my critique partner Polly Iyer for encouraging me to believe in this Kindle Scout winning series. Thanks also to Craig Toussaint for encouragement, brainstorming, proofing, driving, and patience. Lastly, thanks to Gordon Aalborg for his keen eyes.

Chapter 1
September 2065, Earth

The new Guardian of Earth sat in the transmission chair a little before midnight. Zeke wasn't due to make a report for another week, but he felt oddly compelled to connect with the Tamans tonight. In a few moments, the ocean-scented air of his island home faded as his thoughts hurled through space.

The disembodied sensation of this invisible means of communication no longer freaked him out. He'd gotten used to the darkness of extreme telepathy, the shifting shadows of Tween, and the occasional glimpses of orbs of light. He'd even made his peace with reporting conditions on Earth to his distant relatives.

In short, he'd accepted his role as Guardian of Earth.

Trouble is coming.

Like thunder across the ocean, his late father's message boomed through Zeke's mind. In the shuttered darkness of the Taman mindlink, his thoughts iced. Instinct demanded he leave the thought plane and take cover, but he couldn't disconnect without knowing more.

He didn't doubt his Taman ancestors. He believed them. Trouble *was* coming to Earth. The terror piggybacked on the message radiated danger loud and clear. His thoughts scrambled in fear, and he wrangled the paralyzing emotion to the corners of his mind.

He wasn't a superhero. Except for his intellect, most people thought him average. Dr. Zechariah Landry, hydrologist, and coastal Georgia beach bum. Just your average, every-day alien, though that last part was a closely held secret.

Trouble? He shot back, as if he weren't quaking in his mental boots.

More voices joined in, drowning out his father's voice. *Trouble like you've never seen. Trouble like you don't want on Earth. The Maleem. If we could recall you, we would.*

Recall him? How? That possibility rocked through his expanded consciousness, shaking the tenets of all he held dear. With the

1

retirement of the U.S. Space Shuttle program some fifty years ago, space travel had been abandoned by the entire planet. But the Tamans had mastered space travel, or he wouldn't be embedded in Earth's population halfway across the universe.

He didn't want to be recalled. Earth was the only home he'd ever known.

One problem at a time. He needed to focus on this new threat. The Maleem.

What can I do? he asked.

Look and learn. The Taman link shuddered, jarring Zeke. A flood of stark images arrived. Vegetation on fire. People dead, gaping holes in their abdomens. Like the worst vid of his life, the terrible scenes unfolded at breakneck pace. Structures leveled. Forests crackled with crown fires. Water fouled with bodies. People screamed in mortal terror, others wailed softly as they huddled in bolt holes.

He mentally gagged. The link strobed. The darkness whirled in a dizzying freefall as devastation images blanketed him. This was awful. Beyond terrible. He'd never seen anything like this. Never thought this level of genocide could occur in the modern world. Earth had to be protected. He had to pull it together.

He could analyze and review later. His time in the mindlink was short. He wrestled his emotions aside to focus on the problem. *What is this?* he asked.

The planet Drigil Eight during the Maleem attack. Forty survived out of three million.

Zeke sickened at the horrific images, a ghastly panorama of destruction in the obsidian darkness of the mindlink. The Taman collective intoned the names of the faraway places as the images scrolled across his mental blackboard. *Cantoon. Asphix. Thorian. Xantavian. Agathe. Naum Three. Shomari. Ruiz. Wailea-Molkini.*

Places he'd never heard of, places he'd never imagined.

Places no one would ever see again.

Stop! he begged. *You've convinced me. The Maleem are destroyers. What are my options?*

They come. They take.

Zeke struggled to grasp the ramifications. These terrible beings were on the way to his planet. *How do they even know Earth exists?*

We know. Others know.

Though only thought energy was present in the mindlink,

Zeke's whole body tensed. *Others? How many others are there?*

Too numerous to count.

The chilling news jarred his careening thoughts to a dead stop. He'd discovered his Taman heritage two months ago, the same time he'd learned there were sentient beings in the distant universe. He'd love to have his quiet life again, but he was the Guardian now. He needed to do his job. He needed to guard Earth.

Are the others destroyers like the Maleem? he asked.

The lightning-fast exchange faltered, worrying Zeke. What weren't the Tamans telling him? Were worse people than the Maleem out there?

The reply came in an eerie monotone laced with doom. *Tamans seek advanced civilizations to join the Alliance. Others have different goals.*

After the horrific images he'd seen, Zeke had no doubt of the Maleem's intentions. *We have to do something. Can we deflect the Maleem? Can we bargain with them or threaten them?*

His father's voice blasted through the group link. *They have no honor. You're forbidden to contact the Maleem.*

Forbidden? Was he a child to be scolded? So what if these Maleem were the bullies of the cosmos? Even bullies had weaknesses. They weren't invincible. He needed a plan of action.

You can't tell me Earth is doomed and leave it at that. There must be a strategy we could employ to make a difference. Can we taint our resources to make them unpalatable? Can we shield the planet? Can we give them engine trouble?

Once again, the exchange faltered. The edgy silence taunted him. Were they conferring about a solution? Were they debating about cutting him loose? Would they abandon him and Earth?

Shadows flickered in the darkness, black on black, his mental gaze keenly attuned to the dark nuances. Frissons of dread peppered his thoughts, rattling his senses. He floated in the timeless void of space. Cold. Alone. Afraid.

Without warning, a line drive of thought energy socked him. He struggled to hold the link. The vermillion-tinged darkness reminded him of primordial ooze from which there was no escape. Was his planet destined to go the way of the dinosaurs?

Several voices spoke in uneasy unison, adding to Zeke's disembodied sense. *We have not been successful in dealing with Maleem. They take. They do not negotiate. They do not compromise.*

His spirits plummeted. There had to be a way. He couldn't give up on his planet without a fight. Someone, somewhere must have beaten the Maleem before. Earth needed to build on that success. He fired a query across the vacuum of space. *Wait! What about those few stragglers on Drigil Eight? How did they survive?*

The link hummed with energy. It buzzed bright in his head as if hundreds spoke at once. Zeke allowed himself to hope. All wasn't lost. It couldn't be. More than seven billion people lived on Earth. So many innocent lives at stake.

We have sent a query, young Zeke. We will advise you in due time.

The link started to fade. That was it? He needed more information. *How long do we have? When will the Maleem arrive?*

Soon.

Chapter 2

Under starry skies, Zeke hurried through the muggy heat of his island home. Urgency fueled his steps, sweat beaded his brow. Though it was after midnight, he couldn't dismiss the hellish images he'd seen. He had to think of a way to save Earth from these destroyers. He needed to take action, and his brightly illuminated laboratory drew him like a shark to spilt blood.

He pounded up the stairs, dropped in his office chair, and nodded over his shoulder to his assistant. Data streamed in a blue haze from the wall com to the robot's forehead. Great. Now he'd have to be circumspect about his extraterrestrial research. He couldn't let Forman know what was going on. Not without blowing his cover and revealing his off-world information source.

"Didn't think you'd be here," Zeke said.

Forman ducked his head as if he was ashamed. The data bridge winked out, and two wall screens of scrolling data activated. "I wanted to review the projections one last time before we send them on to the Institute," Forman said, his gaze on the data sets. "I'm testing the outliers against the hypothesis with greater and lower statistical confidence levels. Wouldn't want your analysis called into question."

They'd checked the water distribution matrix more than a dozen times now, but old habits die hard. Another check wouldn't hurt anything, though it wasn't necessary. Still, for Forman to be in the lab when Queen Bea had only been on the island for six hours wasn't a good sign.

"Your girlfriend kicked you out?" Zeke asked as he thumbed the power cell on his vid system and typed his password. With the end of the world looming large in his head, he marveled at his ability to make small talk.

"Worse than that. She banned me from her house. Said she couldn't write songs about the end of the world if she was happy." Forman ran his fingers through his wavy blond synhair. In addition to his nerd guy module, his entertainment programming complemented his buff, muscular physique. "I satisfied her sexual needs, but afterward, she asked me to leave. She told me not to return. In eight of eight previous reunions, we spent the entire night lovemaking."

Zeke quit pretending to work and rolled back to study Forman. His robotic assistant had the looks, body temperature, emotions, and sexual appeal of a human Adonis. He also had a major crush on Bea Stemford, an international pop star who'd recently moved to Tama Island off the Georgia coast. The singer had been fascinated to have an entertainment model android to pleasure her. "She'll change her mind."

Forman's shoulders slumped, his head tilted forward. "How can I even hope she invites me back into her life if my presence destroys her career? I want everything for her, and if my staying away makes her life better, that's what I'll do."

Romantic love wasn't Zeke's forte, and with the Maleem coming to destroy the planet, he didn't see the point of this conversation. No one's love life mattered if the Maleem landed.

Even so, his robot was fond of Bea. "I'm sorry Bea isn't what you'd hoped, that she doesn't reciprocate your feelings. Fame must have gone to her head."

The robot shrugged off Zeke's sympathy. "Bea isn't your typical superstar. She's not superficial, and she really enjoys her work. I admire the passion she brings to her music. She rallies millions of people to help each other and the environment. Who am I to stand in the way of that? I could screw up history by keeping her from writing the most important song of her life. Her lyrics rock my world, and I'm not even human."

Unless Bea wrote the song of her life and released the tune tomorrow, it wouldn't matter. Hell, given what he'd learned tonight, nothing related to everyday life mattered. But he couldn't dash around like Chicken Little of fairy tale fame proclaiming the end was near. He had to pretend nothing had changed until he could prove his claim of impending global doom.

"Sounds like you're doing the right thing by giving her some space," Zeke said in a neutral tone.

"Being right sucks. What about you? What happened to you and Jessie?"

Zeke griped the arms of his swivel chair. His first impulse was to brush off the question, but Forman was the closest thing he had to a best friend. What would it hurt to reveal the truth? Sharing his thoughts about Bea's sister might clear his head, and he needed clarity for the invasion issue. "She's nice, and I like Jessie, but I don't obsess over her the way you do about Bea. Jessie and I are good friends, that's all."

Forman cocked his head to the side, as if he were a bird listening to voices on the wind. "Since when are you certain of your emotions? Did you visit a shrink when I wasn't looking? Jessie worships the ground you walk on."

Zeke groaned aloud. Talking about his feelings invited more conversation. It made him uneasy. And if he didn't answer appropriately, he'd be a wuss. He surrendered with the flag of truth.

"Jessie is the marrying kind. She wants a large family." He picked up an old-fashioned ink pen. His fingers worried over the end of the pen, clicking the top button. According to the Tamans, he would reproduce in the same manner as his father and grandfather by having one male heir. "I don't see a large family in my future."

"Weak." Forman clucked his tongue. The surfboards on his colorful aloha shirt fluttered as he put his entire body into the conversation. "You have a great job here at the Institute, a large house on the island, and you're heir to billions. You can afford as many children as Jessie wants. Admit it. Commitment scares the hell out of you."

This conversation scared the hell out of him. He'd taken it slow with Jessie for a reason. Learning he was Earth's Guardian and being ordered by the Tamans a few months ago to find his true mate changed the course of his life. He wasn't the man Jessie thought he was. Worse, he couldn't tell her he was an alien. He couldn't tell anyone. "Leading her on is wrong. I respect Jessie. I won't crush her dreams."

"Get over it. Life comes with a side serving of crushed dreams no matter what path you take. How's the sex between you two?"

Chagrined, Zeke turned back to his vid screen and tossed the pen aside. Forman had the command modules of four robots inside his shell, including the adult entertainment series. Consequently, he considered himself an expert on romance. Zeke didn't want his advice. "We are not having this discussion."

Forman edged closer. "Your pulse is elevated, your pupils semi-dilated. You're avoiding this question on purpose." He continued to study Zeke. "You haven't slept with her yet, have you?"

"It's none of your business."

"Damn. Didn't you utilize any of the techniques I shared with you? Jessie would accommodate you in a heartbeat, I know she would."

"Change the subject," Zeke growled. He'd blocked that previous conversation with Forman from his mind, same as he'd block this one.

The android's console beeped, and he swiveled to study the data. "Aw, boss. You're no fun. We were just getting to the good stuff."

For the robot, maybe, but not for Zeke.

He didn't want Forman's voice in his head when he made love to anyone. But right now he couldn't focus on dating or bringing a child into this doomed world. His planet's survival depended on him. With the advent of the Maleem, his role as an observer had changed into a protector. He'd never felt so inadequate.

Why wasn't there an instruction manual with this job?

He could duck the call to duty and let his planet's military tackle the problem on their own. They'd do that anyway. Judging from how citizens of Earth responded to on-world crises, they'd shoot first and ask questions later. But the fight wouldn't be fair. The Maleem explored the universe in starships. Earth would be seriously outgunned.

The invasion had to be stopped, but how?

Zeke called up several satellite images of Earth, mulling the problem from different angles. He had to save the planet, and he had to do it fast. Between the super computer system the Institute provided, his multiplex robot, and his genius IQ, he had virtually unlimited deductive power and a burning desire to help.

Smarts plus drive equals solution, or so his university mentor used to say. Zeke rolled up his mental shirtsleeves and boned up on the latest trends in astrophysics. But the knowledge set felt foreign to him, weighty, too, when compared with his specialty in hydrology. And too difficult to absorb in a few moments of study. The enormity of the issue bowed his shoulders.

He could get a message to Uncle John right now. On paper, John Demery was the local manager for the Institute on Tama Island. In reality, his uncle headed a vast network of privatized everything. Their think tank role was to take on the battles that needed fighting. This enemy needed to be fought, but Zeke didn't even have a timeline. He needed solid proof they were coming. Something that would legitimately raise the subject with his uncle.

But, even if Zeke gave the warning, what could Uncle John do to stop a powerful galactic horde of killers? He needed a plan, needed something that he could bring to the table as a solution.

How could he do this? A complex matter of this nature required a panel of bright minds and the absence of a ticking clock. He had neither, but he'd played a game or two of chess in his lifetime. He could devise a winning strategy.

Any battle necessitated two fronts, offense and defense. Without protection, an offense wouldn't last long. Defense first, then. The Earth needed to mount a strong defense against the intruders. For starters, he would need a barrier of some sort. A force field or a cloak. Assuming he pulled off the impossible, would a barricade be enough to save them?

Could he make the planet invisible?

Could he deflect the Maleem?

Chapter 3

Though island sunshine drenched her bright kitchen, Jessie Stemford felt lousy. Worse, she had only herself to blame for her foul mood. Why couldn't it be raining? Why wasn't the sky laden with gunmetal clouds shooting out barbed lightning bolts?

Her sister groaned and shuffled over to the counter for coffee. "God. Another crappy day in paradise." Bea no longer sported the fancy Parisian lingerie she'd modeled the night before. Instead, baggy cotton favorites adorned her lithe figure. "Who'd have thought great weather and an island location could be miserable?"

Steam rose from Jessie's coffee cup, making the morning tolerable. She glanced over the top of her fogged sunglasses. "You could still be cavorting with Forman. Then you wouldn't notice you were so unhappy."

"Miserable or happy – there's no wiggle room in between." Bea carried her coffee over to the sunny table where Jessie sat and slid into a plastech chair. "I love Forman. He's everything I ever wanted in a man. No one could be more attentive or perfect. He even goes away when I tell him. Not many men do that. They have to exude dominance. Forman rises above those primitive caveman instincts."

The entire world had put Jessie's younger sister on a pedestal. Consequently, Bea thought her needs mattered more than anyone else's. Jessie had given up a career in science to be her sister's manager. A decision she very much regretted now. "He's not a man."

"He's my love machine. He stopped having sex with others because he's devoted to me. I should be thrilled by his loyalty. Instead, I feel trapped. Smothered. As if part of me can't take a deep breath without being accountable to him. I'm not promiscuous, but monogamy feels like a spiked choke collar. I'm not cut out for it."

Jessie sipped her coffee and shifted her weight to sit on one pajama-clad leg. She understood about conflicted feelings. She'd had high hopes for love, but she'd been mistaken about Dr. Zeke Landry. Falling for an emotionally frozen but brilliant man who wouldn't know an orgasm if it slapped him in the face had been a big mistake.

At least Bea had a love life. She'd never gotten Zeke past the point of handholding and a few steamy kisses. To make matters worse, she ached for him.

He didn't call.

He didn't come over.

He was a jerk.

Her turbulent emotions made her snarky. "Can't be that bad. I saw how you lit up last night when he gave you those orchids. You were delighted he'd gone to so much trouble to find your favorite flowers."

Bea shook her manicured fingers as if she were trying to fling toxic water off them, her mussed blond hair falling over her intense eyes. "Don't you get it, Jess? I can't be happy. Not and be creative, too. I need to write new songs or my career is over. Without new material, I might as well start booking community theaters for my greatest hits tour."

The downside of being Bea's sister and manager was that Jessie gave twice as many pep talks. If Bea had another manager, they could share the responsibility for the woe-is-me talks. Lately, Bea seemed more erratic than usual.

Was she going nuts like their mom?

The terrible possibility worried Jessie to no end. But she couldn't indulge her worries now. If she didn't pull Bea back from the edge, no telling what would happen.

Jessie exhaled slowly, infusing calm into her voice. "So what if you didn't write a hit song in the last month? Your career isn't over. You hit a dry spell. It happens to everyone. You'll get your mojo back. I'm sure of it."

"The only lyrics I write now are sappy drivel. Who wants to hear how much in love I am? I'm supposed to be the world's social conscious. I'm supposed to sing about the fragile environment and how people are messing it up. I can't sing happy songs. Those love ditties are for teenyboppers. The world needs doom and gloom to rally around."

"If you don't want to record your new songs, sell them. No reason you can't make a mint from someone else singing your happy tunes."

Bea's head snapped back. Her eyes blazed with heat. "No way. Those are my songs. I'm not selling them. That would be like giving a child to a stranger to raise. I couldn't do that. Not ever."

If only life were so cut and dry. Unlike Bea's black-and-white world, Jessie lived in a world of grays, where nuances meant something or nothing depending on who uttered them. Or didn't utter them, in the case of her scientist. A vein throbbed in her head.

Damn. She had to quit obsessing over her unrequited feelings for Zeke. But she *wanted* to dwell on it. Wanted to wallow in her feelings.

Rotten bastard.

"Earth to Jessie." Bea's palm smacked the gleaming tabletop. "I'm having a crisis. I need your help. We need to do something different. To shake things up."

Her sister's voice rose an octave as she talked. Jessie fought the rising tide of resentment. Trust Bea to have a breakdown when Jessie needed to have her own. She'd have to bottle everything up again. But why should she always be the one to give?

Suddenly, it was too much to take. Jessie leaned forward into Bea's personal space, and her feelings intensified. "I'm tired of boosting your spirits. I'm tired of The Life. I'm not in the mood to discuss your troubles."

Bea's mouth dropped open. The look of horror passed, followed by grim determination. "You think to distract me with your misery? You can't trump my distress. My career matters. My career bought this house. It put the clothes on our backs."

Her sister's ugliness cut deep. Jessie was intently aware her income was dependent on Bea's. But the cost was too high. "I don't want that anymore."

"Well, I do. I want thousands of fans calling my name. I want to soar high as a kite over a stage and have people sing my songs. I want to write more hits. But I can't. And you're not helping."

Jessie's headache intensified. "Grow up. I helped you get started. I want out. You want the songwriting, traveling life? Fine. Go right ahead. But I'm done with it."

"You think if you stay here, Zeke will notice you?" Bea sneered. "Is that what this is about? Because I got laid and you didn't?"

Jessie barely stopped herself from slapping her sister. She worked to draw in a breath. "That was mean."

"It's the truth. Face the music. You're invisible."

"I'm not. Don't say that."

"You're invisible, and I want to kill myself."

Jessie's hand crept to her aching heart. Despite her personal problems, a latent fear of suicide throbbed in her veins. Her flagging sense of purpose revitalized. Bea was all the family she had. "You don't."

"I do. I think about it every day. It would be easy to drown in a pool of pills."

"Think about something else."

"I can't. I'm not strong like you. I'm weak. Like Mom."

"Take that back. You're not like her."

"I am. I've been hiding it for a long time, but I'm exactly like Mom."

"We need to get you some help. I'll find a facility. We'll hush it up."

"I don't want help. I want to go to Japan."

Fresh horror curled through Jessie. Bea wasn't lying. She was suicidal. If Jessie didn't stay on top of this, Bea would yield to the darkness. History would repeat itself.

She made a stab at appealing to reason. "They've had three tsunamis. People are rioting in the streets. Japan isn't safe."

Bea nodded, a faraway look in her eyes. "Exactly. Raw emotion. I need it to feel alive. Come with me or stay here and mope. The choice is yours."

Chapter 4

Newscaster Connor Bronsen gazed into the heart of camera two. "Coming up live after the break, an interview with Dr. Browning Charles, the world's premiere dolphin expert. And later today, a chat with the zillionaire who plans to launch his entire cryo-frozen family into space."

"And, cut!" the news director said. "Back in five."

"You look great," co-anchor Pauline Curran purred as she worked out nearby. She powered the thigh machine with a vengeance, enjoying the wide-eyed cameraman fixated on her yellow bikini bottom. While she kept his attention, she made the requisite strokes to her co-anchor's ego. All men were putty in her hands. "With that dark tan and your incredible green eyes, it's no wonder people fall in love with you."

Connor flexed an arm muscle for her. "My eyes don't draw them, babe. It's my pecs, and the sex we have on air. Our nontraditional broadcasts are killing it in the ratings. We're pioneers, babe, and our names will go in the record books. People want to see the nasty. And we were the first to bring it to the world live on the news from our home studio. Do you want to do it while I talk to the dolphin man?"

"Only if he's hot." They'd had cameras following them around the clock for months now. Sex on the air at Entertainment News had been Pauline's idea, and it brought her international notoriety. Now she needed a new idea to stay in the forefront of world news. She giggled as another idea popped in her head. "But, I'd rather do it with the dolphins. Will the producers go for that?"

"I like how you think." Connor pumped more iron, his oiled skin glistening under the hot lights. "We'll take riding the dolphin to a whole new level."

"I like. I'm getting excited thinking about it."

He ogled her gleaming thighs. "Me, too."

"Back in five, four, three, two, one," the director said.

Connor straddled the weight bench. "We're back live and have we got a nice feature for you. I know you're tired of hearing about the water riots, so Pauline and I are bringing you a feel-good feature on dolphins. We draw your attention to coastal Georgia and the smiling, frolicking sea creatures who are making a comeback from the endangered species list."

The director cued the vid clip of dolphins swimming and splashing in the ocean and then cut back to Pauline. With a generous boob thrust forward, she read her lines off the prompter. "Atlantic bottlenose dolphins such as these trained by Dr. Browning Charles play key roles in national security, and they do it all for a bite of fish. Tell us about your pets, Dr. B. How are they saving the world?"

An intense man in a rumpled suit coat hit the airwaves in a boxed inset on the screen of Connor and Pauline working out. Behind him on the pier several people clad in loose-fitting orange robes milled about. "Yes, hello. Dr. Browning Charles here. My research confirms sentinel species like dolphins demonstrate innate and adaptive behaviors which are passed to their cohorts in unique ways."

Pauline laughed and plumped her hair to fluster the professor. To further the sexual play, she reached for the overhead weights and worked her chest. "I know you suits are smart, but the rest of us don't have a clue of what you just said. English, please."

Dr. B's expression soured. More orange-clad people gathered behind him. "Dolphins are born knowing how to survive. They learn other behaviors during their lifetime. Because of their social nature, these new skills are taught to their peers and offspring."

"For a smart guy, your translator's not so good. Let me try." She leaned forward, forcing Fred the camera guy to retreat to keep her cleavage from dominating the screen. "These sleek fishies are born knowing how to play and eat and sex it up in the big bad ocean. Some of them get caught up in human war games with bombs and shit. These sea soldiers come home all messed up and teach their family how to explode ships."

Dr. B tugged at his shirt collar. "Not quite. Our humane research—"

"Humane? Are they people?" Pauline released the overhead weight handle, allowing the weights to clatter down behind her. She leaned into the camera, concern etched on her made-up features. "Did I miss something?"

Connor spooned up behind her. "Bug, zoom in on the crowd behind the science dude. Something's happening."

"Wait a minute," Dr. B said as the camera panned away from him to the robed crowd. Placards shot in the air. "This is my interview. I bought and paid for it."

"Earn your money, then," Connor taunted. "Tell us what you see."

"Greenies, about a hundred of them," Dr. B muttered. "Now about my research—"

"Greenies?" Pauline laughed. "Given their orange attire, shouldn't they be called orangies?"

Dr. B sighed quite loud. "They wear orange to honor their fallen comrades on the nearby island. These robes are the traditional garb of the natives on Tama Island. Greenies in our region and across the world have unified their protest movement behind this clothing choice. Can we talk about my dolphins now?"

"We want our water," a woman shouted. Another echoed the sentiment, "Our sons and daughters demand our water. Give us our water. We demand our fair share of the water."

"Water! Water! Water!" the crowd chanted. The placard-wielding people elbowed each other, jostling for space in front of the camera. Soon a punch was thrown. And another. Through it all the cry prevailed, "Give us our water!"

"Ooh," Pauline cooed. "A rabid protest and lyrics from Queen Bea's hit song. I wish we were there. Protests make me hot."

"Everything makes you hot, love," Connor stated as he reached for her bikini strings. "I'll make you sing with pleasure. Come here."

"Yee-haw!" Pauline said as he went right for the honey spot. She fluttered her augmented eyelashes at Fred the cameraman, and he obligingly framed her transcendent expression. God, she loved screwing on the news. This was the best job, ever.

Chapter 5

Forman caught Zeke's eye as the office vid screen mercifully blanked. "That went well."

"Your sarcasm is wasted on me." Zeke unfolded from his swivel chair and stretched his knotted shoulder muscles. The thirty-minute video conference on water distribution had turned into a grueling three-hour debate. He reached over and grabbed a water pouch from the chiller. "I'm going to be forced to go to New York, I just know it. I hate New York."

"You hate everywhere that isn't here."

"What's not to love about Tama Island? Why the hell can't the world leave me alone?" Zeke paced the lab, pulling at the tie he'd had to wear for the online summit, untucking the dress shirt from his swim trunks. "I never asked to be the world's water expert. Rossi and Li are up to something. Why didn't they nominate Gruber or Ivanov to brief the world leaders about the global water distribution plan? The only thing I hate worse than New York is politics. No one owns the planet's water. Why can't they understand that?"

"People revert to an 'us' and 'them' mentality when their backs are pressed to the wall," Forman said. "If you're not 'us' then you're 'them.' One group invariably has resources the other group wants. They refuse to share and bingo, war breaks out."

The android's pleasant demeanor further dampened Zeke's spirits. It wasn't fair that anyone could sit through hours of political posturing and maintain a genial outlook. The weight of the world was closing in on him. He didn't need upheaval in his work life, not when he had a major off world crisis to deal with.

He tried a deep cleansing breath. It didn't work. "You think I don't understand a blasted thing about social dynamics, but I don't need a crash course in sociology. I need a reason to say no when the travel orders arrive. These off-island jaunts never work out well for me. Politicians always shoot the messenger."

"Time to grow up, Dr. Geek. No one wants to be the messenger. By being the person who stuck his neck on the line with a water distribution plan, you are the logical one to explain everything to the ruling authorities and the Global Water Federation."

"Great. I did it to myself. That's a comfort. I can't help it if others don't see what I see. Intelligence is a rugged cross to bear."

"You could get a lobotomy," Forman pointed out.

"You could be reprogrammed," Zeke shot back. He took a long swig from his water pouch and studied his friendly nemesis. "I don't need a smart-mouthed sidekick."

The parakeets on Forman's lime green shirt shuddered. "Standing around pointing fingers of blame isn't productive. You need to get laid, and you need a new problem to wrap your brain around."

"Thanks for your opinion, Dr. Evangeline." Since Forman had mimicked the tone of a notorious sex counselor on the vid screen, Zeke laced his retort with scathing heat. "Knock it off with the sex talk, or I will alter your programming."

"You'd have to catch me first." Forman smirked like a teenaged boy with just the right touch of invincibility and self-delusion. "You don't need a yes man. You need someone to challenge you. Consider where you'd be right now without me in your life."

He'd be dead, and it wouldn't matter that aliens were on their way to destroy the planet. Zeke exhaled heavily. "You're a lousy debater."

"About that new work problem from last night," Forman began. "I noticed you accessed satellite maps of the planet and beyond. You're holding out on me."

"Nothing is private around here," Zeke grumped. "That's a side project I'm thinking about, not a work issue."

"And?"

"I don't know where it's going. All this talk about who owns the water made me realize how defenseless the planet is. What if an outside threat approached us? How would the Earth defend herself?"

"Cool. Do we have access to the current world defense systems?"

"We have access to nothing, and I don't want you tripping wires on the net and getting us in trouble. This is strictly off the books and unauthorized. An intellectual exercise – like a crossword puzzle."

Forman's eyebrows waggled, and his face lit up. "Even better. I get to out-snoop the top security systems on the planet. Where do we begin? With the U.S. systems?"

"We can get in a shit-load of trouble if we get caught," Zeke cautioned.

"Trust me. I'm that good. They'll never know we've been poking around in their files."

"You better be right. If the feds get wind of this, not even Uncle John can help us."

"I'm looking for bombs and missiles?"

"I don't know what we're looking for. I thought I'd inventory what we had and figure out how to make it better."

Forman sang softly about the end of the world as he began accessing secure systems. The haunting lyrics caught Zeke's notice. "Is that one of Queen Bea's songs?" he asked.

"It is. No one sings about the end of the world better than my Bea."

"The tune is catchy."

"One moment." Forman's fingers flew over the keypad. An image of Bea in leather and lace concert finery flashed on vid screen four. Her soulful voice sang of the end of the world, a world with no water and food for sons and daughters.

As he listened, an idea occurred to Zeke. Bea's end-of-the-world songs had been inspired by anonymous communiques from a secret society bent on world domination. The Chameleons had been vanquished, but their method of heightening world awareness of global issues through an international pop sensation had been a golden idea.

One he could put to good use.

Chapter 6

The end of the world. His boss thought he had him fooled with his weak story about bombs and missiles, but Forman had the intelligence of four robots in his memory banks and nearly unlimited processing capability. Zeke had insider knowledge of a planetary threat. It was logical. Why else would a hydrologist inventory the planet's defenses?

Thank the heavens the man had gone off for a swim so Forman could snoop through his office com.

Maybe the physical exercise would work out Zeke's kinks or maybe he'd sit next to the lighthouse to meditate, a practice he didn't like anyone to know about. Which made Forman very curious as to why Zeke wanted his relaxation habit downplayed. But if communion with that place brought his boss peace of mind, it was worth respecting his desire for a semblance of privacy.

Forman unlocked the virtual bridges, and data streamed around him from the supercomputers in the room. But instead of open lines of inquiry in Zeke's recent computer log, he found roadblock after roadblock. He whistled at the complexity of the encoding. His boss was definitely up to something.

Flurk.

This would take serious digging to gain access to the encrypted files. He'd get in, but it wouldn't be quick. While he worked on that problem, he accessed the security cameras at Bea and Jessie's house. Bea didn't know he could do that, and he wasn't about to tell her. It wasn't stalking. He needed to know she was alive and well for his peace of mind. Zeke might be his job, but Bea was his heart. Or what passed for a robot heart.

With each cam shot, his fingers and thoughts quickened. Her house was dark. Room after room. No movement. No people. His fear for her safety warped into overdrive. Where was she? He broke com silence and called her.

No answer.

He dialed Tank, the bodyguard she'd employed to tour with her.

No answer.

What the hell?

He shut down the inquiry into Zeke's files, focusing his entire attention on Bea's whereabouts. She wasn't scheduled for a concert for a month. This was supposed to be her tour break to recharge. She was supposed to be recharging with him.

Except she'd kicked him out.

And now she'd gone.

Without telling him.

Why would she do that? She wouldn't, would she? As he mulled the problem, a sinister idea popped into his processors. Had someone taken her against her will? Please, whatever God there was in the heavens, don't let that be the case.

Moments later, he had his answer. Bea, her sister, and her bodyguard had caught a flight to Japan. He stilled. Why would anyone fly into the maw of trouble? Everyone on Japan was trying to get off-island. Between the tsunamis and earthquakes, Japan was the most dangerous place on the planet right now. Was Bea such a thrill seeker that she had to live on the edge to write her songs?

At the crisp rap on the door, he shut down the virtual data streaming bridges. The blue tinge in the air faded quicker than his tumultuous thoughts. Bea was in danger. He had to go help her. But what if she'd gone to see another man in Japan? That uncertainty multiplied exponentially through his processing modules.

A dark-skinned woman in orange robes entered the lab. A canvas satchel was slung over one shoulder. "Forman?"

He rose. What did Zeke's cousin want? At one time, they'd exchanged flirty looks, but he'd given up casual sex to be with Bea. He kept his glance strictly professional. "I'm here. What can I do for you, Angie?"

"John wants a report. You haven't filed one in days."

He'd been romancing Bea in his down time. Not easy when she was jetting across the globe. He'd had lots of chats with her, sent flowers, and sighed over her picture. He'd been too busy with the things that mattered to follow through on daily reports.

Though the Institute and John Demery created Forman for Zeke, Forman's loyalty was to his scientist. It felt wrong to be accountable to anyone when Zeke was such a private person.

"We've been busy," Forman hedged. "The water crisis. Now Zeke is freaking out over being sent to New York to talk with the politicos. He's gone for a swim."

She nodded. "I saw him leave the lab. You'll accompany him to New York. The travel orders came through today."

"But?"

"But John wants me to install a tracking chip in your circuitry."

Trackers were trouble. They couldn't go off-grid if he was chipped. He needed to maintain flexibility to keep his boss safe. "Those things are traceable. Zeke and I step through one security gate, and the chip will red-flag. My logs could get downloaded by any child with a security app."

"This chip is different."

She showed him the chip. It felt light in his hand, small to his artificial eyes. "I don't recognize the design."

"Nola devised it per John's orders. Should you two get in a bind when you're off-island, we can find and extract you."

"How does it work?"

"If I tell you, I'll have to kill you."

He shot her a quelling look. Angie was maybe one hundred and twenty pounds soaking wet and female. He could bench press her all day long.

"Seriously," Angie said, taking the chip from him. "It's better if you don't know. If danger should befall you, and your programming was accessed, knowledge of the chip could endanger your chance of survival."

She meant Zeke's chances of survival. Forman had already been through physical death once before, and while it had been gruesome and embarrassing, he'd do it again to save his boss. Zeke's welfare was his prime directive.

"I don't like it, but I will allow it." He turned his back to allow access to his central processing unit in his head.

Angie sighed happily. "Thanks. This won't hurt a bit. You're doing Zeke and this country a great service."

He heard the ear panel swing open. The country? What was she talking about? Too late he remembered the satchel she carried and her status as John Demery's top operative. The world went dark.

Chapter 7

A foaming wave surged over Zeke's bare feet. His toes gripped the wet sand as he strode into the surf. Breakers built, crested, and spilled over in all their magnificent glory. Zeke took a deep breath of the salt air and smelled home.

The water deepened, and he perversely tried to stand up as long as possible until a strong wave plowed into him, knocking him off-balance. Seawater rushed over his heated skin, cooling him down. Underwater, he enjoyed the rough ride, timing his ascension between wave troughs. He edged out waist-deep, diving through powerful monsters, bodysurfing to shore when it suited him.

In the presence of the mighty ocean roar, his troubles paled in significance. So what if he was supposed to find a mate and reproduce to carry on the Taman Guardian line? So what if his water distribution options found no favor with politicians? So what if aliens were coming to destroy the planet?

He snorted at the so-whatness of that last point and treaded water. A wave curled, crested, and surged into him, knocking him sideways. He thrashed in the powerful hydraulic, fighting the current because he didn't take a deep breath before he went under. A few agonizing seconds later, the swell thundered past, and the foaming underwater chaos released him.

With an eye to the eastern horizon, he crested the water surface, realizing he needed to swim out past the breakers if he wanted to focus his thoughts. In the trough of the incoming waves he could still touch bottom, so he pushed out another ten feet. The only natural challenges out here were rounded waves and a whitecap or two.

Dolphins surfaced and frolicked a hundred feet away.

He drifted with the current parallel to shore, buoyed by the salt water. As he floated on his back, thin wispy clouds sailed overhead in the blue sky. Water lapped at his ears. He tasted salt on his lips. He sculled the water with his hands to stay afloat, freeing his thoughts to wander at will.

Everything looked so normal, as if nothing were wrong. In such a perfect world, his only worry would be finding a mate. Damn

Forman for reinforcing his subconscious need to get laid. He'd dated casually but sex had been a physical release, nothing more. He hadn't developed lasting attachments with any of his lovers.

Would it be different with his true mate?

How would he recognize her?

Until then, how would he handle Jessie? She wanted him. He wanted her. So what if she wasn't his mate? Did that detail matter when the world might end tomorrow? The only reason they weren't sleeping together was his reticence to lead her on. He needed a new approach, one that made both of them happy.

Something bumped against his right leg. Something else rubbed his left arm. He glanced around in alarm, fearing a shark attack, but instead he saw he'd come upon the pod of Atlantic bottlenose dolphins. Or they'd joined him. He straightened, lowering his feet and treading water. They splashed around him in joyous abandon. One bold dolphin nudged him with her slender nose as she swam by each time. He put his hand out, and the pushy dolphin swam under it, rolling onto her belly. She did this several times before Zeke recognized her behavior pattern. Did she want him to be horizontal again?

Hmm. Why not?

He stretched out parallel with the water surface, gazing at the sky. Two dolphins idled nearby. When he raised his head to glance at him, they made chucking sounds. He lay back down. How odd. Clearly, they wanted him to float in the water. What else did they want of him?

What he wouldn't give to have a picture of him swimming with the dolphins. But maybe these dolphins weren't wild animals. Were they Browning Charles' trained dolphins?

There was no way to tell, but he should do something.

What?

Doing nothing seemed to be what they expected, so he floated with the pod, letting his thoughts drift with the water, relaxing and drowsing in the sun. Without warning, the hurling freefall of the Taman mindlink claimed him.

He strained against the link much the same as he'd fought the underwater hydraulic when he was knocked down a few minutes ago. What was going on? How was this possible? This wasn't safe. He was in the open ocean, for Christ sake.

Easy, son.

He knew that voice. *Dad! What's happening? How is this possible?*

You're progressing rapidly, son. I'm proud of you. I didn't access the dolphin hyperspace link until you were nearly grown.

I thought I had to be in the transmission chair to link with you. Please, explain.

Nothing to explain. These dolphins and their descendants have lived near Tama Island for as long as we've been there. They know things. They recognize us. They help us by amplifying our signal.

They're friendly, all right. But I never noticed them before. I never saw them when I swam.

The link pulsed with high-octane energy. Unlike in the transmission chair, this signal was so clear and true, he didn't strain at all. Another voice commanded the link. His grandfather. *They recognize your brainwave pattern, little Zee. It identifies you as one of us.*

Zeke craned his head to see in the stygian darkness of his mind. *Grampa? Where are you? Am I dead?*

We don't have time for this. A harsh authoritative voice echoed through the watery link. *The dolphins are in trouble. A man is enslaving them for evil purposes. You must stop him from harming the dolphins. One of their podmates was captured three days ago.*

Dr. Charles? Are you talking about his dolphin research?

A nervous man, they say. He inserts a sonar disruptor under their skin. They have to follow his signal, or they become too disoriented to surface for breathing.

Zeke recoiled. *I had no idea he was disrupting their survival mechanism. That's not right. How can I help?*

Swim with the dolphins. Rescue their podmate. Remove the disruptor. They will show you the way.

The link faded, and once again Zeke felt the warmth of sunlight on his face. He opened his eyes and blinked against the brightness. He allowed his feet to submerge so he could get his bearings. But instead of becoming clearheaded, his thoughts raced with his heart. Tama Island was nowhere in sight. The sun hung low in the sky.

How long had he been out?

The only landmark for miles was a distant buoy. He could drown out here in the deep ocean, and no one would know. He could die. He didn't want to die. He had plenty to live for, and he was no quitter. He'd agreed to help the dolphins rescue their friend, so that's what he would do.

They'd propelled him offshore during the mindlink. He gazed into the watchful eye of a dolphin that surfaced beside him, wishing he could read the animal's mind.

Another dolphin, the one with a small nick on the front of her dorsal fin, bumped him again, urging him to swim toward the buoy. The bell atop the floating platform tolled mournfully as it rode the three-foot swells. He stroked straight for it, hoping his hybrid physiology would give him superhuman endurance to survive this ordeal.

Finally, he reached the buoy and climbed it, shaking with effort. The dolphins splashed and chittered like angry squirrels, or at least that's how they sounded to him. On rubbery legs, he stood, scanning the water nearby. A pen of sorts was tethered by a thick rope to the buoy. A heavy log snagged on the mesh pen, weighting it down. An opposite corner of the pen broke the water surface between swells, but not often. From his above water vantage point, he saw a small dolphin taking a quick breath before being pushed back underwater by the bobbing pen.

No wonder the dolphins were frantic. Their podmate in the pen was drowning. Damn that Browning Charles. He should know better than to put such a beautiful creature in harm's way. Fueled by righteous anger, Zeke dove underwater and swam to the pen. He shoved at the log, but it was stuck fast. Waves crashed into him, knocking him into the pen.

The dolphin inside the pen brightened at the presence of his podmates. Two dolphins worked cooperatively to lift a corner so the little one could catch a full breath. Time for him to help. How did the pen open? Zeke dove under and tried to figure it out, but the visibility in the dark water approached zero. He surfaced and studied the dolphins. They were at the other end of the pen. The end with the log.

"I can't move the log," he said. "Already tried that."

The dolphin with the nicked fin, or Nicola, as he'd decided to call her, swam under him again, urging him forward. With no better plan, he followed her. After two dives at their location, he saw what he'd failed to see before. The log obstructed the gate to the pen. Damn. He dove down again and realized that the hinged side of the opening was held in place by nylon twine.

Three dives later, he'd made progress unraveling the hinge. On the fourth dive, he got it. The little dolphin swam free. It leapt and splashed with clown-like abandon, nudging its podmates, splashing in great circles like a circus performer. What a freewheeling Bozo!

Zeke swam to the buoy, exhausted by the effort. He'd freed the dolphin, so his task was half done. How the heck would he remove the radar disruptor? As far as he could tell, there wasn't a noticeable bulge under the animal's skin.

Nicola swam up to him, with the little one by her side. With her bottle-shaped nose, she nudged the small dolphin forward. Her luminous eyes seemed to plead with him to fix this.

Zeke touched the little guy, and it shuddered. He tried again, gentling it with his voice. "Easy, Boz. I've got you." He felt along the back. There. A small ridge under the smooth skin behind the fin. Saltwater splashed in his eyes. He wiped his face. How would he remove the implant?

Luck was with him. The nearby skin had abraded by rubbing against the surfacing pen. "This won't hurt but for a second," he promised, knowing it was silly to talk to a dolphin. He reached in, grabbed the chip, and flung it in the ocean.

He could have sworn Nicola smiled at him. Little Boz swam away and circled back. This time all the dolphins swam with him. Zeke clung to the buoy. He felt happy to have helped. Screw Charles and his dolphin researchers. This remote setup was terrible. Dolphins shouldn't be isolated. Anyone could see they were social animals.

He sagged against the buoy. Mission accomplished. Success felt great. But diving to free the dolphin drained his energy reserves, as had swimming out here in the unrelenting rollers. The sun crept closer to the western horizon. How would he get back to shore?

Should he hang onto the buoy until someone came looking for him? Bad idea. Charles might arrive first, and Zeke wouldn't be able to control his reaction to the man. He didn't tolerate cruelty to animals.

Nicola nudged him off the buoy. She splashed in his face when he struck out in a direction, turning him in the direction of sunset. Oh, yeah. Land was to the west. He should have started that way instead of wasting twenty strokes swimming further out to sea.

He swam for home. Survival resolved to five basic thoughts. *Stroke, stroke, stroke, stroke, breathe.* Then he'd start the sequence again. The dolphins stayed close, nudging him ever westward. After a while, little Boz swam directly in front of him, giving him a moving target to follow.

Never had he realized how important it was to swim with a buddy. No one even knew he was out here. *Swim or die*, he thought.

Chapter 8

In the thin light of sunset, Forman pounded down the beach, splashing through the shallows to reach the seemingly lifeless form. As he approached the body, he optically scanned the radiant heat signature and realized it was too low. Damn. Why hadn't he paid better attention to the time?

"Zeke!"

His boss didn't respond.

Like every robot on the planet, he had a cardiopulmonary resuscitation program embedded in his start-up routine. He reviewed the basics of compressions and breaths as he hauled Zeke from the tidal zone. Beyond the beach, four dolphins splashed in the lackluster low tide waves. Nothing else marred the watery horizon.

"Come on, doc, don't die on me." He dropped to his knees in the sand, checking and finding a faint pulse in his boss. Zeke was alive. Thank goodness. Forman scooped him up and ran all-out for Zeke's house, which was half a kilometer closer than the lab.

What happened?

Zeke was a strong swimmer. Had his body malfunctioned? Had he encountered trouble in the water from an external source? Why was the man unresponsive?

Priorities. Zeke's core temperature needed to increase. He needed medical attention. Fluids. He needed a bodyguard who didn't lose track of his whereabouts. He needed to pull out of this so he could tell Forman what had happened.

He pulled the metal house key from his pocket, unlocked the front door, and headed for the master bathroom. With Zeke still in his arms, he stepped into the hot shower. Carefully shielding Zeke's breathing zone, he let the warm water splash over them both.

His boss barely stirred as his body warmed. Forman checked for a pulse again. Sure and steady. Zeke was alive, but he still wasn't conscious.

"Computer, call John Demery," Forman said as he wrapped Zeke in a thick towel and carried him to bed.

Zeke's uncle appeared on the bedroom vid screen. His thick

white eyebrows were beetled together. "Demery."

Forman turned to face the cam. He couldn't keep the hitch out of his voice. "There's been an accident, sir. Dr. Landry is alive but unconscious."

Demery leaned closer to the vid camera. "What happened?"

"Don't know. When he didn't return to the lab this afternoon, I searched the island for him. I found him in the shallows on Goat's Head Beach. He had a pulse, but his core temperature was low."

Forman angled the cam so Demery had a full view of Zeke. "I warmed him in the shower, but he didn't revive. He needs medical assistance immediately."

Demery nodded. "On it." Forman heard the faint sounds of data entry. Demery looked up again and called his name.

Forman stepped back into cam view, ready to be busted all the way back to a house droid for not performing up to expectation. "Yes, sir?"

"No sign of foul play?"

"Nothing, sir."

"Stay put. A med team will arrive in ten minutes."

The image winked out. Help was on the way. Forman tucked an extra blanket tight around his boss before hurrying out to change into dry clothes. Would Demery send him back to Supply Central? Would his unique four-in-one processing capability be detected?

Would he be junked?

He couldn't worry about that now, not with Zeke's welfare on the line. He stepped into tan trousers, buttoned up a sunset-themed aloha shirt, and jammed his feet into boat shoes. Returning to Zeke's room, he quickly filled a backpack with apparel and essentials for his boss.

When he ran out of tasks to do, he sat beside the bed watching Zeke's chest rise and fall, wishing he hadn't messed up. If only he could remember what happened this afternoon. He'd been at the lab. Checking on Bea instead of working. She wasn't where she was supposed to be. She'd hopped a flight to Japan with her sister.

The news had floored him. But he'd returned to work, according to his personal logs. He'd run several simulations of water distribution profiles to prepare for the upcoming trip to the Global Water Federation in New York. Realizing Zeke was overdue, he'd searched the beach for him. If he'd tagged along, none of this would have happened.

But Zeke didn't want him tagging along on his beach trips. He'd dismissed Forman on previous beach outings, saying he needed time alone with his thoughts.

I should have insisted on accompanying him.

Had Zeke been swimming for hours? Did he get swept offshore by a dangerous rip tide? Forman gripped his hands. Ye gads, he was in so much trouble.

A chopper approached, and Forman hurried outside to meet it. Until two months ago, the island had three hundred year old trees, but a forest fire took down the ancient oaks and everything else with it. Without the thick canopy of vegetation, there was plenty of room for a med chopper to land anywhere on the island.

"In there," he said, pointing to the open front door. "Down the hall and first bedroom on the right."

Two white-clad attendants with medical satchels hurried inside. As they checked Zeke's vitals and blood levels, Forman waited in the living room with Angie, who'd piloted the chopper.

"Didn't know you could fly." He gazed at Zeke's cousin with new respect.

"I'm a woman of many talents," she shot back. "What really happened out there?"

"Same as I told Demery. When Zeke didn't return from his swim, I went looking for him. I didn't realize he'd been gone for so long. He always returns within two hours."

Angie blushed. "It wasn't your fault."

"Well, it certainly wasn't your fault, so that leaves me to take the blame."

"The incident will be investigated. If you are found negligent, there will be repercussions."

"Such as?"

"Such as you don't want to know right now."

The attendants wheeled out Zeke's gurney. "You better have room on that chopper for me. I'm not letting Zeke out of my sight."

"Good response. You can ride in front with me."

Chapter 9

Bea whirled in a circle. "God, I feel so alive. There's so much conflict here."

Jessie checked that the iron bars were secure in the windows and double-locked the door. She made a security sweep every time they returned from an excursion. The local news was full of travelers being assaulted by scavengers.

She regretted accompanying her sisters overseas. "Coming here was the biggest mistake of my life."

"How can you say that?" Bea kicked up her bare heels in the minimalist two-room apartment. "People are rioting in the street. We couldn't purchase dinner. That's real hardship. That's living on the edge. That's what it takes to write hit songs."

"I'm hungry, and I stink," Jessie grumbled. "I didn't think about water shortages and food rationing when you booked the trip. We've been here three days, and you haven't written a single word, much less a song. I want to go home."

Bea stopped jigging around the room and stared at Jessie. "Home to Richmond or home to the island?"

Jessie's hands rose in the air. "We sold our place in Richmond. Home is where our stuff is, and right now that's on Tama Island. I want to sit in a real chair, sleep in my own bed, and not have to worry if the next earthquake will bring twenty stories of apartments crashing down on my head."

"They build 'em to withstand quakes." Bea crossed to the window, grabbed hold of the security bars, and tugged with all her might. "See? Not even a wiggle or a wobble. The building is fine. We should hop a bus tomorrow and sightsee."

"I'm fresh out of energy. Not eating does that to me."

"Snap out of it, Sis. You made your own decision."

"It isn't safe here. I've requested departure airline tickets, but we're on standby due to everyone trying to leave this rock. If you're so energized, why aren't you cranking out songs instead of arguing with me?"

"It doesn't work like that. I can't sit down and write on

command. I need to be afraid."

"Go stand in the crowd of people outside protesting the lack of dinner. That should do it."

"You're not coming with me?"

"No. I had enough of that craziness when we tried and failed to procure dinner." Jessie fired up her vid link, accessing her mail account. Was there something from Zeke? Nope. Damn.

"I can't do it without you," Bea said.

"Yes, you can. Hey what's this?" Jessie clicked on the message with a subject header of new global disaster. The document opened in a small font that was nearly impossible to read. She magnified the screen fifty percent.

"What?" Bea asked, stepping closer to read over Jessie's shoulder. "Make it bigger. What does it say?"

"Something about a world disaster." She glanced at Bea. "Uh-oh. An anonymous communiqué. I thought we were done with that."

"Is it from the Chameleons?"

They'd run up on the Chameleon secret society a few months ago. Jessie clicked on the sender tab, but the identity and all the properties of the sender were not available. "It's anonymous. I don't know who sent the message."

"What kind of disaster? I thought we'd seen it all, what with food, water, transportation, and governments being at risk. There's nothing left on Earth to be a disaster."

Jessie made a half squeak-half laugh. "Nothing left on Earth? Did you read this already?"

"No. I haven't seen it before. What? What did you learn?"

"A threat is approaching from outer space. Is this some kind of joke? Who would possibly think we'd take that seriously? Why didn't they send this to the newsrooms if it was a true disaster? Who would believe little green men from Mars are coming to invade us?"

"Do little green men exist?"

"It was a figure of speech. I don't know what color they are or even if they're men. They could be radiated ants for all I know. This has to be a prank. Who would have my private address? It has to be someone we know."

"Forman says nothing is private anymore. Computers and technology have digitized everything. All of our so-called private information is not the least bit private."

"Why would they go to the trouble of erasing the sender info if it was a prank? That had to be a major pain in the ass."

"Tell me more about the little green men."

Jessie synched her wrist com with the wall com. A moment later, the entire document displayed across one wall of the apartment. "Read it for yourself. All we need are some drinks with parasols and a good imagination to flesh out the coming alien invasion."

"Alien invasion." Bea grinned, reaching for a pad of paper. "I love it. Let's dance with the little green men, dance all the way to their spaceship."

"Careful what you wish for. Those aliens might eat you alive."

"We'll be thinner, we'll be dinner. That's great, Jess. Keep the ideas rolling."

"It says here they'll take what they want, and we can't stop them. We should be very afraid."

"Be afraid. Be afraid. They're not coming for trade. Hide the lemonade, prepare for the raid. Little green men are coming."

Jess shook her head. "Is that the refrain?"

"I think so. It's catchy, right?"

"If this is serious, we could be in a world of trouble for making fun of the little green men, who may or may not be green."

"Or men. They may not be men." Bea grinned. "Not a man. Not a fan. Just a hit me with a pan kind of being. Close your doors, hit the floor, this is not a drill."

"Funky and catchy. Probably not what our silent sender had in mind, but what the hay? A hit song is a hit song. We're telling people to be aware. That's all we need to do."

"Be aware. Be aware. If you dare, cuz the gov'ment doesn't care." Bea trilled, hitting sky-high notes and bottoming out in her low register for the end of the phrase. "I can hear this song, with lots of techno riffs to sound like space aliens. I'll get this written, but you know what? I think this would be more effective as a duet. Do you think we can get Dylan James? He's on the island somewhere."

"Dylan James hasn't had a hit single in at least ten years. You thinking to put a little uptown swagger in the melody?"

"Yeah. Nobody does uptown swagger better than James."

"Cool."

Chapter 10

"This method of travel is obsolete," Forman announced as they snugged into a tandem pod the morning after Zeke's hospitalization. "We should be jetting through the sky like everyone else."

"Nothing wrong with the tunnels. Lots of people still use them." Zeke belted himself in the seat, wrestling with his traveling fears. With the altitude-negating implant in his neck, he shouldn't experience any of the displacement symptoms he'd felt prior to receiving the implant a few months back, but even so, he couldn't shake the brooding mood that had settled on him.

Between nearly drowning from rescuing a dolphin, knowing the Maleem were approaching the planet to annihilate it, and having to talk to a bunch of world leaders in New York, going through the everyday motions of life seemed meaningless. He wanted to sit on his beach and enjoy the play of light over moving water for as long as he could.

"No need to carp at me, boss."

"Sorry." As the lid snapped shut and the pod gained momentum, Zeke glanced at his traveling companion. "I'm not looking forward to this trip."

"What's not to like? We're heading straight to the Big Apple. Everything happens in New York. It's the center of the known universe."

"Yours maybe, not mine."

"You'll get back to your beloved island in a few days. Meanwhile, I get a chance to experience city life. Ooh-la-la!"

"If you hate being stuck on the island so much, Uncle John will wrangle you a new assignment."

The grin fell from Forman's face. "I wouldn't. I mean, I couldn't. Leave that is. You're my mission."

"Someone programmed me to be your mission. You could get new programming. You'd never miss me."

"I don't want that. I want to keep the memories I have, thank you very much. You have no idea how disorienting it is knowing people are messing with your thoughts, erasing memories, inserting new ones. I like the man I am right now. So what if I dream of the big city? I'm allowed to dream, but my heart is in our work. You and I are a team. A great team."

"What about Bea? Where does she fit in the picture?"

"Bea's special. She'll always be special to me. She asked me to stay away, and I'll respect her wishes. She's writing a new song in Japan."

"You're tracking her?"

"I can't help myself. I love her." Forman glanced slyly at Zeke. "Jessie's in Japan, too. There are riots in the streets. Food shortages. Earthquakes. All sorts of trouble. We should rescue them."

"Agreed. Don't those women have any sense?"

"I've been analyzing their rash action. Chances are good this is your fault. Jessie did this. Because you ignored her."

"Jessie's smarter than that." But she'd gone anyway. Where was the sense in that?

"We could swing by Japan on our way home from New York."

"Japan isn't on the way."

"It could be. Please?"

Rescuing Jessie appealed to him. He'd rather do that than go to New York and discuss water distribution plans. He'd love to be Jessie's lifeline. She'd love it too.

Love. Was that where this was headed?

His parents—

Forman interrupted his train of thought. "Zeke?"

"Yeah?"

"You all right? You look pale, and your respirations dropped. I told your uncle this trip was too soon after your hospitalization. You should be resting."

"Sorry. I'm fine, really. I was thinking about my parents, about the love they shared. I want that for myself. Jessie wants that same level of commitment, but I don't feel the same way about her that you do about Bea. Would I rescue Jessie if she was in a flaming pod? Sure, but I'd do that for anyone. How do I know when the right woman comes along?"

"Love is different for everyone. Some experience love at first sight. Others fall into it gradually. Just because you and Jessie haven't set a forest ablaze with passion doesn't mean you shouldn't try a relationship on for size. It's not like a horde of females are knocking down your door. Only Jessie. She's crazy about you, man.

Loosen up, live a little."

"You could follow your own advice."

"I can't relax while Bea's in trouble. Please say we'll rescue them. After New York, of course."

"They need help, that's for sure. I want Jessie to be safe. We'll do it."

"Thanks. You're the best boss ever."

Zeke waved off the uncomfortable praise and sought a new topic. "What do you know about Browning Charles?"

"The dolphin dude?"

Zeke nodded, his hands fisting. He'd never liked Charles, and after the dolphin episode, he'd lost all respect for the man.

The air softened from a dusky twilight of the pod to the blue of a streaming data bridge as Forman interfaced with the grid. "Browning Charles graduated from Florida State University with his doctorate in oceanography. He interned at the Baltimore Aquarium and was at Woods Hole before he came on staff at our Institute. He's divorced, no kids, no pets. He's published a dozen professional papers on dolphins."

Damn. The man had quite a resume, but his actions revealed his true nature. "He wants my lab."

"He can't have it," Forman exclaimed. "We're doing important work in that facility."

"Where is he? I don't trust him. What if he tries to stake a claim while we're away?"

"One minute." The pod throbbed with streaming blue data then cleared abruptly. In the twilight of the travel pod, Forman turned to Zeke. "No worries, pal. He's on the west coast. At a dolphin conference."

Zeke's fingernails bit into his palms. "The guy's a jerk and a user. Plus, he mistreats his test subjects. I'd love to expose him as a fraud."

Forman shrugged. "Do it."

"Can't. But I can dream about it."

"I can do more than that." The air in the travel pod turned blue.

Alarmed, Zeke waved his hand through the data stream. The energy parted around his hand and integrated on the other side. "What are you doing?"

The bridge faded. Forman grinned, his teeth flashing bright in the pod. "All done."

"Forman."

"What?" The robot shrugged. "I merely posted a question about him to an animal rights bulletin board."

"Devious. But take it down. I don't work that way."

"This guy deserves whatever he gets. You said so yourself."

"I won't destroy his reputation on my gut feeling. Undo what you did."

"All right already. Don't have a cow about it."

Zeke studied the data stream. Was Forman obeying him or making it worse?

Forman turned to face him, a worried expression on his blue-tinted skin. "Uh-oh."

"I don't like the sound of that."

"My anonymous post is down, but several related threads have spun off."

"Remove them. The man's professional reputation is at stake."

"Can't. I didn't post them. The data's gone viral."

"Uh-oh is right." Zeke followed the action-reaction chain backward. "Can the original post be traced back to you?"

"No way. I bounced it off hosts around the world and ran it through three scrubbers."

"You shouldn't have been so impulsive. What got into you?"

"I thought I was helping."

"Promise me you won't do anything like this again."

"I won't." At Zeke's sharp glance, the robot shrugged. "I won't. I promise. Want me to pinkie swear too?"

"You want to take this to the playground level? Fine. I've got four choice words for you. Are. We. There. Yet."

Chapter 11

Connor Bronsen finished his laps in the estate pool and sat on the swim-out step in the deep end. Where the heck was Pauline? She said she'd be downstairs in time to film the breaking news segment. That was fifteen minutes ago. He was crazy about her, but lately he'd sensed she was pulling back from him. Sure, they were a television couple, but they could be together in real life as well.

For weeks, he'd thought about popping the question. Asking her to be his wife. He'd stopped every time, worried she might decline his offer. Then what would he do?

It was no secret to anyone that he was nearing the end of his news career. Younger guys with hotter bods and less crooked smiles all wanted his anchor slot. They all wanted the chance to get their hands on Pauline.

Not on his watch.

He'd pushed harder on fitness to make sure Pauline had no complaints in that department. He loved her. But did she love him? The question ate at him.

The sliding glass door opened, and Pauline appeared. With eyes for the camera, she pranced in her stilettos all the way to the pool.

About time. Connor pushed off from the step and breast stroked to the shallow end and Pauline. Did he have enough time to get her all wet in the pool before the segment? That filmy lingerie she had on would be transparent if wet. The thought of it made him hot. He waited.

She stopped a few feet away, slipped off her spiked sandals, and dipped her toes into the sparking waters. She shivered with enthusiasm. "Don't you just love a pool? I find it incredibly sexy."

"Almost as sexy as the hot news from outer space." Connor emerged from the pool, moisture streaming off his oiled, tanned body. Pauline knew how to work him but good. They had another short segment to tape before he'd get some action, but sex was all he could think about right now. Sex and Pauline.

"Yes!" Pauline quipped as she neared their outdoor recording studio. Connor's camera swung over to capture her undulating walk. "Word on the streets is that company is coming. Isn't this news ultra-exciting?"

"NASA scientists came out with an official statement this morning," Connor added, noting with satisfaction that both cameras swiveled to focus on him. He stretched a bit to ripple his abs. "At first, the goobers with the big telescope in Hawaii believed a trio of asteroids were headed our way. Tumbling space rocks come along all the time, and it's no big deal."

"But," Pauline interrupted with a coy flutter of her false eyelashes, "the asteroids slowed down and changed formation. Space rocks can't do that. Which means – wait for it – intelligent life is out there, and it's coming here to party with us. We're like galactic ambassadors or something. Woo-hoo!"

Connor cleared his throat and ignored the canned text on the teleprompter. Their best ratings came when he and Pauline ad-libbed. She'd been off script all morning, needling and cajoling him. Time for him to add a little spice to his lines. "The suits are all cautious about what's coming. Sure, they could eat us or blow us up, but why would they? We've got so much here to offer."

"Yeah," Pauline sighed happily. "I hope our space nerds are laying out the welcome mat. I'd like to personally be on hand to welcome the new arrivals. I've been studying sign language in case they don't speak our language." She flashed the 'I love you' sign at Connor.

The chance of the aliens knowing sign language were slim, but he didn't want to discourage his lover. He wanted her to keep smiling at him, to truly fall in love with him. "I'm sure our network will do all in its power to add us to the welcoming committee."

"Let's hope so. Those guys wouldn't know fun if it socked them in the pants."

Ah, his pants. He hadn't forgotten about the bonus of his job, getting paid big bucks to make love to the hottest woman in entertainment news. Life continually amazed him.

"Fun is what we're about, that's for sure." He nodded to the tech in the nearby control booth to cue the music. He cupped Pauline's hips, drawing her close. "Listen to this brand new duet from Queen Bea and Dylan James."

As the lyrics of "Dancing with the Little Green Men," played over the airwaves, the camera zoomed in on Pauline shaking her booty to the hot beat. Connor matched her undulation for undulation until he lost himself in the moment. Dancing and kissing and thrusting.

Screw the aliens.

Pauline was his girlfriend.

Someone else would have to cover the aliens' breaking news story. He had more important things to do.

Chapter 12

Halfway through his presentation to the task force scientists in New York City, Zeke scanned the scowling faces in the posh conference room. Not a smile in the lot. His water disbursement options were viable and fair, but no one in the Global Federation cared about equality. Not when more water meant more population growth and more world clout.

Everyone believed the water was theirs, and they'd beg, borrow, and steal to get more than their fair share. Alliances being what they were, the outcome was predetermined. China would align with Italy, Austria with Russia, and the rest would throw in with the winning faction.

No one wanted to hear him rhapsodize about water models right now, not even him. He had other priorities and the sooner he could leave here, the better. There was an air transport to Japan this afternoon that he and Forman planned to catch, and they'd make it if they left soon. Once they rescued Jessie and Bea, then Zeke could focus on the larger problem of the Maleem.

With that thought in mind, he skipped to the end of his presentation. "My recommendation is Option Two."

"Not so fast. Statistics can be made to say anything," Dr. Rossi countered with a fluid Italian hand gesture. "If we took a month to study Dr. Landry's analysis, we'd have a better handle on his recommendation."

"We can't wait another month. England needs that water now," Dr. Davies said, his cultured English tone suggesting he knew best. "Stalling allows Italy time to procure a Papal mandate to commandeer the water for the church. Leave religion out of this. I say we vote today."

Everyone spoke at once, and Zeke gazed longingly at the guard posted by the double doors. Even though he represented the United States in this matter, he didn't mind if they duked it out without him. Water rights didn't mean much if you were dead, which is what the Maleem had planned for the inhabitants of Earth.

Peoples Republic of China representative Dr. Ming Li's

accented voice rose above the fray. "If we follow Dr. Landry's recommendation of using population density as the deciding factor, who will oversee the process? Who will check data veracity?"

"Good question," Zeke said, relieved the discussion had steered to safer ground. He might get out of here in time to catch that transpo. "I suggest a neutral third party to administer the plan."

"Where will we get one of those?" Austria's Dr. Claudia Gruber snickered. "Everyone here has nationalistic goals at heart. If we want unbiased, we should ask the little green men from outer space."

The energy brightened in the opulent room as laughter flowed around them. Zeke smiled as someone hummed the catchy refrain from Queen Bea's latest hit. Thanks to the wonders of modern technology and Bea's catchy style, his coded message to Jessie had produced immediate results. No wonder a secret society had employed this strategy to create global environmental unrest. There was no lag in response time.

Plus, he loved the refrain with its "be afraid" lyrics.

Pop music culture was positively viral in nature. A political statement would not warrant as much play or discussion as a hit song. A point to ponder later when he had time on his hands.

"Are we ready for a vote?" Chair Anika Fischer rose and motioned for silence. "All in favor of Option Two, raise your right hand."

A clear majority raised their hands. Zeke allowed air to seep into his lungs. Hallelujah. His job was done. They'd approved his recommendation. The chair banged her gavel. "Done. Our recommendation will be passed along to world governments within the hour. Now about this new matter, the approaching ships. What's our recommendation on them?"

"Mount an offensive and a defensive strike force." Zeke's insides hummed at this found opportunity. He cued up another presentation on the vid screen behind his head. His cartoon of a dark-haired man on a Vesper air scooter firing at a silvery saucer-craft got a big laugh.

"What the hell is that?" Rossi's head reeled backward. "Isn't it enough that thieves stole our water? Now you make a mockery of Italians? We'll show you how tough we are. We'll show those little green men. My Polizia will shoot the invaders out of the sky."

"Down, boy. No one knows if the approaching beings are law-abiding or dangerous," Gruber said. "We should exude peace and harmony during diplomacy. We want to make a good impression."

"Rossi is right," Dr. Li stated. "We must show a strong offense. We must present a powerful united front to ward off danger and to engender peaceful negotiations."

Ivanov leaned forward and stated, "We don't know what kind of weaponry these people will have. We don't even know if they're human. Our long-range scopes on the space station can't see inside their ships. Since they've mastered space travel, we can assume they are of superior intelligence and their weapons are more advanced than ours are. We would lose in a frontal assault."

Ah, the perfect lead for Zeke. "It can't hurt to have a defensive strategy in place. We could be facing total annihilation. The NORAD strategy of deter, detect, and defend is perfect for this situation."

Claudia Gruber leveled a manicured finger at Zeke. "Don't encourage the Russians. This is our chance to extend hospitality to our first space visitors."

Ivanov inclined his bald head toward Zeke. "Landry makes good sense. Grube can have tea and cookies with the aliens. But the Roscosmos will be ready to defend Earth."

Chair Fischer paled visibly. "I sincerely hope the Russian Space Agency exercises restraint."

"The ships," Rossi persisted. "Reports have varied on their numbers. I've heard three, four, and five ships."

"I can help with that." With a few deft keystrokes, Zeke called up the live feed from Earth's most distant space satellite. "Looks like three ships to me."

Rossi rose to study the blurred video. Three ghostly images marred a field of black. "Is that really them?"

Zeke nodded, not trusting his voice to speak. He'd probably pushed his luck as far as he should take it regarding educating the world about the Maleem.

Rossi whistled his appreciation. "You've got mad computer skills, Landry. Definitely three ships. Can you sharpen the image?"

Play it safe or go for broke? He inhaled a shaky breath. Time was short. Might not get another opportunity. "This is the best I can do. Any minute now, the space spooks will notice I tapped into their feed. Ladies and gentlemen, these aliens halted their speedy approach to our planet. I suspect the worst of them. They're preparing for an offensive strike."

"What proof do you have?" Ivanov asked.

Zeke shrugged, and the sat feed clouded with static. "Not a shred of proof. Just a feeling I have. A very bad feeling."

At the crisp rap on the door, Chair Fischer nodded to the room security agent. He opened the door, and Forman dashed to Zeke's side at the podium. He leaned close to whisper, "There's an emergency at home, Dr. Z. It's your uncle. He collapsed. A heart attack."

His uncle? Zeke clung to the podium as a thick band of dread constricted his chest. His vision narrowed to the ragged edge of his thumbnail. "Is he alive?"

"Nola got help immediately, but you never know in these situations." Forman disconnected Zeke's com and stuffed the notecards in his jacket pocket. "Your uncle asked for you."

Zeke caught Dr. Fischer's eye. "Please excuse me. I must leave. A family emergency."

"Of course," Dr. Fischer said. "Give John my regards."

Neither the elevator nor the ground transpo they flagged down went fast enough to suit Zeke. "This is taking too long."

"Not to worry. Nola chartered an air unit for us. We'll be there as quickly as is humanly possible."

Zeke tried to clear his jumbled thoughts as they threaded the crowds at La Guardia. With this new development, he couldn't commit to helping Jessie and Bea. His uncle came first. He pointed at a ticket kiosk. "You should go to Japan as we'd planned. I'll stay with Uncle John."

"No way." Forman clamped his hand on Zeke's arm. "I'm not losing you in transit. Been there, hated that. I'll get you settled in Georgia, then I'll fly to Japan for the Stemfords."

Zeke breathed a little lighter. "On second thought, if Uncle John is coming out of heart surgery, we could take the tube instead of flying. We don't need to fly."

"Forget it, buddy. We're flying and that's that. Time is short."

No kidding.

The Maleem could attack any minute.

Chapter 13

"How much longer?" Zeke asked with a fearful eye to the wide-open sky around them. With each passing moment, the certainty he'd made a mistake intensified. Both hands clamped onto the armrests.

Forman made a show of glancing at his wrist com. "It is precisely three minutes and forty-three-point-six seconds until our chartered flight arrives at John Demery's house."

Zeke tugged the collar on his dress shirt. "I feel too exposed. The aliens might perceive a flight as a threat. They could incinerate us at any moment. I should've insisted on using the underground pod system."

"Nonsense. We can't bank on what a group might or might not do. We shaved eight hours off our travel time. That's what family does in an emergency – hurry home."

Forman was right. He had to quit obsessing over the Maleem. They'd come when they came. He shouldn't invite trouble. Not when his uncle's life was on the line. Uncle John was his only living blood relative. His cousin Angie had come to the family through a second marriage of her parents, so even though he called her family, they weren't related genetically.

Hell. He cared equally for Uncle John and for Angie. Truth be told, he cared for Forman, Bea, and Jessie, too. Were they becoming his family? What was family anyway? Shared bonds of DNA or a unified outlook?

He wished Jessie were here. She'd know what to say, know how to make him feel better. She'd been by his side through a previous ordeal, and he'd taken her gutsy competence for granted. Now she was in Japan doing God only knows what, and he missed her companionship.

What kind of man was he that his best friend was a robot?

He wasn't a man.

He was an alien.

An alien living in stealth on a planet that was about to be invaded by unfriendly aliens. Sobering thoughts, those.

"Sorry. I'm overwhelmed by this sea of change," he said,

wishing he could at least confide in Forman about his alien status. But no one was allowed in on the secret.

Forman studied him speculatively. "How did you know?"

Outside the window, jet engines roared. Zeke regarded his companion steadily. Regret and caution entwined in his bloodstream like serpents on a medical insignia. Keeping secrets was hard work. "Know what?"

"About the spaceships. You knew before it was announced. Before Bea wrote her little green men song. How'd you know?"

"You won't believe me."

Forman leaned forward. "Try me."

He resolved to tell the truth, or at least a partial truth. "I dreamed about approaching spaceships when I nearly died in the ocean."

"A vision derived from your near death experience?"

"I know it sounds lame. I require proof for scientific conclusions, but I have no proof. Worse, given my professional reputation, I didn't feel I could mention such a spurious source." He glanced at Forman briefly before scanning the sky-scape outside the window. "I'd appreciate it if you'd keep this between us. I don't want anyone to know I'm a whack-job."

Forman relaxed back in his seat, crossed his legs, and donned a cheesy grin. "You going to run off and join the greenies?"

"Why would I do that?" Zeke felt heat rush to his face as his voice cracked. "I have to figure out how to save the planet."

"Lollapalooza and kiss my foot. You know more about the aliens? They don't come in peace?"

Zeke hesitated for a moment. If he kept the rest to himself, he would only appear slightly crazy. However, if he took a risk and invited Forman into the circle of knowledge, he'd have Forman's help in continuing to study the problem. It was worth the security risk.

"They come," Zeke whispered harshly, "to cleanse the Earth of human infestation. They will burn and rape and plunder and take anything they want. They're exterminators and usurpers. They are every nightmare rolled into one highly intelligent and mobile attack squad."

Forman jumped out of his seat and swore like a submarine full of sailors. "You sure?"

"As sure as I was that they were out there."

"How long do we have?"

"I don't know. Not long."

"The scenarios we ran before New York. Those were real?"

"Yes. If my vision is accurate, and again, I'm putting all my faith in something I can't prove, the chance of anyone surviving an attack from the Maleem approaches zero."

"Maleem?"

Zeke winced. He hadn't meant to let that slip. "That's what they're called."

The robot sat down again and fastened his lap belt. "You got all of this in a vision?"

"I know it sounds unlike me, but I can't shake the urgency of that vision. It's as real as you and me sitting here in this sleek airbus."

"You've made me a believer."

"Thanks, I think."

"No problemo." Forman leaned forward. "What's our plan?"

The engines changed tone. The vessel's nose angled down to the Georgia coast. "I'm working on a plan. Logic suggests the best way to avoid annihilation is to keep them off our planet."

"Can we blow them out of the sky?"

"Doubtful. We don't know the composition of their ships, or if they have any shielding capability, and we lack capable long distance weaponry."

"Sounds like a challenge."

"Why are you smiling? This is serious. These invaders plan to kill us all."

"That's their plan. But we've got one thing they don't have."

The air transpo touched down, jarring Zeke physically. "What?"

Forman grinned and pointed at Zeke. "You."

Holy hell.

Talk about pressure.

Chapter 14

Feeling helpless, Zeke watched Uncle John press the remote and raise the head of his sick bed. Machines beeped in the cozy room, adding to Zeke's out-of-phase feeling. He didn't know what to expect, but the doctors hoped for a miracle from the postsurgical nanites they'd injected in his uncle's bloodstream.

Throughout Zeke's youth, Uncle John had been a jovial, outgoing, compassionate man with a fondness for aircraft. He'd bought Zeke any number of small, mechanized planes, but Zeke had taken them all apart to see how they worked. Interestingly, a model plane sat on his uncle's bedside table.

Uncle John's pain-dulled eyes drilled into him. "We've got aliens coming."

"Not your problem, sir," Zeke said, wishing he had magic healing skills to cure his uncle's heart. As it was, he had no choice but to trust that the surgeons and the nanites would repair the problem. "Stress isn't good for you."

"Nonsense. Stress makes the world go around. Tell me more about the situation."

The med team had told Zeke to downplay world news, to keep his uncle isolated from current events. But he'd want to know if their positions were reversed. "There's not much to report. The ships stopped at the furthest edge of our detection radius. Officially, that's the sum of our knowledge."

Silhouetted by the darkening windows on the other side of the bed, Forman made a circular motion with his hand, urging Zeke to confide in his uncle. Zeke shook his head. His *vision* was to remain private.

"But?" Uncle John asked, his fingers curling into the sheets, the knuckles on his hand gleaming like pearls on the vine.

He was treading in dangerous waters here, trying to tell the truth without lying or revealing how he knew things. "But I have a feeling they are trouble."

Uncle John studied Zeke for a very long time. "Your father used to get feelings about things, too. I never understood it, don't want to know the how of it, but he was correct one hundred percent of the time. I'll take those odds to the bank every time. What else can you tell me? What do you need?"

Zeke's breath caught in his throat. "The Institute has already provided beyond my wildest dreams. My setup is state of the art."

"Yeah, you've got a great lab, but I'm talking about the aliens." John struggled to sit, raising up from the pillow, his body swaying like a palmetto frond in the wind. "How will we stop them?"

Zeke and Forman caught his uncle and nestled him back into the support of the bed. "I don't know that part yet, sir. When I do you'll be one of the first I tell."

"I expect to be the first to know. Got that? I need you to step up and take control of this situation. I'm out of commission."

Feeling cornered, Zeke retreated. The glass of water he'd downed on the flight felt as heavy as the planet. "I'm out of my depth, Uncle John, but I'll give it my best shot."

"Do that. You need any scientist on this planet, I'll get 'em for you. Same for technology. You ask, and I'll make it happen."

Zeke's heart raced triple time. As the head of the Institute's covert operations, John Demery was a powerful man. If he asked his uncle for a long-range Oakmont rocket launcher, four Russian cosmonauts, and a troupe of dancing elephants, he had no doubt they'd be on the island first thing in the morning. Barely five hours out of surgery and his uncle was hell-bent on preserving world order.

"Sure, Uncle John. Get some rest. We'll talk in the morning."

"You'll be here?" John's eyes searched both their faces. "You'll both be here?"

Forman edged closer to the bed. "I'm catching the red-eye to Japan tonight, sir. Bea's over there, and she's in trouble."

"What about that bodyguard fellow? Tank. What happened to him?"

Forman made an expression as if he'd sniffed pure hydrogen sulfide. Noxious stuff, that. "Bea fired him for being stoned on the job. I expect we'll hear from Tank when he runs out of dough."

"Stay with Zeke, Forman. That's an order. He's your mission, not the singer."

"Sir, I planned to stay here with you on the mainland," Zeke said. "I don't need to go to the island tonight. Besides, I've already missed the last ferry."

"I can resolve the transpo issue. I want both of you on the island

50

tonight. Promise me that."

Forman shot Zeke an imploring look. Zeke gulped. Everyone wanted something different. How would he navigate through this emotional maze? "You need to get some rest, sir. Forman and I will manage."

Uncle John bolted upright. This time his body did not tremble. "Your father needed to go to the island at times like these. I expect you benefit from the same sort of mental clarity over there. It's in my best interest, hell, the world's best interest, that you are at home tonight, sleeping in your own bed."

Damn if Zeke's knees didn't tremble. His mouth went dry. How much did his uncle know about his alien heritage? John Demery was his mother's brother and not of the extra-terrestrial Taman line. But the man seemed to realize the island held special powers for his species.

He shot a glance over at Forman. What would the robot decide? Would he follow his heart and get Bea? Or would he let Uncle John dictate his whereabouts?

"As you wish," Forman said, with a curt head bow and a hasty exit.

"Excuse me." With a respectful nod to his uncle, Zeke followed the A.I. unit out to a computer station down the hall. "Look, you don't have to stay with me. I'll be fine. Uncle John doesn't have to know where you are until later. Much later. Go get Bea. I've got Uncle John's Nola and a house full of weaponry the likes of which most people have never seen. He's well protected."

Forman shook his head and his fingers flew over the keys. "No. He's right. We're headed to the island. Your safety and the world's future are more important than my unrequited feelings for a woman. My duty is to protect you. I won't let you down."

Zeke's shoulders bowed under the burden of added expectation. "I'm not almighty or infallible. I'm one person. The world has thousands of security experts and space jockeys. You and Uncle John believe a hydrologist is smarter than all of those people combined?"

"I believe you aren't constrained by staid, linear thinking. I believe you are open to possibilities. I believe you can do this. You can save the world."

"Because I confided in you about my, um, episode? That's crazy."

"Not my words. I believe in you. Besides, positive is as positive does."

Zeke groaned. "Now who's talking crazy?"

Chapter 15

Bea danced around the tiny apartment, kicking up her bare feet. "This is wonderfully insane. People are going bonkers, and we're right in the middle of it. I nailed it when I booked our trip here."

Jessie pried her fingers off the baseball bat she'd bought on the black market and leaned it next to the door she'd just locked. The polished stick of wood was the only thing that made her feel safe walking the teeming streets of Tokyo. "I'm glad you're having a great time because we're stuck here. The embassy was absolutely no help. I wish we had one of the guys here."

"Like your hunky scientist?" Bea asked with a knowing wink.

"Sure, Zeke or Forman or Tank. Any of them would make me feel like we weren't one smashed head away from living on the streets."

"Not Forman. He's too controlling. And not Tank either. He likes to party too much. Come to think of it, your Zeke needs improvement, too. He's too straight-laced. Don't expect any of them to come for us. We're on our own."

How could her sister sound so logical in such an illogical situation? Didn't she see the big picture? "We could die here, Bea. Where would your fans be then?"

"Death is very good for a singer's career."

"Not so good for the singer, though."

"Don't be such a downer. We're tough chicks. We've been through worse."

"I don't think so." The ground trembled, and they both leapt for the nearest doorway. "Between the earthquakes, the high chance of another tsunami from the ground disturbances, lack of food and water, and now no way out, we're stuck on this rock. I hate being stuck."

"Wait. No way out. That's catchy," Bea said. "It isn't only our personal needs at stake here. With the aliens circling like sharks, we're a lousy bait ball."

Jessie thought hard about the familiar idea. "Circling sharks. Wasn't there a singer a few gens back who sang about fins and sharks and schooling the bait around? You'd best think up another song idea; wouldn't want you to copy his. Your critics would have a field day screaming about plagiarism."

"That gives me an idea. I could update his song, adapt it to our times. I'll pull it up in a sec, but first, let's check the news." Bea queued up the vid screen. She flipped to the entertainment channel where Pauline and Connor sat spooned together on a fake-looking missile as if they were astride a mighty steed. There wasn't so much as a sliver of air between the two news anchors.

Connor's arm wrapped around Pauline's narrow waist, his other hand was planted between her bare breasts. His masculine air of possession transcended the vid screen.

"That poor guy," Jessie said, drawing close to watch but hating herself for being a voyeur. "Pauline is using him to get ahead. She'd hump a rhino if it raised the ratings. When she moves on, and she will because I know her type, Connor's going to implode."

Suddenly Pauline leaned forward. Because he held onto her so intimately, Connor also seesawed forward. "Wouldja look at that thing go?" Pauline shrilled as a small craft shot out of a fuzzy spaceship, a blaze of exhaust blazing across the twinkling darkness of outer space.

She touched her ear and nodded at the message she'd received. Then she smiled at the camera. "Yay! The aliens are sending a landing party here. Oh, it's going to be so much fun interviewing them. Fire up our air rover, boys. We'll follow them home to the planet." She glanced over her shoulder at Connor. "What should I wear?"

His face clouded. "Body armor. I don't want aliens ogling your tits."

She cupped herself front and center on the vid screen. "Little late for that, lover. The entire world's seen these puppies. I know what I'll do. I'll guide the aliens to the planet with my personal headlights."

"You'll do no such thing." Connor dismounted the missile, his frontal nudity blacked out on the screen. Funny what the censors allowed and what they didn't.

Jessie groaned, wrestled the remote from her sister, and flipped to the music archive before passing the channel selector back to Bea. She couldn't help but feel a tragedy was in the making. If Pauline or the network didn't crush Connor's romance, the aliens certainly would. "Those news people act like horny teenagers. The world doesn't revolve around sex and especially not theirs. I can't believe Entertainment News doesn't violate decency and morality laws. It makes a mockery out of real news programs."

Bea snickered as she keyed in shark as a search term and scrolled through the search results. "Bet Connor's got a woody right now that won't quit. God, I'd love to do him."

"Thought you were done with real men, that a robot was the only way to go."

"That's what I said before kissing Dylan James during our duet music vid. I didn't plan to cheat on Forman."

"But you did. Cheat on him. You enjoyed kissing someone else and would've slept with the man if I hadn't needed a ride home. Dylan is old enough to be our dad, and then some. What are you going to tell Forman?"

Bea shrugged a shoulder, and her wide-neck top slipped off the opposite shoulder. "He's a robot. I don't have to tell him anything."

Jessie gasped at her sister's callous attitude. "He's more than that and you know it."

"He's a pain in the ass and a thorn in my heart. He'll see the kiss and go apeshit. I can't explain why I did it. I was as star-struck as the next groupie over Dylan James. He's still got it."

"And he nearly had you. Did you know he propositioned me before you taped the music vid? He also hit on every female in the cam crew and two of the guys. Dylan considers himself quite the player."

Bea's face fell. "Thanks for the save. You are so good for me, keeping me grounded. Too many people in show biz get swept away by the chemistry of the moment. It's a wonder we're not rabid with sexually transmitted diseases."

Jessie hadn't been tempted by the aging rock star, but her sister was right. The guy had "it" in spades. Bea's campy song fit right into his music lane, and if early sales were any indication, they would both make a bundle off the tune.

Someone pounded on the door. Jessie's heartrate lurched into overdrive. They didn't get visitors at their apartment. As far as the neighbors knew, they were simply two American sisters trying to book a flight home.

Together Jessie and Bea glided toward the door. As Bea checked the peephole, Jessie grabbed the baseball bat. "Who is it?"

Jessie asked through the locked door.

"We come in peace," an Asian woman said.

Chapter 16

"I don't need to power down tonight," Forman said. "I will protect you."

Zeke yawned and flopped down on his bed fully clothed. Home. He was finally home. He hated traveling. In an ideal world, he'd never have to leave Tama Island again.

"Suit yourself," he said. "I don't know what's coming down the pike at us, and I need to be rested to face whatever it is. I could sleep for the next four hundred years. I can't remember ever being this tired."

"Hmm. I suppose the island is safe enough," Forman said. "The people here have a security clearance or have lived here their entire life. I'll do a quick perimeter sweep, and if all is well, I'll also recharge. You're not going swimming in the middle of the night?"

"Fat chance. I'm exhausted. The only swimming I'm doing tonight is right here, right now."

With that, Zeke curled into his pillow and sank into a troubled sleep. He seemed to be alone in a small craft at night. In the distance, a voice insistently called to him, except he couldn't make heads or tails of it. Breathless and fully alert, he burst the thin veil of sleep.

His heart jackhammered against his ribs. He gulped in a ragged breath and strained to see where he was. A plastech dresser. Blinds on the single window, slanted open. A chair by the bed with a pile of laundry on it. Recognition dawned, and he breathed easier.

Home.

He was at home and in his own bed.

The house was quiet, blessedly so.

Rising, he ambled to the window and studied the familiar terrain to steady his heart rate. A crescent moon added a trace of silvery light to the meager plantings around his new home. Nothing moved. Nothing stirred. He glanced back at the rumpled bed. The smart thing to do would be to sleep around the clock.

But the need to communicate with his ancestors persisted.

He couldn't tell Forman about his Taman heritage or his responsibilities as the Guardian. If Forman had truly powered down, this was the ideal window to sneak over to the lighthouse and link with his ancestors. He bypassed his customary flip-flops, choosing sneakers instead. The lighthouse was about half a mile away. Not very far, but far enough that he should hurry to maximize his time there.

Once dressed, he raised the window and climbed out. He waited to make sure the robot hadn't followed. Alone, he jogged to the lighthouse. The cooler night air felt good against his skin. Wouldn't be long and everyone would be wearing a light jacket for the coming winter. Assuming they survived the alien invasion.

Inside the dark lighthouse, he wished he'd thought to bring a flashlight. Since he'd never visited here at night, he hadn't thought this impulse through. Going by feel, he inserted his father's necklace stone into the access slot in the lighthouse interior wall. The panel slid open, and he descended the ladder to the underground room.

A soft light dawned in the chamber. All was as he'd left it. He strode to the transmission chair and climbed in. Though his thoughts raced at the speed of sound, he dampened the crazy what-ifs and opened his mind to the Taman collective.

Finally, his father said. *We've been calling you for hours.*

Sorry. I didn't know. Things are crazy here. I had to travel for work and Uncle John had a heart attack. I only returned to the island late this evening, but I was too exhausted to come down here at first. What's so urgent?

John will be all right? his father asked.

They say he's on the mend.

He's a good man. Look after him. Meanwhile, we've got a treat for you. A survivor. She wants to share her story with you. Ready?

This mindlink works with other species?

In some cases. We've made an adaptation here. Wait a moment.

Not like I've got anywhere to go. Zeke glanced around the interior of his mind. Wouldn't it be nice if he added décor to this dull waiting space in Tween? A sunny window, a recliner or two, maybe some soft music. No, ocean waves instead of music. Perfect. As the room took shape in his head, Zeke nodded in satisfaction at his handiwork. Sweet.

Zeke?

I'm here, dad.

This is Thoren.

A trembling presence entered the link. Zeke felt the individual's fear. Hell, he could smell it. What did one say to an alien? *Greetings, I am Zeke*, he tried.

You want to know about the Maleem?

I do.

The link shuddered. Zeke clung to his reception room he'd envisioned, but he couldn't hear Thoren or his dad, for that matter. Must be burning too much juice on the fancy waiting room. He winked out the furnishings, and the mindlink hummed with energy.

Oh. That's better. You're stronger now, Thoren said.

You see me? He asked, unable to keep the incredulous note from his voice.

I see nothing. I feel you. You Tamans are powerful, as we once were. Our people were too trusting. The Maleem fooled our leaders. They lured us into a false sense of security with trade agreements; all the while, they transported their death machines down to our planet to zap our brains. I was lucky to survive.

How did you survive? What did you do to escape detection?

My grandparents were survivalists. I inherited their place when they ascended, along with their bolt hole. When I realized the imminent danger, I took my closest friends and my kids and hid out there for two weeks. We accessed the grid through ham radio late at night. That's how we learned of the Maleem's treachery. That's how we learned we were the last of our people.

You went underground?

Not just underground. We hid in a mine shaft. The ore disrupted their tracking devices, and we became invisible.

Sounded credible, Zeke thought. *What did they want from your planet?*

Our precious metals. Our water. And our spleens. They killed eight million of us for our spleens. When we emerged after they'd left, bodies were everywhere, bellies ripped open. It was terrible. I'll never forget that sight as long as I live. I should have done something to help my people. I should have been concerned with more than saving my own skin. Hell, saving my own spleen. Maleem don't care about skin.

Zeke blanched as the horrific image insinuated into his thoughts. The Maleem were indeed terrible. Worse, they were on the brink of invading Earth. There was no way Zeke could hide the entire human race below ground before they arrived. He needed more information.

I'm sorry for your loss. What else can you tell me about the

Maleem? What do they look like? Are they little green men?

You got the green part right, but there's nothing little about them. They are fierce warriors and ruthless enemies. Maleem resemble humans physically but don't mistake them for friends. The destruction and havoc they wreak is beyond anything I've ever seen. Take the worst person on your planet and multiply their flaws by a thousand and you have the Maleem.

Oh, this was not good at all. *Anything else? Any weaknesses you remember?*

Thoren held his silence for several agonizing moments. *Don't give them mafut. It makes them crazy.*

Mafut? Zeke asked.

The link hummed silently. *Candy*, his dad interpreted. *Anything with sugar or a sweet flavor sends them right over the edge.*

Great.

That's just what Earth needed.

Sweet-crazed, extraterrestrial warriors.

Chapter 17

"You left the house." Forman said as he flopped down beside Zeke on the sand. "You left your bodyguard behind without as much as a note."

Zeke winced at the terse, chastising tone in Forman's voice. Waves crashed on the shore, the ebb and flow of water spilling reminding him he'd deceived his friendly bodyguard. He didn't ask for this secret life as the planet's Guardian. He'd inherited the role. The best he could do was beg forgiveness. "Sorry. I didn't think to leave you a message. I couldn't sleep so I came down here to sit for a while."

"Figured as much." Forman looked around the shadowed beach. "What is it about this spot that does it for you? It's scenic, but so is this entire island. The marsh view from your back porch is stunning. Why can't you commune with nature there instead of exposed on the beach like this?"

"I've always come here to think."

"I got that. I don't like it, but I understand. You humans are such creatures of habit. You do the same things over and over again."

The onshore breeze ruffled Zeke's hair, cooled his face. Waves crested and spilled on the beach, the white foam resplendent on the dark canvas. "That's brilliant."

"It is?"

"People follow patterns. We can use the fight over the hoarded water to keep it safe."

"Why would we do that? I thought we wanted politicians to like us."

"We do, but we have another agenda. To protect our planet's water from the Maleem."

"They want it? How do you know?"

"I just know." He turned to study Forman. Time to change the subject. "What would it take to divert the remaining surface waters into the underground transportation corridors?"

"Do you have a fever? That's crazy talk. Those things are

watertight. No way can we dump rivers and lakes in them. People spent years figuring out how to keep water out of the tunnels. Their creation was hailed as the greatest engineering marvel of the twenty-first century. We can't undo that."

"Anything is possible. Assuming we had the means to inject the water quickly into the corridors, they'd hold the water, right?"

"Sure. They're watertight."

"We can't hide the ocean, it's too big, but we might hide the Mississippi River and the Great Lakes."

"That's a lot of water to move." Forman leaned back on his elbows. "I'll say this for you, boss. You don't do anything halfway. Here I thought I was coming to do research on a backwater island, and the stakes couldn't be higher."

"My father always said great men step up in times of trial." His dad had made the statement often during heated discussions with his mom. They usually carried their discussion off to another room of the house where he couldn't hear the rest, but he knew from long experience that his parents often made love after their fiery talks. Lucky them.

"Hell, we're going to save the world. I shouldn't have doubted you for a second. Okay, I'm in a hundred percent. Assuming the rest of the world goes along with your novel idea, how would we get this defensive stratagem up the chain of command?"

"Uncle John will take care of that. I'm wondering about the layout of those pod burrows. Are there maintenance corridors beneath the tunnels?"

"I believe so. Why?"

"I'm thinking out loud, exploring our options." Though the breeze added a chilly note to the air, Zeke knew the water temperature would feel comfortable. It was warm enough for a swim even though it was September.

"Can't fool me, Dr. Geek. Hiding people beneath a tunnel full of water is sheer genius. I should do a recon on the mainland's tube system tomorrow. We'll want to snag a primo spot since we thought of the idea."

"Assuming it comes to that, the decision of who gets to hide under the water-filled tunnels will be out of our hands. It's a defensive strategy to be employed if our offense fails."

"And what offense is that? Will we kill them with broadcasts of old sitcoms? Or maybe our space garbage will block their approach."

"Apt, but not funny. I'm working out an offensive plan in my head. Chances are they've tapped into our broadcast sats. Chances are they'll know the rudiments of our language before they land. Chances are they'll come with pretensions of peace and trade agreements."

"You got all that from sitting in the sand?"

"Been thinking about the situation for some time now. Sitting here helps me articulate it to you."

"If they don't display aggressive tactics and world leaders welcome them, who will give the approval to hide the water? It won't seem necessary."

"I didn't say it was a perfect plan. It's a strategy. Whoever is in charge can evaluate the options and make a decision. We're the idea guys."

"Ideas have a way of becoming guns and explosions."

Zeke chuckled at Forman's derisive tone and stared longingly at the water. "I'll protect you, big boy."

"Not needed. If it's guns and bombs, we'll soldier on."

The urge to take a dip wouldn't leave Zeke alone. He toed off his shoes, stood, and stretched. "I feel like a swim."

"At night? Isn't that dangerous?"

"You're here. What harm can befall me?"

"I'm supposed to be guarding you. Guess I'm going in as well."

"Are you watertight?"

Forman rose and shucked off his aloha shirt and shorts. "All entertainment models are sealed. We're often called upon to perform in showers, tubs, and pools. You're my first ocean gig."

Zeke decided stripping for the moonlight swim would send the wrong message to his bisexual android. As he headed for the foaming surf, the need to swim beyond the breakers intensified. He didn't question the reason, just followed the suggestion.

Beside him, Forman dived and dodged waves and laughed like a kid. "This is so cool. No wonder you like swimming in the ocean."

The dolphins surfaced nearby. Zeke strained to see how many were in the pod. Four. Were they his dolphins?

"Wildlife at three o'clock," Forman said, paddling over to Zeke.

Zeke smiled. "They're friendly. I know these dolphins."

"You do? How?"

"We're swimming buddies," he hedged. "Do as I do."

Forman copied Zeke's back float, and the dolphins approached as before, rubbing up against Zeke's hands. First Nicola, then little Boz and the other two. He needed to come up with names for the others at some point. *Good to see you,* he broadcast through his thoughts.

He wasn't sure if he heard a response. It seemed like he was now thinking *"we missed you,"* so he shot back, *"I've been away."*

"Z, you're like Dr. Doolittle. How come I never saw this ultra-hip side of you before?"

Forman's voice disrupted the narrow band of communication in Zeke's head. He caught Nicola's eye and shrugged. "Got a feeling there's more to all of us than we let on."

Chapter 18

"I can't believe they gave us different assignments," Pauline cooed into her personal vid link. She held the wrist cam close to her face so her surroundings didn't show. It wouldn't do for Connor to know she'd gotten tagged to meet-the-aliens in Nevada. He'd hear about it soon enough. And she'd lie and say she'd been sworn to secrecy.

"How're the water riots?" she asked.

"Rough. People are dying of thirst here. Someone needs to step up and make this right. Water needs to be released, yesterday," Connor said, his eyebrows beetling together in concern.

"Great facial expression," Pauline said. "And the right amount of pathos in your voice. Be sure you do it that way on-cam, and you'll silence your detractors. Connor Bronsen isn't yesterday's news, he's hot and current. Women all over the planet will be thinking of how sexy you are throughout the day and into the night. You totally rock."

Connor's smile faded. "I miss you, babe."

Were those wrinkles on his tanned face? Shame on him. "It isn't the same here without you. Pooh on the morality police. I can't believe Entertainment News caved to the lawsuit. Without sex on the news, our ratings will drop twenty percent."

"It is terrible, for them and for us. People will have to watch vids or porn to get off now. This sucks. I don't want to be in Podunk, Idaho reporting on the water shortage."

Pauline waggled her finger at the screen. "Careful what you say. No telling how secure the link is. You wouldn't want to put your job in jeopardy, would you?"

"Screw the job. I want my old life back, the one where we get paid to get it on every day."

"You're ahead of your time, a true leader in network news." At the coded knock on the window, Pauline jolted. "That's my cue. My ride's here. Ta-ta."

She cut the link and pulled down the vanity mirror to insert vibrant green contacts. Never let it be said that she hadn't done her homework. She'd make these little green men feel right at home.

Angling the mirror lower, she checked the front of her thin blouse. The day-bright body paint on her nipples glowed green through her lacy bra and sheer top.

The morality police may have won this round by banning sex from the news, but sex was her stock in trade. She had to work with the tools she had been given, or her broadcast career could blow up same as Connor's.

Her lime green stilettos and pistachio-green pencil skirt emphasized the curves of her legs and hips. God, she looked hot. Alien, hot. She was banking on the outfit gaining her a scoop on their arrival.

Stepping out onto the Nevada tarmac from her transpo vehicle, she noted the dull suits of the male reporters and the slightly more feminine version the handful of females wore. Amid all these dull wrens, her parakeet-bright coloration really stood out. No way would the aliens overlook her in this crowd.

She looked good.

Damned good.

Alien good.

A Secret Service agent escorted her to the knot of reporters and camera operators sweltering in the desert heat. Pauline spoke to the closest woman, a network news star who'd been on primetime for ten years. "Isn't this fun? I've never met an alien before."

The news anchor turned her back to Pauline. "Bitch," Pauline thought. She fluttered her augmented eyelashes at two men. One dropped his notebook he was so flustered. Another guy lolled his tongue like a wolf.

Cool.

She hadn't lost her sex appeal.

Pauline checked out her surroundings. She'd been whisked here in a dark transpo, same as the other media reps. Rows of soldiers and tanks flanked the cluster of media and a smaller pool of well-dressed men. Soldiers and machines sported very large weapons.

Just then everyone pointed to the sky. Pauline dismissed the unidentified flying object in a passing glance, focusing instead on her lanky cameraman. "Stay with me, Bug. As soon as they touch down, I'm gonna run like a gazelle over to stand in front of the dipshit diplomats." She shivered excitedly.

Bug nodded.

The circular craft set down on the tarmac with a hiss of steam, or what looked like steam. Overhead, funny-looking air transpos buzzed around like angry bees. The diplomats quivered with excitement. First contact with another species was a career-making event for all of them.

Pauline smoothed her hair back from her face. "How do I look?"

"You look hot," Bug said, his smile lingering on her headlights. "The aliens won't know what hit them."

She grinned. "Let's hope not. Oh, lookie there, the bottom's folding down to form a ramp. Here they come, and here I go." She hoofed it across the pavement, but so did every other member of the press corps. A row of soldiers broke formation and created a barricade in front of them, kneeling with guns pointed at the ship.

"Damn," she said, checking and finding Bug with her in the front row. "Give me a ten second lead and then aim the cam at the gangplank. We'll be the first network to show vids of the spacemen. You getting the feed, Roz?"

Her boss's voice hummed in her ear. "It's coming into the station fine. Go get 'em, tigress. Here's your chance to prove to the news world you're sexy and smart."

Everything was riding on this. Her future. Her career. Her chance to make love in private. She signaled Bug to start recording. "This is Pauline Curran coming to you live from the alien landing site. I see big boots. White boots. They're marching down the ramp. The aliens have on white armor of some sort. It's form-fitting, and they are buff, let me tell you. Their skin appears to be green, just like Queen Bea said it would be, but there's nothing little about these guys. They look like Vikings.

"I see six aliens in total, their heads enclosed in clear bubbles, as if our air is toxic to them. Wait, the diplomats are speaking to them." Pauline indicated for Bug to get a close-up of the dips. "Warner greeted them in English, and then the other three dignitaries spoke in Spanish, French, and Chinese. The aliens haven't uttered a word. They seem to be looking around, checking things out on our planet."

Pauline moved her mike to her left hand and shaped the "I love you" sign with her right hand. Her repeated movements caught the eye of the tallest alien. He pointed to her with a small object, and a barely visible green beam touched her head.

"Do you see that?" Pauline tugged on Bug's sleeve. He angled the cam tight on her glowing face and the green light. "The alien favored me because I used sign language. Perhaps they don't have ears and communicate by gesturing."

She tried to signal Bug to swing back to film the aliens but her hands wouldn't work. Her insides felt fizzy like a soda bottle about to blow its lid. A wave of intense nausea gagged her. The light. She had to get away from it.

"Something's happening to me. I'm cold inside, and it feels like a giant magnet is pulling me. I can't hold out much longer. It's stronger now, taking ahold of me."

Her feet moved of their own volition as if she were possessed, climbing over a stunned soldier. The mike fell from her hand, clattering on the concrete. "I don't want to move but I can't stop. Don't shoot," she hollered as soldiers aimed weapons at her. "Bug? Help!"

"I can't move," Bug shouted. "None of us can. You're in some kind of alien tractor beam. It's pulling you and repelling the rest of us. Be careful, Pauline."

If only Connor were here. He'd kick alien butt, for sure. That's what she got for stealing this assignment out from under him. And look what it got her? Trouble.

The charged field drew her to the side of the tallest alien and rotated her like a rotisserie chicken. With ice chilling her marrow, she faced her fellow humans. Tears filled her eyes as she realized she was a marionette in the alien's hands. *I'm going to die, right here, right now, and I never told my Mom how much I care. I love you, Mom.*

Oh, God. I'm so gonna die, and I totally deserve it for dumping Connor. I don't want to be anyone's dinner. I want to be respected and revered. And I want a fat bank account.

Yeah right, like Santa would stop at her door.

A rumble filled her head as the tallest one placed his hand on her shoulder. A deep timbered voice emitted from her mouth. "Greetings, inhabitants of planet ZBY34827. My name is Drok. We have traveled far across the cosmos to come here. We, the Maleem, do not speak your language and have selected this life-form to be our mouthpiece. We seek to establish trade agreements with your leaders."

Ambassador Warner's eyes gleamed with excitement. "On behalf of my fellow ambassadors, governments, and citizens of Earth, we welcome you. I invite you to enjoy our hospitality and see our fair planet. You are our first visitors from space."

The buzzing was so loud in Pauline's head, almost as if there were ten people inside talking all at once. Unable to move, she tried to catch Bug's eye, but he was glued to his cam. Figured.

"We accept your offer." Pauline faintly heard a mechanical sound behind her, then the hiss of lift-off as the alien craft rocketed away. "My bodyguards will accompany me on this visit. I require a life-form as a translator. This human will suffice."

Pauline screamed silently, *No! I don't want to be anyone's mouthpiece. F-this. She wanted out of this assignment right now. No exclusive was worth having her mind invaded by aliens. She didn't want the story this bad. Somebody, please help me!*

Not a sound left her throat. Tears welled in her eyes.

All smiles, Ambassador Warner nodded at Drok. "Whatever you need. Say the word, and it's yours."

Chapter 19

"You come in peace? That's hysterical," Jessie laughed switching her bat to the other hand as she opened the door to Sammie Liu, Dylan James' tour manager. They'd met her when Dylan and Bea collaborated in Dylan's sound studio a few days ago. The Asian woman wore her usual form-fitting leather pants and halter top. Jessie tucked the baseball bat under her arm and waved the woman inside. "Come in."

"Thought you'd appreciate my humor." Sammie's dark eyes and her shimmering waist-length hair gleamed as she flounced in the Stemfords' tiny apartment. "You're not planning to bean me, are you?"

Jessie propped the bat by the door, which she closed and locked. "If I could buy a gun in Japan, you'd be staring down its barrel. A baseball bat was all we could find for protection, and I paid an outrageous fee to get it."

"It's the weapon of champions," Sammie said as she grabbed Bea and hugged her. "There are more baseball bats being sold for security purposes these days than were ever made for the defunct game of baseball."

Sammie hugged Jessie next, but the strong aura of desperation surrounding their guest made Jessie wary. Jessie trusted her intuition enough not to take Sammie on face value.

"You guys ready to get off this rock?" Sammie asked.

Jessie nodded. "Past ready. But flights are grounded. No one's getting in or out."

"Have no fear. We have a way," Sammie said. "Are you in?"

"Yes!" Bea shouted. "You're our salvation! What's the plan?"

"Dylan has one more stop on his concert tour in Japan. He's performing tomorrow in Hiroshima, which is five hundred miles away, so we're hopping on the bullet train tonight. We have a whole train car to ourselves. After the concert, he's arranged a moonlight boat excursion, but it's really a slow boat to South Korea. We can book a flight to the U.S. from there."

Jessie didn't share Bea's excitement. "A boat ride? What about the tsunamis?"

"The Sea of Japan, or the East Sea as the Koreans call it, is protected from ocean. Monsoons and eight-foot swells are the worst we'd face. Those are standard fare around here, and the boats and captains know how to navigate them."

"Why isn't everyone doing this if it's so easy?" Jessie hated the spoilsport look Bea shot at her and wished she could blindly trust everything would turn out fine. But it wasn't in her nature to be so gullible.

Sammie shrugged in a fluid motion that was both sexy and aloof. "Folks in Tokyo can't get through the security checks to the southern city. But Dylan has the right pass with room for more, and he knows you guys are stuck, too. And since Bea sang the duet with him, he could tell the guards she's on the concert program."

The explanation sounded logical and feasible. Still, Jessie didn't trust the woman. She didn't trust anyone who refused to make eye contact with her. "What will it cost us?"

Sammie's eyebrows waggled. She gave a throaty laugh. "He likes Bea a lot."

Jessie's heart sunk. Dylan expected Bea to sleep with him. "We need to discuss this in private."

"Suit yourself," Sammie said. "I'll wait in your lobby for twenty minutes. Then I have to meet the train. You're either with me or stuck here."

Jessie let Sammie out and stared at her sister. "No way are we doing this."

Bea brushed passed her and started throwing clothes at her suitcase. "Why not? I hate feeling caged up in this two-room apartment. So what if we're on a waiting list to leave? We're way down the list and have a long wait once the flight ban is lifted. If I have to sleep with Dylan James to get us off this rock, I'll do it."

"Bea!" Jessie grabbed for her sister's arm, but Bea twisted away. All they'd worked for, all they'd done came down to this moment. "This is a bad decision. We'll find another way. Dylan is … bad."

"He's not the anti-Christ. He's a man. I can handle him."

Jessie trailed after her sister, desperate to make her to see reason. "This is a terrible mistake. You're putting your reputation on the line. I don't approve."

Bea bustled around scooping up belongings and her notebooks.

"Suit yourself. I'm going with or without you."

Jessie heard the rustle of plastic as Bea grabbed her toiletry supplies from the bathroom. "Dylan James is major bad news. You know it. Sammie's not telling us everything."

"Why would she lie to us?"

"I don't know. But she's lying. I'm sure of it."

Bea made a pass through the bathroom. "How do you know?"

"My intuition."

"We're sisters, and we make our own decisions. I respect your opinions, but this is my choice. You can choose to go or stay. I'll respect your decision." Bea snapped her suitcase shut.

Heart in her throat, Jessie edged closer. "We've stuck together through thick and thin."

"There's a difference between us, Jess. I live my life. You sit on the sidelines."

Jessie recoiled as the barb struck home. "That's mean. And it's totally untrue."

"I'm not afraid to take a chance. That's what this is – a chance. I'm grabbing the brass ring. I won't cower in this apartment any longer. I want to live."

She'd never seen her sister so enraptured by an idea. Jessie deepened her voice. "As your manager, I'm telling you this is a bad idea. I've heard ugly rumors about Dylan on tour. Orgies. Injectables. Rough stuff. You're better than that."

Bea paused at the door, case in hand. "My mind's made up. I'm going."

The door slammed, and Jessie's world exploded. Bea was making a terrible mistake. Dylan would chew her up and spit her out in little pieces. In the past, she'd protected her little sister from the rougher side of life. She'd steered her away from bad choices. Bea usually listened to her.

Not today.

Five seconds ago her sister walked out the door, out of Jessie's life, and into the arms of a man who had taken drug experimentation to new heights. Or lows, depending on your point of view.

Her little sister.

Pimping herself out to a wild man.

No way was she turning her sister loose on a slow boat to anywhere with a nasty user like Dylan James. Bea would try anything the rocker suggested, and do it just for the experience.

From what Jessie'd read about the new injectables, one hit and you were hooked for life. She wouldn't let the aging musician turn Bea into a drug addict.

Not while she had a breath in her body.

She grabbed her purse and bolted out the door. "Wait for me!"

Chapter 20

"The Maleem have landed, and they have Pauline Curran from Entertainment News," Forman announced after Zeke silenced his four a.m. wake-up alarm.

Startled out of a dream where he'd been running and running, Zeke gasped for air and context. He sat up, rubbing his head. It was still dark outside, but Forman's bright pink flamingo shirt had a glow of its own. "What? Who?"

"The aliens. While we were swimming with the dolphins and sleeping, the aliens sent a scouting party here. They don't speak our language but somehow they're communicating through Pauline."

Zeke reached for his clothes. How could he mount a defense against the Maleem if they were already here? How could he have slept through such an important event? "Am I hearing you right? Maleem are on the planet? They've got the woman who has sex on the news?"

"Yes and yes. What are we going to do about it?"

"We're going to get some caffeine and protein and digest this news. Why didn't anyone contact us?"

"Power problem. Be right back." Forman left and returned with breakfast goodies. "Here you go. Power grid went down, and there were rolling blackouts across the planet. Plus everything that's bounced up to a satellite and back isn't working."

Zeke accepted the coffee and drew a cautious sip of the steaming beverage. "You think the Maleem did this?"

"It's certainly possible. I'd venture to say it's highly probable."

"How'd they do it? Did all of humanity lay on its back for the aliens?"

"The Institute has rad recovery capabilities. Your uncle pinged me two hours ago on the new high-level encrypted line. We have power restored and access to global news feeds now."

"Damn. Why didn't you wake me?"

Forman handed Zeke a protein bar and motioned him to the vid setup in the great room. "Your uncle said you needed to rest, but he's expecting to hear from you as soon as you're fully briefed."

In front of Zeke, three screens of news flashed. Banners of news flitted across each screen along with flickering images. Where to start? "God, I wish I was a robot like you and could plug into the grid for instant information."

"You finally acknowledge I'm a more advanced being than you?"

"The judge and jury are still out on the humanity versus artificial intelligence debate. I don't know which one of us is smarter. I'm pretty damned smart. So are you."

Forman cued up the first contact footage. "The best feed is from Entertainment News. The cam guy was right beside Pauline when she came under their control."

"What's that green beam?" Zeke asked, walking closer to the large screen. His disappointment at missing the big event was eclipsed by the mystery of the pulsing light. How did that thing work?

"Don't know. It appears to have taken control of her body and mind. If Pauline's still conscious, she's being totally suppressed by the alien entity."

"Complete mind control? How's that even possible?"

"With an alien gadget and stolen power from across the globe," Forman quipped back. "From what I can glean snooping through various intelligence sites, the CIA spooks are pissed because the aliens block all monitoring devices around them."

"This is not good. Our enemy has boots on the ground in our territory. How many are in this forward party?"

"Six are all anyone has seen. That's Drok and five bodyguards."

"Someone must have flown their ship back into orbit."

"Not necessarily. They could have an A.I. component on board. Or some version of autopilot."

"Given their electronic scrambling and power-sucking ability, how would a robot function in that hostile environment?"

"Maybe they've got carbon-based life forms running the ship. We have no data."

"Good point. We need data to assess their strengths and weaknesses."

"They look strong. They must be smart to travel this far. They seem to be savvy about diplomacy. I'm not seeing any obvious weakness."

"What do they eat?"

"No one's seen them take off the helmeted spacesuits. They don't appear to eat anything. Even the food sent to their room for Pauline remains untouched. Perhaps they're A.I.'s like me."

"Trust me on this, they are carnivores, and humanity is this group's next banquet."

"You sound like every bad science fiction movie ever made."

"I wouldn't know, but I need to get close to the Maleem to study them. Why are they green? Is their blood iron-free? Do they have symbiotic algae in their nervous system? Let's catch the first ferry back to the mainland. Uncle John can arrange for me to get close to Drok. I have something else I need to discuss with Uncle John anyway."

"Like giving me a free pass to Japan to bring Bea and Jessie home?"

"That, too."

Forman clicked a few keys. "Bad news. The ferry is down this morning, and the choppers are grounded due to the power outages. We're stuck on this sand heap."

"We can row back to Uncle John's house. I've done it before."

"Great. Manual labor. Maybe your dolphin buds will grab hold of the anchor line and pull us to shore." Forman fiddled with a few more keys. "What's this? Oh, no!"

"What now? Isn't it enough that aliens have set foot on our soil?"

"Bea and Jessie left Tokyo on the bullet train to Hiroshima. They're traveling with Dylan James. He's giving a concert there tonight."

"So?"

"Jessie's very worried. She said if there's any way we can get over there we should come immediately. I have to leave right now."

"This is a bad time to be in an airplane. Rolling power outages and aliens in orbit – the sky is the most vulnerable place on the planet. You wouldn't want the engines to fail while you were aloft."

Uncle John's face flashed on the vid screen. "You're up. About damned time."

Zeke moved to stand in front of the vid cam, wishing he'd had a moment to shave his beard-stubbled face. "Good morning, Uncle John. You look very alert and peppy for someone recovering from heart surgery."

"Nothing good about today. The Maleem are here, and the

76

power grid's fried."

"We think the events are related," Zeke began.

"I need proof."

"How about a beam of power leading off planet? Would that be proof enough?"

His uncle leaned in close to the cam. "Did you find something like that?"

"We're looking, sir," Zeke said. "But you were right about the island clearing my head. I feel certain that everyone should get underground as soon as possible."

"Why?"

"Protection. Quietly move as many people as you can to safety. The deeper underground, the better. If possible, divert surface water to fill up the transit pod corridors. People can hide in the maintenance sections beneath the tunnels."

"Easier said than done. It took a generation to build those corridors."

"If the aliens stole our power without our permission, they'll help themselves to our water. If they take it, we won't have it. We can't survive without water."

"Still. Flooding those tunnels is a drastic measure. It will be noticed."

"Not if the outages are passed off as routine maintenance."

"I expect a detailed implementation plan within the hour."

"It'll have to wait. We're headed to the mainland by rowboat. Forman wants to go to Japan to rescue Bea and Jessie. I'm coming over to work at your place."

Uncle John's bushy eyebrows rose. "Both of you stay put. I need you at your best to fight this global threat."

"I need to get close to the alien to learn his deficiencies, Uncle John. I can't study him remotely. I need to make personal observations. See if you can obtain his travel schedule before I arrive."

"Damn."

The coffee in Zeke's stomach churned at his uncle's thunderstruck tone. "Come again?"

"The aliens are touring the planet. From Nevada, they flew to Paris and Cairo. They're in Mumbai, India now and reportedly headed to Beijing. Or Japan. My sources can't confirm. After that, it appears they will fly to Sydney, Australia and Sao Paulo, Brazil."

Zeke grinned. "Sounds like I'm headed to Asia with Forman. One-stop shopping. Piece of cake."

"Any chance you'd stay home and let me send someone in your stead?"

"No way."

Chapter 21

Connor Bronsen wished he could strip out of this constricting suit and tie and don an orange robe like the protestors he was featuring on a news segment. A few months ago he'd thought members of this back-to-nature group were complete idiots; now he identified with their cause. He wanted to save his planet and his girlfriend who'd been kidnapped by the galactic visitors.

"Zoom in on the girl with the thick braids, just left of center, second row," he urged Marni, his cam operator. "She looks the most passionate about the cause."

Marni obligingly zeroed in on the dark skinned woman. In a field of people who seemed to be on autopilot, this woman lit up the screen. "She's fantastic," Connor muttered for Marni's ears only. "After I intro the story, transition to the hot black chick for a few seconds then pan out to show the size of the crowd. If I don't win an award nomination for this clip, the bosses are deaf, dumb, and blind."

His producer Roz rumbled in his ear. "Nice choice. You're on the air in three, two, one."

Connor turned on the charm as the cam light shone in his face. "We're here in Birmingham, Alabama, the site of one of many unified protests across the globe. The greenies, as they're commonly known, are against negotiations with the space visitors. This grassroots organization has fueled a worldwide protest to focus awareness on the danger of sending our products and resources off world. They've refused to speak with us individually and instead want their collective voice to be heard."

Marni swiveled to focus on the expressive woman. Her orange robe billowed as she jabbed a poster into the air. "Save our resources," she chanted with her peers. Her poster read, "Aliens, go home." All the posters had negative messages about the aliens.

The fury in the protestor's eyes seared into Connor's soul. What was he doing in Birmingham? He should've quit his job to rescue Pauline. But Roz had told him there was nothing he could do, that the diplomats would make sure Pauline received humane treatment.

He didn't believe the dips could do anything.

"Close it out, Connor," Roz hissed in his ear.

He jolted back to the reality of news reporting. "This is Connor Bronsen reporting to you live for Entertainment News, the network that's first with news, first with views."

"It's a wrap," Roz said. "Catch the tube to Nashville and interview that aging country singer tonight. I'll see you here at the station first thing in the morning. We need to talk about your future at E News."

Connor's flagging spirits revved three notches. "You're moving me back to an anchor slot?"

"We'll talk tomorrow," Roz said before she cut the connection.

Connor caught the mobile transpo to the tube station with Marni. As he went through the motions of commuter travel, his unfortunate lifestyle now that he'd been busted back to roving reporter, his thoughts whirled like transpo tires. Which was more important, his job or his heart? He wanted to say his heart, because his heart was broken and he felt like shit, but he'd never been one to hold on to his money. If he didn't work, he'd be flat broke.

Life sucked.

That thought stayed with him during his tube ride to Nashville and throughout his interview. Millie Carterman, the aging country star, caught his hand as he was leaving. "I'm sorry to hear about your girlfriend," she said in her trademark whiskey-roughened voice.

"I'm lost without her," Connor admitted, feeling relieved to speak about his heartache, even though Millie was a stranger. "I want to marry her, but I don't even know where she is."

"Love's got a dark side, and it wallops us regularly. You and Pauline have good chemistry together, and I see how much you miss her. Why aren't you going after her?"

"I can't. My job. The aliens. What can one person do against so many?"

Millie smiled sadly. "People have been asking that question throughout time. One person can make a difference. One person can literally move mountains. You want Pauline? Then you better go get her or she'll be forever lost to you."

"My boss won't be happy if I walk off the job."

"When are bosses happy anyway? Get a new boss. There's plenty of them to go around."

"I want to go after her, but I don't know where to go, where to look."

"Seems to me those aliens are getting the star treatment. They've been to New York, Rome, Jerusalem, and Bombay. I suspect they'll visit Beijing next."

"How do you know?"

"Through history and especially in the last thirty years, those cities have served as religious Meccas. The Maleem claim they're here for trade agreements, but they seem to be searching for enlightenment. If I was searching for Pauline, I'd head to Beijing."

At the suggestion, Connor's blood rushed to his wobbly knees. He'd already done a bit of investigating on transports, with negative results. "It isn't safe to fly. Air transpos are falling out of the sky. Twenty planes crashed today."

"Never said it would be easy, kiddo. But you want her, go get her."

It was a hare-brained stunt even for him, but the more he thought about it, the more he wanted to make a bold move. "Good idea."

Chapter 22

Forman worked the oars as fast as he could, pushing the small craft across the choppy sound with mighty strokes. Facing backward to row, it was impossible to miss the rise and fall of fins behind the boat. "You want to tell me why the dolphins are following us?"

"Nothing to tell," Zeke said with a glance at the darkening sky as his hand trailed in the water. "Storm's coming."

His boss had a droll sense of humor. "No kidding. But is the storm human, alien, or Mother Nature?"

"Likely some of each. We're still in hurricane season for a couple more months. I wouldn't be surprised if a large storm system is headed this way."

Forman accessed the weather information he'd downloaded before they left the island. "There are several events south and east of us with hurricane potential, but none are predicted to come ashore in Georgia."

"That's one of the best kept secrets of my state. The Georgia shoreline is recessed from the ocean. Most major storm systems bang into Florida or head for the Carolinas. With a very few notable exceptions, we get through hurricane season with only some high winds and heavy rain. Let's hope that's the case this year."

Was Zeke talking solely about the weather? Or was Forman supposed to read between the lines? It was hard to tell with Dr. Z. He tried the direct approach. "What about the aliens? How will we stop them?"

"Too soon to tell. We haven't detected any vulnerabilities. They're a formidable foe."

"I'd rather have a hurricane come this way than the aliens. At least we know what to expect from a hurricane."

"Careful what you wish for." Zeke glanced around the sound again, his hand still in the water. He froze in place.

"What is it?" Forman asked.

Zeke leaned forward, his voice just loud enough to be heard. "I have the strong sense we're being watched, but I don't see anyone."

Forman heaved the oars up through the air and down into the water. "Could be the dolphins following us."

"Nah. The dolphins feel different."

"Really? You're a dolphin whisperer?"

Zeke blushed and settled back into his seat. "Don't read too much into our swim last night or their presence here today. I've coexisted with these dolphins for years. I am very comfortable around this pod, that's all. But the feeling I have of being watched isn't going away. It's the way I feel when someone glances at me across a crowded room. Only there's no one in sight."

Forman felt obliged to point out the obvious. "Don't forget the satellites orbiting the planet. Spook technology being what it is, any one of them up there could count the hairs in your nose."

"Through the cloud cover? That's impressive."

After a few more beats of oars in water, Forman had a blinding revelation. "We're not thinking this through. Maybe the aliens have some super-snooping capability. Maybe the aliens are watching us."

"How would they even notice us in the ocean? Why would they notice us? Nothing too special about the pair of us."

Forman laughed at the absurdity of that statement. He was the most advanced robot ever built, and Zeke was the smartest man on the planet. "You're a riot." A few raindrops started to fall. Forman applied himself to rowing. They were almost out of the sound and into a tidal creek. The nautical chart of all the creeks surfaced in his head. "About Bea and Jessie. There's a commercial flight out of Atlanta we can take to Japan if we get there in the next three hours."

"We'll get there."

"Your uncle..." Forman's voice trailed off. So much depended on the humans making the right call. He didn't trust them to get this right.

"I'll convey the urgency to Uncle John, don't worry about that. We're making good time across the water."

Because I'm rowing my buns off, Forman thought privately. What was with Zeke anyway? He seemed distracted and agitated. Was it the alien's proximity to Jessie? Was it because he couldn't reach Jessie?

The rain fell steadily, accumulating in the bottom of the craft. The dolphins surfaced back at the mouth of the creek. They hadn't followed the boat to shore. And Zeke had withdrawn his hand from the water as soon as they crossed into the creek. Something was definitely up with Zeke and the dolphins. But what?

"Did you check my messages before we left Tama Island?" Zeke asked.

"I did. You had a message from Dr. Anika Fischer of the Global Water Federation during the night. Seems there's a problem with the water distribution system."

"We voted already. It's out of my hands. Fischer is trying to make an issue of this to prolong her status as leader of the water alliance. If you get a moment at Uncle John's send her a query asking for more details. That should stall her for a day or so."

"Will do." He glanced over his shoulder to see the dock coming up fast. "We're there."

Zeke secured a bow line around a metal cleat. Forman did the same with the stern line. They stepped on the dock, Zeke bending first to gather his gear sack. Forman carried the other two bags for their trip.

Before they'd gone five paces, John Demery's assassin robot, Nola, stepped out of the shadows, a blaster in her hand. Forman dropped the bags and tried to block her access to Zeke. She was too fast for him.

The red targeting light of her weapon glowed over Zeke's heart. "You will come with me."

Chapter 23

Water.

Must have water.

Pauline felt too weak to move off the cot in the dark room. For two days straight, she'd been a puppet for the Maleem. They'd finally put her in this tiny cell and taken away that awful green beam. For the first time in what seemed like forever, she could think her own thoughts, and all she wanted to do was sleep.

She was so tired. She couldn't even lift her head to try to escape. Sleep swallowed her whole. In her dreams, she fell from a great height, hurtling through the air to certain death. She awakened later, coming out of her troubled sleep into full alertness. Her pulse pounded like tribal drums. Where was she?

Fragments of the last two days careened through her head, banging into the side of her brain like crashing race cars. So many international cities, so many people fawning over the damned Maleem. Fools, one and all. She couldn't read the Maleem's thoughts, but she'd felt enough of their unspoken intent during the link to know that the Maleem planned to scavenge every marketable resource they could from the planet.

She drew in a cautious breath. The room smelled stale, but the air smelled like Earth. Hopefully, she still had a chance of obtaining her freedom. Those damned dignitaries had thrown her under the bus to curry favor with the extraterrestrials.

She'd cry if she had any moisture to spare, but that wouldn't help her escape. Every muscle in her body ached from the strain of being a captive. She needed water and food and she'd give anything for a shower and a toilet. Slowly, making as little noise as possible, she sat up. Nothing jumped out of the dark at her.

So far, so good.

She pushed her discarded stilettos out of the way. If she ever saw another pair of heels, it would be too soon. Fuzzy pink slippers were what she craved, slippers and a gallon of drinking water. Please, dear God, let there be food and water in this room.

Her fingers encountered a light switch. Did she dare flip it on?

Would it signal she was awake? That wasn't a risk she was willing to take. With one hand on the wall, she tiptoed around the enclosure. It wasn't very big, possibly a closet? There was nothing in the room but her and the cot. She tried the door, ever so quietly. Locked.

Damn.

She slumped back on the cot. Her eyes were so dry and tired. Wait. She could take out the green contacts, and she didn't even care if her hands weren't clean. She pulled them both out and threw them on the carpet. Perversely, her eyes still ached.

Stone cold reality hit like a sledgehammer. She was a prisoner here. Without water she would die. From what little science she remembered, a person could go about three days without water, longer without food. Obtaining water was her top priority.

Where are you, Connor?

Aren't you coming to rescue me?

What was she thinking? The big goof had probably already stepped into her news anchor shoes and was likely making his way into the beds of the entire female crew. That had been his M.O. before she teamed up with him in the reporter pool. He'd been her ticket out of obscurity, and her plan had worked fine until these damned aliens showed up.

She curled into a tight ball, her heart and spirit so fragile that it wouldn't take much to break either one. Her head ached, and she wanted to go home.

She wanted her mother.

Was she a woman or a wimp? She had options. Those stilettos, for instance. She could write a message on the wall with the heel of one shoe. Heartened by that idea, she summoned the energy to sit up and scratch the word help and her name into the wall.

She'd just settled back in the cot when the door opened, and the green beam ensnared her again. She screamed as she went under, hoping her protest would be heard. There were rules about this sort of thing. The Geneva Convention. Yes, that was it. Prisoners had rights and rules.

She arose from the bed as if in a trance as her mental processes dampened to near zero. Shit. She hated this. Though she wanted to stop moving, her bare feet plodded forward, out of the small closet of a room, and into the main room. She'd learned that if the green beam was employed to make her move, it couldn't dampen her entire brain and she had access to her own thoughts.

She didn't have the tall alien this time, merely an underling operating the green beam. He matched her height but he was muscled through the chest and arms like Connor. Why didn't these Maleem take off their armor or their helmets? Was the air here lethal to them?

Dear heaven, she hoped so.

The first thing she'd do if she got away from the beam would be to break those damn globes on their heads. She'd love to see them suck wind. And explode. Yes. They deserved a most painful death.

On a table near the door sat a pitcher of water and a basket of fruit. Her mouth watered. She tried to speak, but couldn't. Instead, she did her best to mentally shout her need of water to the minion holding the controller beam. He didn't respond, forcing her to stand at the other side of the door like a statue. He placed the beam on a table across from her and lounged in a soft chair.

The beam flickered a bit, and her thoughts strengthened. The water was so close she could smell it, but she couldn't move a finger to get it for herself.

It was so frustrating to be paralyzed like this. For most of her life, she'd used sex appeal to get her way. These Maleem had robbed her of that. They appeared not to notice that she had a great body. They were not interested in her as a female, only as a mouthpiece.

Another guy came in the far door, still not the head honcho, and her guard hopped to his feet and stood soldier straight. The new guy punched him in the shoulder, and they both sat down. Why didn't they talk so she could figure out what they were all about?

Sensation flitted painfully through her fingers and toes. The beam pulsed intermittently. Her heart pumped faster. Could she be so lucky? Could the beam need new batteries or whatever made it go?

She snatched in a deeper breath and inhaled the fruity aroma of grapes and apples. And heavenly water. What should she do? Try to bash both their heads in? Run as fast as she could? Scream?

With two of them and one of her, her chances of escape weren't great. Chances were this place was isolated. No one would hear her cries for help. Without water, she wouldn't be able to go very far.

Water was her top priority. If the beam went out altogether, she'd run to the table with water and fruit. Little by little feeling returned to her body. As inconspicuously as possible, she shifted her stance, flexing her knees, rounding her shoulders. The beam's light grew fainter until it winked out.

Her thoughts roared back.

She was free.

She hurried to the refreshment station and drank greedily from the pitcher. The rustle of clothing behind her alerted her that her guards were nearby. A thick musk pervaded the room. It was their smell.

She hated it.

She hated them.

Without conscious thought, she whirled in her bare feet, pitcher in hand, and coshed the nearest guard on his fishbowl of a helmet. To her delight, the clear material splintered. The man's panicked reaction of trying to hold onto the growing cracks made her laugh hysterically.

His companion also tried to plug the holes. She dashed to the nearest door. Locked from the outside. Damn. She tried the other door. Locked as well. This was not happening. She ran to the window and looked out. No balcony and they were high in the air. A skyscraper.

Her hopes crumbled.

She couldn't leave the room.

Fear returned, and with it the urge to see what the guards were doing. The one she'd hit lay still on the Oriental carpet, the other one cradling his head. Through the clear viewing visor, she noticed tears rolling down the helmeted guard's face.

Intrigued, she crept nearer. The musky smell intensified, and she inhaled deeply. The more she breathed, the more she craved. Whatever was in that helmet had leaked out into the room, and it was the most wonderful smelling thing in the world. She had to have more.

The guard shoved her away.

He couldn't do that.

She had as much right as anyone to smell that enchanting fragrance. If she didn't get more, she'd die. Emboldened by the aroma, she pushed the guard away, sniffing at the man's pale green face. His mouth lay ajar as if he'd been trying to say something. The alluring scent pervaded his skin, his mouth. Sniffing like a hound, she peeked inside, seeing blackened teeth and a stub where the tongue used to be. Gross.

No wonder these green guys didn't talk.

They couldn't.

Double gross.

She shoved away from the dead guy, and a faint whiff of the scent rose from his deflating clothing. She leaned down and inhaled deeply. Ah. What a rush. Her head cleared, and she seemed to be dancing in the most beautiful ballroom in the world. Swooping and turning in a glittering gown.

Then the music stopped. The image faded to the luxurious chamber. She grabbed her spasming throat and fell to the floor, the ornate ceiling spiraling further and further away. Her body shuddered and twitched. It convulsed.

A shred of consciousness remained. She clung to it for as long as she could.

The light flickered.

A shadow passed over her.

Drok.

He wasn't wearing a helmet.

His jagged smile followed her straight down into hell.

Chapter 24

Zeke glared at his uncle's robot. "Is there a problem here?"

Nola lowered her weapon, stepped aside, and waved them through. "No problem. Merely a precaution."

"Understood." In these uncertain times, folks had a right to be jittery, and his uncle more than most. As head of the Institute's clandestine activities worldwide, any number of people wanted John Demery out of commission. Which only made his uncle more determined to survive and outlive them all.

While Nola moved their small boat to cover, Zeke strode under the shielded canopy to the big house. This meeting with his powerful uncle had the potential to blow up in his face. His needs conflicted with his uncle's needs.

"Whew. That was close," Forman said in a church whisper. "I thought she was going to shoot us."

"My uncle is cautious. I would do the same in his position."

"We need to be in and out of here in record time, or we'll miss the flight."

Zeke eyed the stately columns in the shaded garden. It wasn't too long ago that this colonnade had hosted a deadly battle. "I am well aware of that need."

"The girls are depending on us."

"The girls never should have gone to Japan," Zeke groused.

"We'll find them and bring them home. If anything happens to my Bea, I don't know what I'll do."

Zeke walked faster and prayed his uncle was in a reasonable mood.

Uncle John met him at the door in a motorized scooter and ushered them into the living room. His color was much better today. "I'm surprised to see you."

Zeke remained standing. "Not that surprised. We told you we were coming. Plus, you had Nola ambush us at the dock."

A fleeting smile crossed Uncle John's lips. "A test to see if you were on your toes. What did you discover?"

Might as well give the man what he wanted. "Last night I

thought about the visitors some more. If it was water they wanted, they could have stopped at several moons on the way to Earth. They're after something else, something that's extremely valuable to them."

"What?" his uncle said. "If I knew the target, I could initiate protection."

"I need to get close to them, but first I need to get to Japan."

"The Stemford sisters?"

Aware of his uncle's steely gaze, Zeke hardened his reply. "Yes."

"They're not mission-critical."

"They are to us, sir."

"We have to save them," Forman added. "They made a mistake. They shouldn't have to pay for it with their lives. But we have to hurry to catch a commercial flight, or all is lost."

"How touching. Two of my top personnel sidelined with girlfriend issues. I never would have thought I'd say that about the pair of you."

"I respect your differing opinion, Uncle John, and I hope you can respect my decision. I have my travel screen, and we can remain in close contact on the alien problem. As soon as Jessie and Bea are safe, I'll focus on the visitors one hundred percent."

His uncle said nothing for an eternity of seconds. "Figured you'd say that."

Forman tugged Zeke's arm. "We have to go."

Zeke hesitated, sensing this was a critical turning point in his relationship with his uncle and boss. Would his decision cost him his job? Would his uncle become vindictive over Zeke's temporary defection?

"Not so fast," Uncle John said. "I have a proposition."

"I'm listening," Zeke replied.

"Certain perks come with my job, including transpo. Very fast air transportation. If I get you to Japan posthaste, will you abide by my authority and work on the alien problem?"

"I will."

"In that case, Nola will fly you to Atlanta in my Gull, then you'll travel to Japan via my ML4. You'll be there by nightfall."

Forman whistled. "How'd you get a ML4? I thought only the President had one of those superfast jobbies."

"I have connections." He fixed Zeke with a stern look. "I'm

counting on you. We're all counting on you."

"I won't let you down."

"Anything I should get started on while you're jetting off to Japan?"

"One thing I wondered about. If the Maleem are here to restock their pantry with people, they might've begun harvesting them from the planet. Could you check in Nevada, Paris, and Cairo to see if there is an unexplained rise in the number of missing persons?"

Alarm flared in Uncle John's eyes. "Wouldn't we know if they invaded our air space?"

"Maybe. But maybe not. They may have shielding technology we can't detect. They may be able to sit in a shielded vessel, get a lock on their prey, and transport them to their ships without us even knowing. It won't hurt to check to see if my suspicions are on track."

"Can do. Anything else?"

"We need to be ready for any kind of attack. Military. Biological. Or even a manipulation of our climatic events. Assume they will strike our communications and power grids. Stockpile basics. Move key personnel to safety deep underground. Do this without the public's knowledge, or you'll have mass panic on your hands and the aliens will learn our plans. Stealth is important."

Uncle John beamed. "Now you're talking my language."

Chapter 25

Jessie hunched over the coffee pot, listening for the dripping to stop. It seemed like the only constant in her life was coffee. She stifled a yawn and stretched, glad to be on the move again.

Despite her worst fears, Dylan James hadn't pulled any surprise punches. Sure, his private car on the bullet train from Tokyo had been a wild party with plenty of booze and drugs for the taking. Jessie had kept a watchful eye on her partying sister during the trip, and her vigilance paid off with a disaster-free trip to Hiroshima.

Upon arrival, they'd followed Dylan onto a people-mover to the Royal Atom Hotel, three blocks from the concert venue. He'd invited them to stay in his suite, but Jessie had insisted on separate rooms. Thankfully Bea hadn't fussed about that.

"Morning," Bea said, wandering out of the bedroom to the tiny kitchen area. "Do I smell coffee?"

"Yep. It's almost ready."

"I checked out a few things on the com last night. There are lots of places I want to explore today. What sounds like the most fun to you? The Atomic Bomb Dome, the peace site, the history museum, or the Five Story Pagoda?"

Jessie liked this plan. Sightseeing would keep Bea occupied and out of Dylan James' clutches. She poured out two cups of coffee and handed one to her sister. "They all sound great. I'm most interested in the peace site and the museum, if that suits you."

Bea sipped her coffee. "Agreed. Just need my caffeine infusion and a shower and I'll be ready to hit the streets."

She sat and activated the tabletop com to check her messages. With traveling and getting settled last night, she hadn't accessed her combox messages for a few days. She scrolled through the list, intending to go back and read them all more closely, but one message stuck out.

"Uh-oh," she said.

"What?" Bea asked.

Jessie transferred the view to the wall screen. "Look. Between my electronic bank statement and my history ezine. Anon sent us something new."

She disliked the anonymous aspect of these messages. "Why can't Anon use his or her real name? Is she a fugitive?"

"Who cares?" Bea sat up straighter, her attention riveted on the wall. "Let's read the message."

Jessie clicked through, bringing up the full text onscreen. As she read, her jaw dropped. "This is end-of-the-world scary. Global devastation, catastrophic casualties, and a war humanity can't win. I feel like I'm going to throw up."

"Un-frickin-believable," Bea said with a sense of reverence.

You'd think her sister had seen the Holy Grail, Jessie thought, aggravated by Bea's awestruck reaction. "This isn't good news. We're going to die."

"We all die sometime, but this is big. Historical, even. Assuming good ole Anon has it right, we're on the verge of extinction. Humans are going the way of the dinosaurs."

"We should take everything we have and go hide somewhere. If we're out of circulation, we might survive."

"What fun would that be? We'd be stuck there, the two of us. No men. No fans. And we'd have to clean up the mess from everyone else dying. No thanks. If it's time to get our tickets punched, believe me, we should be in a crowd and go out together."

"We'll make it a party down below. Whatever it takes to keep you safe." Jessie studied the message again. "There's a lot of omissions. Like a timeline. If we knew when this would happen, we could prepare better."

"Has Anon ever been wrong?"

"No. But that track record has little value. This has to be a new sender. We don't know what his or her track record is." Jessie's thoughts raced as she tried to put this in context. "How will it happen? Will it be an act of nature? Will our human enemies escalate a war of words into lethal weapons? Is this because of the aliens?"

"I can wrap my brain around the concept, but I can't quite picture that level of devastation."

Jessie's fingers flew over the entry pad. Mass destruction was surprisingly easy to find. "Somalians did their best to wipe each other out a coupla gens ago. Total destruction would look something like this." Horrific pictures of mass graves and bombed structures scrolled across the screen.

"Turn it off!" Bea shouted, jumping out of her seat and turning her back on the wall screen. She shook her hands as if she were trying to fling the spilled blood from her fingertips. "I can't get those images out of my head. I don't know if I can write about it. The music to accompany an act like that would definitely be minor key. Mournful. Filled with loss and regrets."

"You don't have to write about it," Jessie offered in a soft voice. "No one appointed us bards of the free world."

"I have a responsibility," Bea said. "I can't shirk my duty as the voice of the people. Anon sent us the information for a reason, so that I'd write about it. I can't let her down. We've received tough messages before."

"But none so final. The end of the world." Jessie pondered the thought. "Not saying I really believe it will happen, but going along with that train of thought, how will it happen? Will we see a cataclysm? Will we go out in a flash of light?"

"Reading between the lines, the time is near but not under our control," Bea offered. "To face death, you'd want to gather your loved ones, and everyone you held dear. You'd want to mend fences, and tell friends you love them."

"I like that sentiment," Jessie said. "If we only consider the unspoken need for reconciliation - that would be a great song. You could write about making peace in the family. Each verse could expand on the premise on getting things right in your world, whether it's your household, your neighborhood, city, country, or all of Earth."

"I need pen and paper," Bea said. "The song is coming in hot."

Jessie ordered breakfast through room service and grabbed a shower while Bea wrote. She washed out her only clothes but donned a metallic blue outfit of Bea's while hers dried. A glance in the mirror revealed the stretchy tank top hugged her curves and emphasized her narrow waist. The slacks fit like second skin.

If only Zeke could see me, she mused as she applied lipstick and mascara. He wouldn't be able to resist. She snorted. Like that would happen. Zeke didn't burn for her.

If the world was ending, she had to forget about the scientist. She needed to focus on her survival. But if she found a new boyfriend along the way, so much the better.

Chapter 26

"I'm coming for you, baby," Connor Bronsen muttered. In the dimly-lit space of the two-man travel pod, he clung to his sense of purpose because he had little else. His press credentials and credits had gotten him across the Atlantic, across Europe and midway to China. Then Entertainment News froze his expense account, and he'd been bumming his way across Asia ever since.

He'd sold his jewelry, clothes, shoes, luggage, and self-respect. The itchy robe and rustic sandals he wore were the sum total of his personal possessions. Among other lewd acts, he'd danced naked for a Saudi Arabian princess, and she'd granted him permission to fly in her air transpo. The rest of the space was occupied by bulky containers that he was pretty sure held weapons. If something went wrong during the flight, he'd catch the heat for the illegal arms.

But he had no choice. He'd run out of options several thousand miles ago. All he'd been, he'd given away to get Pauline back. How he wished he'd treasured their time together. Their good times on network news seemed like they would go on forever, and he'd taken her for granted.

He wanted to marry Pauline.

He'd messed up by waiting to ask her and now he was paying the price. Some said Pauline had been playing him from the start, but he didn't believe them. Pauline was kind and decent and honest. He'd save her or die trying.

Once his air transpo landed in Beijing, he'd leave the travel pod, access a com in the terminal, and find where the aliens were holding Pauline. If he rescued her within two hours, they could ride the plane on to Japan and then back to Saudi Arabia. Otherwise, he was on his own.

As the transpo touched down, he wondered if Pauline would even recognize him. He hadn't shaved in days, and he certainly wasn't a clotheshorse any longer. In fact, the untamed look he sported these days made most people take a step back from him. Before, in his news anchor life, he would have been appalled at annoying potential fans; but today, he didn't have time for niceties or grooming. Only Pauline's safety mattered.

Finally, the pod safe-exit light activated. He shut off the green glow and opened the hatch. Fierce dark-haired men swarmed the containers beside the pod, but they paid him no attention. Connor hurried away from the landing zone. Inside the transpo terminal, he found an open com unit, changed the language to English, and searched for his love.

A few minutes later, he had her. The aliens had finished their visit to China and had hopped over to Japan, reportedly to see the Dylan James concert tonight. Queen Bea was also on the program. That singing duo was a real hot ticket event. No wonder the aliens wanted to catch the show.

Lucky for him, he already had a way to Hiroshima. Connor scurried back in the travel pod and locked himself in. Hunger pangs stole his breath, but he couldn't afford food, and he wouldn't eat until he rescued Pauline.

Money couldn't buy happiness, but it surely helped. He'd never traveled so far with so little. He didn't know what he would do for money once he rescued Pauline, but he couldn't worry about that now. She needed him.

The transpo engine roared to life. His mantra welled up inside until he could no longer hold it. "I'm coming for you, baby," he shouted in the sealed travel pod.

Chapter 27

As they followed the sun westward, Zeke turned off the deluxe com station where he'd been searching for a loophole or a miracle to stop the Maleem. The idea of a brick wall kept popping into his head, but how could he do that? He stretched and walked over to where Forman sat calculating the probability of their rescue mission's success. He studied the stats and shook his head. "Those odds aren't good enough. We need hot disguises to make sure we get close to the Stemford sisters."

Forman growled at him. "You want hot? Put on a sweater."

The robot's flip remark rubbed him the wrong way. "Not that kind of hot – oh, you're kidding, aren't you?"

Standing, Zeke felt the barely discernable vibration of the ML4 engines. According to the nav tracker, they'd be on the ground in less than ten minutes. He didn't know what he'd say to Jessie, how he'd convince her to return with them.

He exhaled slowly to release the coiled tension in his shoulders. It was hard to concentrate on two problems at once. "I need for this to go smoothly so that the womenfolk are safe, and we can focus on the aliens."

"You think Jessie and Bea will reject our offer of assistance?"

"They'll be glad to go home. But the two of us are persona non grata with them. We need an edge, a way to get close and then whisk them away. That's what disguises will do for us."

Forman's head cocked to the side like the orange parrots on his aloha shirt. "Are we talking skin color, hair, and eye color? Or will I be updating your geek central wardrobe?"

There was nothing wrong with his natural fiber suit and tie, but why not humor the robot? "Whatever it takes. Like I said, I don't want to stand out."

"In a Dylan James crowd, it would take a lot to stand out. Let me see what's available in shops near the Hiroshima transpo center."

A flurry of images paraded across the screen. When Forman lingered too long on one poor choice, Zeke had to say something. "Not pink. I don't wear hot pink."

Forman's fingers zipped over the data entry pad. "That's precisely why it's such a good color for you. This pink on pink shirt is perfect. I'll dye your medium-toned skin darker, add trendy glasses, trekkie boots, delish jeans, and a righteous hat. You'll be smokin' hot. Jessie will jump out of her seat to grab you. And if she doesn't, I can guarantee you'll have Asian chicks going crazy over your bod."

"What about you? If I'm stuck in flaming pink, how will you disguise yourself? Will you go the old man route again?"

"Not this time. I'm trying to get my girl back, so I'm amping up my sex appeal. I'm emulating Johnny Cash with all-black attire. As for the rest, wait a minute."

Though Zeke watched the minute-long transformation, he still found it hard to believe. Forman's tanned "skin" lightened several shades. His blond hair, eyelashes, and eyebrows darkened to ebony. His blue eyes changed to a chestnut brown.

Zeke whistled his appreciation as the transpo angled toward the runway. "That's amazing. If I hadn't seen you change, I couldn't pick you out in a crowd."

"Being a super robot has its advantages. I scored us the best seats in the house for the concert. Some diplomats outbid us for the last skybox, so I arranged backstage passes and front row seating for us."

"I thought this concert was sold out."

"Took care of that, too. Different rules for VIPs."

"You didn't break any laws, did you? Uncle John wouldn't understand a call from a Japanese jailhouse."

"We're square with the law. Things work differently over here. Fortunately, I speak their language."

The ML4 touched down. Moments later, the attendant robot, a Jenna, brought Forman's purchases on board. Forman shooed Zeke back to the sleeping quarters. "I've added the skin dye to the water res for the shower. Sit for a moment while I apply the highlighter to your hair. Five minutes in the shower, and you'll be a new man. Keep turning so the skin coloration applies evenly. When the timer rings, rinse your hair."

As Forman tucked his shaggy hair in a watertight cap, Zeke reminded himself that it was his idea to wear disguises. The water smelled like crushed almonds, and he was careful to keep it out of his eyes. After the shower, his skin was a perfect match for his cousin Angie. Gazing in the mirror, his eyes seemed whiter, his teeth brighter.

Forman burst into the bathroom and grinned. "Nice. You look like a soulful brother. Just the right amount of blond in your hair now. You should consider this clubbing look on a full-time basis."

"I'm not ashamed of my natural appearance."

"No one said you were. This is more of a statement of who you can be – someone who takes pride in his presentation."

Zeke held his tongue and dressed in the clothing Forman provided. The first thing he noticed was how much taller he felt in the boots. The pink shirt was hideous, but fortunately, it was out of his line of sight. The white hat made him smile. Altogether, he looked and felt like a different man. A man on the prowl. He liked that.

"Ready?" Forman asked.

"Ready as I'll ever be."

Chapter 28

Fools.

Pauline Curran stood at Drok's side above the milling crowd assembled under the stadium's domed roof at the Dylan James concert. She'd seen Dylan's show twice before. She'd even gotten off on his music. Now she knew music for the lightweight gimmick it always was. Music couldn't compare to true power.

Tonight, music would focus the world's eyes on this venue. Later, the after-the-show celebration would be life-changing for everyone. And thanks to the Maleem, she'd be part of the entertainment. Pauline had found nirvana, and she intended to share the wealth with everyone.

With reverence, she stroked the jeweled necklace resting on her bare skin. Drok had offered it to her to stop the gas-induced nightmares, and she'd taken it without hesitation. He'd been crystal clear on this point. The jeweled collar was hers to wear or remove. He hadn't forced it on her; he hadn't even placed it on her.

Thank goodness for the necklace. The nightmares faded away, so however the pretty stones worked, she was grateful. Very grateful. And hyped up about spreading the good news of the Maleem. She couldn't wait to demonstrate what the Maleem offered.

Drok's hand gripped her shoulder, and his thoughts invaded her mind. *You have the ultimate power, Lia. You choose who benefits the most from our trade agreements. You will shape the future of your planet. You bring honor and glory to the Maleem.*

Lia was his pet name for her. His thoughts burned into her brain, always sharp and a bit caustic. Somehow, in their first meeting, he'd sensed her intelligence and competitiveness. He'd selected her over the ambassadors and newsies. She alone had full access to the top Maleem. She alone controlled the fate of her planet. Her face would be on all the broadcast vids. She'd be internationally famous. They'd know her throughout the universe. She would be that special.

About damn time.

All her life she'd wanted to be a superstar, and the Maleem launched her right into the stratosphere. Talk about being in the right place at the right time. After this gig, she could have any news assignment she wanted. They'd probably give her the entire news network in honor of her service to the planet.

Drok's hand pulled away, and she exhaled her tension in a series of panting breaths. Funny, since she'd worn the necklace, she'd begun to breathe differently. Faster. Lighter. It gave her a heady, powerful sensation.

She wanted to touch Drok, but she'd learned the hard way not to initiate contact. The first and only time she'd tried, the jolt had knocked her out cold. Good thing these Maleem were friendly. No telling what sort of havoc they could wreak on humankind if they weren't. They were physically stronger than any male she'd ever met, and they could control a mind with a mere touch. They literally charged the air around them.

What she wouldn't do to be so powerful. She'd sure like to mentally Taser a bunch of network executives, her sleazy stepfather, and all the news snots who thought they were better than her.

The door clicked open and she whirled to see who had the audacity to enter the private skybox. A uniformed attendant wheeled a cart of food and booze toward her. Drok's cadre of bodyguards immediately circled the lithe young man. Drok shot her a universal take-care-of-this look.

Pauline stepped forward to block the cart. "Thank you. Please don't come any closer. The Maleem are on edge in such a large crowd."

"Are you all right, ma'am?" the attendant asked in perfect English, his gloved hand extending toward her. His bronzed lapel pen stated he was Eito from Concessions. His perfect English suggested he might be more than a stadium worker.

"I'm fine. Please leave the cart, and I will take care of it."

Eito's gaze sharpened. His voice dropped to a confidential whisper. "Are you being treated fairly? The entire world knows you were forced into this role."

With a glance at Drok who nodded his approval, she motioned Eito outside to the quiet backstage corridor. "I'm fine. What's the problem?"

"I'm not with the venue, ma'am," he said apologetically. "I'm here to escort you to safety, if that's what you desire."

She retreated toward the open doorway. "No. I'm staying with the Maleem. I could leave at any time. See? I walked out of the skybox with you. I'm staying with them of my own free will."

"Begging your pardon, Miss Curran. There was that 'help me' message in the Beijing hotel. We assumed you'd written it."

"I did." She frowned and flicked her wrist to show how inconsequential the message was. "A small disagreement among friends. I'm a volatile, high-profile media star. I'm allowed to change my mind. The Maleem and I resolved our differences."

Eito's eyes narrowed. "Tell me about the Maleem."

"They don't speak, but they haven't hurt me, as you can clearly see."

"You look like you've lost weight."

Food wasn't a priority. She didn't care if she ever ate again. She'd never felt so fit, so healthy. "I needed to lose a few pounds. I'm fine."

"We'd like to have a doctor examine you, to see if being with the Maleem has adversely affected your health or well-being."

She felt a stab of fear in the pit of her stomach. She couldn't miss her starring role tonight. Everything depended on it. On her. "You can't. I won't. I mean, they need an interpreter. I'm their spokeswoman. Their visit here is nearing an end. You will set back diplomatic relations severely if you insert another person in my role at this late date."

Eito nodded toward her sparkling collarbone. "Tell me about the pretty necklace. That's new."

She touched the necklace reverently and smiled. "You like? Drok gave it to me." With bravado, she unclasped the necklace and handed it to him.

He turned it over in his gloved hands and snapped photos with his wrist com. "I've never seen stones like this before. I'd like to examine this in the lab."

"You can't have it. Drok would think I didn't value his gift," she said in a sharp tone. When he gazed at her in alarm, she held out her hand for the jeweled collar. "There's plenty of time to examine the crystals after he leaves."

As if she would give anyone her necklace. It was all she could do not to snort out her disbelief. When Eito returned the necklace, she settled the jeweled nirvana back in its rightful place. The edgy sensation subsided.

Much better.

"Is there anything you need? Anyone you want us to contact?"

Eito asked.

Thoughts of Connor flashed through her head. She'd love to see him again, to let him see what he'd lost, but there was no going back.

Connor was her past.

Drok was her future.

"I'm fine," she stated firmly. Rock and roll swelled through the open door, quickening her pulse. "The show's starting. I need to get back inside."

Eito pressed a card into her hand. "If you have a change of heart."

Drums banged and guitars wailed as she closed the skybox door behind her. She sauntered to Drok's side. His green fingertips grazed her cheek in query.

Electricity pulsed through her, but this time it didn't hurt. When she didn't recoil, his thick vermillion lips parted, revealing jagged teeth. He drew her under his arm and for the first time ever, she wrapped her arm around his waist.

Beneath her skintight leather clothing, her skin smoldered, but still she clung to the alien. Her auburn hair snapped and crackled with current, but every eye in the place was on her. On them.

She used sign language to shout out her sentiment to everyone there. I love you.

Pauline grinned in triumph.

Eat your heart out, Dylan James.

You may be center stage, but I'm the real show.

Chapter 29

All around him, the crowd writhed to Dylan James' uptown rock beat. Forman gyrated with the best of them, scanning and dismissing nearby concert-goers for danger. With his disguise in place and his ID collar secured on the transpo, his true identity was concealed. Even Zeke said he wouldn't have picked Forman out in a crowd.

He was good at his job.

The best.

On stage, the aging rock musician swaggered and sang and rocked out. Lights flashed, a giant vidscreen of Dylan played behind the stage. Leather-clad cuties jiggled and jostled at the back-up vocal mikes. The hot number on keyboards winked at him. Twice.

The sultry brunette didn't have anything he wanted. Bea was his ticket to happily ever after. If she didn't come out soon, he'd die.

At his side, Zeke remained board-stiff.

No way did his boss fit in with the concert crowd.

Forman leaned over to speak directly in Zeke's ear. "Normally I tell my concert dates not to inhale, but you need to take in a puff or two of what's going around the crowd. Loosen up."

Zeke spoke so softly Forman asked him to repeat his words.

"They're here," Zeke whispered.

"Of course they're here. That's why we came. To rescue Bea and Jessie," Forman said. For a brilliant guy, Zeke often said dumb things.

"The aliens. The Maleem." Zeke bobbed his white hat toward the skybox hovering beside stage left.

Forman danced around, recording the three-dimensional scene in his processors. He was careful to conceal his stunned reaction to the tall green man hugging news anchor Pauline Curran. From memory, he assessed Pauline in a microsecond. Gaunt face, thinner body, greenish cast to her skin. Drok, the alien, stood a head taller than Pauline. He still wore his form-fitting body armor and helmeted breathing apparatus, but Forman detected a strong electrical field around the Maleem.

The field encompassed Pauline.

"I don't like it," Forman said as he danced around to face Zeke. "There's enough power surrounding that alien to light up the entire city."

"He's a killer," Zeke said. "We have to destroy him before he kills us."

"We can't get close to the guy. He has bodyguards, an Earthly protective detail, and diplomatic immunity. It would be a death sentence to shoot him, even if we had weapons, which we don't."

"He sees me," Zeke said. "How did he pick me out of the crowd?"

"Look away and dance for your life," Forman said, edging them behind a mother and daughter with bright blue hair. When the older woman zeroed in on Zeke, Forman danced with the twenty-something daughter.

No matter what they did, Forman noticed Drok's gaze locked on Zeke. Not cool. Zeke had been so focused on repelling the Maleem attack of Earth and now the head Maleem couldn't take his eyes off Zeke. This was not good.

Why hadn't he smuggled a blaster in his hollow core? He was already playing fast and loose with the law by not wearing his ID necklace. What would it matter to break one more rule?

The song ended, and amidst welcoming cheers, Queen Bea made an entrance in a pistachio green bodysuit. She blew kisses to the audience and joined Dylan center stage. Forman stilled, his cyber heart on his black sleeve. She looked good. No. She looked great. Didn't look like she'd missed him one bit. And that welcoming kiss from Dylan set his teeth on edge.

With a nod to their extraterrestrial visitors in the skybox, Bea and Dylan sang "Little Green Men." Forman watched, unable to tear his eyes from the scene. He loved Bea with everything that was in him.

At the roar of the crowd, he looked up to see Pauline Curran had separated from Drok and was dancing to the song. Everyone in the audience copied her wild gyrations, even Bea and Dylan. Only the band members wearing headsets seemed immune to the lure of Pauline's movements.

Forman went on full alert. What was happening? Was the alien controlling ten thousand people? Or was it a sort of group-induced hysteria? What party drug were they piping into the stadium?

He turned to ask Zeke about it, but Zeke wasn't there, only the

Japanese mother and blue-haired daughter stood at his side. He whirled to scan the crowd, using his superior facial recognition software to track and record every face in the vicinity. But it was no use.

His boss had vanished into thin air.

Chapter 30

Connor sighed with relief. He'd made it to the concert. Pauline was still alive and somewhere inside this stadium. He didn't have a ticket. Hell, he didn't even have a pocket, but nothing would stop him from saving his girlfriend.

At the gate, the guards shooed him away. Like Joshua circling Biblical of Jericho, Connor trudged to the next gate. He'd come too far to give up now. Pauline needed him. He would be there for her.

Hunger gnawed at him. The world spun a little off its axis. He staggered and held onto the fencing until the disorientation passed. He'd eat as soon as he rescued Pauline.

Luck was with him at the next gate. The guards seemed to be in a strange thrall, gyrating together to that stupid song about little green men. He hated green men, and if he had the chance, he'd throttle Drok with his bare hands.

"Thank you very much," he said as he strolled past the dancing guards. Everywhere he looked, people were making the same jerky movements.

How odd.

He shook his head to clear it and chanted "I'm here to rescue Pauline." He didn't waste time on the concert. His best bet was to grab Pauline after the show, so he headed to the skybox area. Though he'd never been in this stadium before, he'd reported from many stadiums in his former life.

Connor caught a glimpse of himself in the mirror. He barely recognized the man with the scruffy beard, matted hair, and rustic Middle-Eastern style robe. He prayed Pauline would see through the lack of grooming and hygiene and recognize salvation when she saw it. Because that's what he was – her salvation.

He hid in an alcove in the skybox corridor. Pauline and her alien would walk right past him on the way out.

Sleep threatened. He fought it. This was the moment he'd been waiting for.

Pauline was here.

He had to save her.

Chapter 31

From Stage Right, Jessie enjoyed a bird's eye view of the alien and Pauline Curran. The woman repeatedly made the hand gesture for 'I love you,' prompting Jessie to wonder about the silent message. Who did Pauline love? The world? The alien? Her co-anchor?

Was it a coded transmission?

Bea elbowed her and nodded. "Look at that."

"I see them," Jessie said. "How odd that the alien came to this concert on his planetary tour. One would think he'd be schmoozing with heads of state. They keep hinting about trade agreements in the news, but I haven't heard what they want from us or what we'll get in return from them. I don't trust Drok or the Maleem."

"You don't trust anyone these days."

"With good reason. The world's gone crazy because of resource shortages. The last thing we need to do is ship our limited supply off-planet."

"Maybe they'll sell us food," Bea countered.

Jessie blinked twice at the absurdity of that statement. "Would you eat alien food?"

"Heck, no."

"Good girl. Let's hope Drok blasts back off into space and leaves us alone. I feel like I should join the greenies and start chanting 'alien go home.' Earth may be messed up, but she's ours. We don't need outsiders making things worse."

"No one knows what effect the Maleem will have. Things could get better, so you can cut them a little slack."

"Suit yourself."

"Drok must have great taste in music. Maybe Dylan and I will go platinum across the universe," Bea said with a nervous laugh. "Drok's done wonders with Pauline. She looks biker hot in all that clingy black leather. She takes that retro urban fantasy look to a whole new level with her gaunt face and high-end breast augmentation. And boy can she dance."

Bea could think what she liked, but Jessie seethed with suspicion. Had her sister forgotten the basic rule of survival?

Strangers were not to be trusted.

That's why her nerves wouldn't settle tonight. The alien. He was a big unknown. If he liked Bea, that would be bad. If he disliked Bea and tried to harm her, that would be worse. Bea's appearance at the concert was lose-lose.

Onstage, Dylan transitioned to a mellow number. During the practice set earlier today, this song was the one before his second duet with Bea. She'd give anything to whisk her sister away from the sold-out stadium so the alien never came within two feet of her.

"Do you think they're sleeping together?" Bea asked.

Jessie jolted back to the present and replayed the question in her mind. Her teeth clenched together in disgust. She pried them apart. "Why?"

"He's a guy. She's a girl. Pauline enjoys sexual experimentation on the news, so I'm guessing yes. If he's got the right equipment, he's doing her."

Jessie shuddered. "Gross."

"Oh, come on. They're a cute couple. See how close she's standing to him. They're shimmering."

The air around them looked different. Like heat waves rising off desert sands. "Probably some publicity stunt. Pauline is all about her career. Who knows what the Maleem have in mind for Earth?"

"Lighten up, sis. You're full of gloom and doom. After the concert, we're on our way home. That's where our focus should be. We're getting off this stupid rock."

"I am focused on going home. I'd love to wake up in my own bed tomorrow morning."

"We'll be there soon, I promise. You can relax, and I can finish my new song."

Applause rocked the stadium. As Dylan began Bea's introduction, Jessie hugged her sister. "Your first song went great. The second one will bring the house down."

Bea squeezed her and some of the warmth returned to Jessie. "Love ya."

When her sister walked on stage for the finale, the crowd roared its approval. During the number, Jessie kept one eye on Bea and the other on the alien. She didn't trust the Maleem.

A familiar-looking man appeared in Drok's skybox. Jessie shook her head, not trusting her eyes. She dared to hope she wasn't seeing things.

Could it be?

With her heart pumping in slow motion, Jessie studied the newcomer. Same profile. Same build. Skin tone seemed different. But the dark curly hair gleamed with blond highlights. And the clothes were wrong. She'd never seen him in blinding pink.

But she knew this man. Knew him and wanted him to be hers.

Her hands fisted in fury. The alien couldn't have Bea, and it damn well couldn't have Zeke.

She rushed offstage.

Chapter 32

Scarcely believing his run of good luck, Connor followed the dark-skinned man in the bright pink shirt into Pauline's skybox. She'd lost weight, but she looked even hotter than usual. Seeing all that prime flesh in motion stirred his every desire. God, how he'd missed her. His heart pounded in his ears.

Mine.

None of the spacesuit-wearing guards moved to stop him or the pink-shirted man. Connor stared at their helmeted faces with surprise. They looked human, but their straight-ahead gazes never flickered. Were the guards were turned off? Was that possible?

Were they men or machines?

Not that he cared.

The aliens could rot in hell as long as he got Pauline back.

He crept forward, growing braver by the millisecond.

Mr. Pink approached the armor-clad alien and bowed deeply. The man's fawning infuriated Connor, and he stumbled. The room spun. He grabbed onto a chair until the spinning stopped.

Drok wasn't royalty. He didn't deserve anyone's fealty. He didn't belong here. For taking Pauline, he deserved a bullet in the head, though Connor had only his fists for weapons. He'd take the alien down and free Pauline. He'd crossed continents for her.

A shout burst from his throat. He rushed toward the alien. Within a step, the ends of his matted hair stood on end, and his heart fluttered like a drunken butterfly. Rage and fury powered his fevered steps. He lunged forward and slammed to a full stop two feet from Drok, who'd merely lifted a hand. Connor's face ached as if he'd run headlong into a brick wall. He slid to the floor beside the alien's thick-soled boots.

He roared in protest, but not a whimper left his throat. Damn it. He couldn't fail. He was so close. Pauline was less than four feet away, but she might as well have been on another planet.

The alien had done something to her.

Grossly unfair.

Drok couldn't have Pauline. She belonged to Connor.

112

He tried to roll to his feet, but he couldn't move a muscle. He couldn't even blink an eye. His heart thumped slowly, and his lungs managed a few shallow respirations. He trembled. A dry sob rose in his throat. He couldn't die now.

Drok flicked a wrist, and Mr. Pink backpedaled to the wall where the guards stood. When the man in pink stepped over him, Connor poured his distress into his gaze, but his efforts were for naught.

The music stopped, and the audience clapped wildly. Pauline turned and smiled. Not at him. At Drok. Connor fumed. She didn't see him on the floor. He tried to thump his heel, to alert her to his presence, but his limbs were pinned by an unseen force.

Pauline, he screamed silently. *Down here. It's me. Connor. I love you.* Mentally, he mimicked the sign language she'd taught him, the I-love-you sign.

Drok nodded toward Connor, and Pauline's gaze slid to the floor. A small sound died in Connor's throat as their eyes met. Finally, she saw him. Now they could go home and spend the rest of their lives together. She'd be his wife.

He put everything he had into his gaze, beseeching her to see beneath the strange clothing, facial hair, and road grime, to see him. His flaring hope extinguished as she dismissed him with a cursory glance.

Connor's fingers twitched. His toes spasmed. What had they done to her? He pushed up onto his elbows.

"Pauline!" he cried, his voice cracking with effort. "It's Connor. I'm here to save you."

When she didn't respond, he scrambled to his feet, tottering like an old geezer. He stared into her dilated pupils and died a little. "Pauline? Honey, it's me, Connor. I've come to take you home. Let's go now."

Pauline's eyes widened in fear. She touched her jeweled necklace and retreated. "I can't go."

"You can. Let's walk out that door and back to our old lives."

"I want to stay with the Maleem."

Though she continued to retreat, he matched her step for step, hoping and praying to reach her. "You love me, Pauline. Come home with me. I need you." He motioned I-love-you in sign language.

Her expression remained blank, and Connor's hair electrified again. Uh-oh. He'd sensed crackling energy when he slammed into an invisible barrier. Something bad was about to happen. The alien was amping up for action. Too bad. He'd had enough of this guy controlling his girlfriend.

Connor grabbed Pauline. Electricity arced lightning-fast from her arm to his heart. His life flashed before his eyes. In every scene, Pauline gazed at him in awe and wonder. The old Pauline. Not the alien-loving, leather-clad bitch standing over him as he flailed on the floor.

Though she didn't say a word or lift a finger, twin trails of tears rolled down her flame-red cheeks. *Pauline*, he cried soundlessly. *I love you.*

His vision faded first. Sound died next. The last thing he remembered was the pungent scent of burning flesh.

Chapter 33

Zeke strained against the mental shackles. Once the Maleem switched focus to the guy in rags, he regained a modicum of human brainwave activity. He could see, but hearing, vocalization, and movement were suppressed.

How did this happen? One moment he'd been on the concert floor, and the next he'd been unwittingly drawn to this skybox. A single glance from the alien, and he'd been powerless to act on his own. He'd been enslaved.

By a look.

How could he have been so stupid? The Tamans warned him about the Maleem, but he didn't heed their warning. He'd never encountered a problem he couldn't take on. His superior intellect solved any puzzle he'd tackled.

Until now.

Blood still flowed to his limbs, but his limbs were not his to command. He couldn't move without Drok giving the order. If the Maleem warrior wanted him to dance naked on the narrow skybox railing, he'd have no choice. Drok's musty brainwaves overwrote his every thought.

He had to break free.

He had to destroy Drok.

But how?

How could he sever the invisible link that bound him to humanity's agent of death? The invisible link had worked across the distance of the stadium. It endured through the maze of walls and corridors as he walked to the skybox. He'd been surrounded by others, and yet they had not been affected. This entrapment was personal. The Maleem culled him from the crowd for a reason.

Did the Maleem know he was Taman?

It was the only line of reasoning that made sense. Standing beside him were others in spacesuits, allegedly Drok's bodyguards. It dawned on him that the guards could be unwilling servants like him.

Would piercing the Maleem's spacesuit end his life? Would

human air poison him? Zeke clung to that hope.

If he got the chance, he'd rip Drok's suit.

Zeke watched the dirty man in a middle European robe try and fail to escape. His green eyes didn't fit the ethnic nationality his clothing suggested. What was going on here? Zeke wished he could hear what was being said. The news anchorwoman acted as if she was also in Drok's thrall.

Which meant the guy on the floor came for her.

Was it Connor, her former co-anchor?

Drok appeared to be toying with the man, but it didn't matter. No one could move in this skybox without Drok powering the action. Pauline was as much the alien's slave as everyone else. Only the man on the floor seemed immune to the alien's mind control.

Zeke tucked that oddity away until later.

The tableau played out as he'd predicted. The raggedy man reached for Pauline. The alien's heavy-handed presence intensified in Zeke's mind. His body throbbed as if he were being ripped apart. In the same breath, an overwhelming blanket of fatigue bowed his shoulders.

The man on the floor jerked and twitched in a powerful electric field. He stopped moving. Was the man dead? When the fierce pressure in Zeke's head eased, he wept silent tears.

He was so tired he could barely stand. What had happened? He had to make sense of this, or he'd meet the same fate as the raggedy man.

Think, Zeke.

Where did that energy to shock the man come from?

Humans didn't discharge strong electrical fields. They couldn't shock each other to death. Therefore, Drok had done it, not Pauline. Like a parasite, the alien siphoned energy from the minions he'd sidelined, including Zeke. He remembered the mental latching sensation in his head prior to the energy surge.

That's why the other space-suited aliens weren't moving. They couldn't. Drok held them hostage in this high-stakes game. The bodyguards weren't guards at all; they served as energy reservoirs for the alien.

Bile gathered in his throat. This would not end well. Worse, he'd failed to safeguard anything. He'd let everyone down.

Forman charged in, and Zeke silently shouted a warning to him. *Get out! Save yourself. Save Jessie and Bea.* But even though

Forman stood right in front of him, Zeke couldn't communicate with him. All he could do was stare straight ahead. He couldn't blink or wipe his tear-stained cheeks dry.

He groaned in mute agony and struggled to move, but he couldn't control his body or his mind.

If only he could read lips, he'd know what Forman said. If he got out of this, no, when he got out of this, he'd learn to read lips. That was a promise. He would never be this defenseless again.

Could Forman vanquish Drok? He was the most intelligent robot on the planet. A stunningly complex assemblage of four of the most advanced artificial life forms ever created. He knew every form of combat known to man. If anyone could stop Drok, Forman had the best chance.

Or did he?

Zeke felt a mental shudder followed by an over wash of gut-kicking dread. Oh, no. This was a terrible mistake. Forman's systems ran on self-contained power. Though Forman wasn't plugged into the grid, his activity was powered by electric current.

Get out! Zeke screamed silently. *You're going to die. The Maleem will fry your circuits. Get out of here, Forman.*

But the robot turned from him, walked to the front of the skybox, and appeared to be addressing the crowd below. He pointed at the Maleem. The musty mindlink hummed again. Zeke recognized what that meant and fought the power lock with all his being. Not this time. Dear heaven. Not this time.

Run Forman.

But it was too late to run.

His thoughts whited out as another burst of energy was extracted. Despite the electrical assault, Forman remained standing. His black clothes steamed with heat. His disguised dark hair reverted to its normal blonde color.

Zeke died a little more inside. With Forman's appearance changing in such a public setting, he was doomed. A.I. units weren't supposed to wear disguises. And his robot wasn't wearing the mandatory A.I. identifier necklace. Even if Forman survived the alien attack, the robocops would destroy him. Gross misconduct was not tolerated from machines.

To Zeke's horror, Pauline opened the access panel and revealed Forman's inner circuitry. The smoke thickened in the skybox. Zeke's hopes failed. He was doomed to a life of slavery, and Forman was toast. He'd failed himself, his friends, and his planet.

Sparks shot from the robot's open headpiece. Pauline's look of triumph glowed vulture bright. She flung smoldering parts of Forman's circuits into the crowd below.

No.

He needed to wake up from this very bad dream.

Forman was his friend. His best friend. He'd already sacrificed himself for Zeke and been rebuilt. He didn't deserve this pubic humiliation.

Zeke strained against the mental shackles, pulling and tugging and twisting to no avail. *Stop!* he yelled in oblivion. *Don't hurt him. I'll do anything you want.*

Surely someone would help.

But no help came.

He raged against his captors. *I'll get you. Count on it. You'd better flurking kill me because I'm sure as hell coming after you if I get the chance.*

Though he couldn't feel his limbs, the room spun. His stomach writhed. Sweat beaded on his brow and slicked down the bony channel of his spine. Bile burned his throat.

He had no options. No way to help his buddy. No way to save himself.

He was a slave.

Worse, he'd succumbed without a fight.

He let his emotions roll and wailed his grief in the chasm of his mind. *Forman. My friend. I'm sorry.*

Cold fingers grabbed his hand.

His nerves jangled.

What?

Out of the corner of his eye, he saw Jessie.

Jessie?

Time bent. Not Jessie. Please, not Jessie.

What was she doing? *Run, Jessie! Get away from here. From me. Save yourself.*

She didn't hear. She couldn't. He hadn't spoken a word. He had to do something. He couldn't let Jessie sacrifice herself.

He fought Drok's mind control link and managed to make his fingers twitch. That wasn't the universal sign for get the hell out of here, but he hoped like anything that's how Jessie interpreted it.

She squeezed his hand back, and he wept silently for them both.

Chapter 34

Pauline admired her new meal ticket from across the party boat's stateroom. Drok epitomized everything she wanted in a lover. He exuded power, strength, and authority. His body seemed perfectly formed, and even though she hadn't seen his reproductive package, from all appearances things looked to be smoking hot down there, too.

Definitely an upgrade from her previous hookup on Entertainment News.

Bigger and better was the way to the top, and she'd had her fill of being on the bottom. The view from the top suited her better.

The euphoria when everyone in the stadium began copying her dance moves still coursed in her veins. Granted, the dance choreography came from Drok, but everyone saw her grooving to the music. She'd been broadcast around the world. She was famous. A superstar.

She smiled in triumph. Dylan James had invited them aboard his midnight cruise, and now she was partying with two rock stars and the sexiest alien this side of the Milky Way. This was definitely the hottest ticket in the universe.

She'd been concerned when that sly robot tried to upstage Drok, but Drok had turned the tables on the rogue A.I., exposing him for the cybercrime of impersonating a human. The robocops hauled the machine away. They'd also disposed of that worthless pile of rags on the skybox floor. What nerve! Connor thought he could waltz in here and mess this up for her, but she'd set him straight.

She'd fried his ass.

The only remaining glitch on her bright horizon was Mr. Pink Shirt. Out of the blue, he'd arrived and joined the retinue. She glanced over at the wall where pinkie and his girlfriend stood with the guards. She wanted to kill him for stealing Drok's attention, but the Maleem warrior had lost interest in the man as soon as he appeared, so she'd left pinkie alone in the skybox. But his potential worried her. Was he her replacement?

That would not be tolerated.

Stoking her jeweled collar, her priceless gift from Drok, she strolled over to learn more about Mr. Pink. She extended her hand to the woman beside him. "I'm Lia," she said, using the name Drok gave her. "And you are?"

The tricked-out brunette in do-me pumps ignored her outstretched hand. She clung to Mr. Pink as if he were a lifeline to salvation. "Jessie."

Bitch, Pauline thought, tucking her rejected hand back to her side. But she wouldn't zap the hussy yet. She needed information. She damn well wouldn't leave without it. "Who's your boyfriend?"

"Zeke."

"Not much of a conversationalist, are you, Jessie?" Pauline nodded at the man. Except for walking from the skybox to the boat, the man had barely moved. "What's wrong with him?"

"He doesn't say much," Jessie whispered with a nervous glance toward the Maleem.

Pauline stroked her necklace again, feeling more invincible with each caress of the shiny stones. "You're with the band?"

Jessie's face tightened, but she favored Pauline with a slight nod.

"Tonight, I'm awarding two more of these collars as gifts from Drok. The choice is mine alone. What will you give me for one of them?"

"I'm not interested."

Liar, Pauline thought. Who wouldn't be interested? The jewels alone were worth a fortune. She reached up and unclasped her necklace, intent on showing the woman what she was missing. "Let's see how it looks on your neck."

Jessie pressed against the wall behind her. "I don't want your necklace."

Her refusal annoyed Pauline. She decided to turn the tables on the woman. "All right then, I'll put it on your silent friend."

"No!" Jessie stepped forward, wide-eyed with fear. "My boyfriend doesn't want your gift either. You may try it on me."

"Good answer." Pauline settled the collar on Jessie's neck. In seconds, the woman's pupils dilated. Her breathing changed. "You like how it feels?"

Jessie's face relaxed into a satiated smile, infuriating Pauline. The longer Jessie wore the collar, the more irritated Pauline became. Nightmares flickered at the edge of her consciousness. "That one's mine," she said, taking it back. "You want one of the others, you have to pay for it."

"I want the pretty collar." Jessie grabbed for Pauline's coveted trophy.

"Uh uh uh." Pauline cinched it in place and felt much better. She waggled a finger in Jessie's direction and gloated. "Mine."

Jessie released Zeke, stepped forward, and raised her voice. "I want it."

Drok signaled his guards to protect Pauline. "Can't have it," Pauline said. "And I don't want you in here. You offend me. Guards, throw them overboard. They aren't welcome on this boat."

The guards looked at Drok, who motioned them with his fingers. After that victory, Pauline danced her way around the room, sharing her necklace with ambassadors and Dylan James. She'd learned her lesson with Jessie. Only a moment of jeweled glory was allowed to her adoring fans. She wouldn't chance someone making a grab for her coveted prize again.

Queen Bea, looking disheveled, youthful, and much too sexy to Pauline's way of thinking stepped in Pauline's path. She glared at the singer. "Step aside."

"What did you do with my sister?" Bea demanded, staggering sideways.

The sex kitten was stoned out of her mind. She posed no threat. Pauline laughed in her face. "Be gone."

Drok caught Pauline's eye and inclined his head. Pauline moved to his side at once. She exulted as all eyes turned to her. His hand rested on her shoulder, and she felt his brooding presence inside her mind.

"My time here is near an end," Drok said through her. "I have sown the seeds for our future trade relationships. Lia has selected two men to wear the valuable necklaces from my home planet. Dylan James and Ambassador Warner, please step forward."

The men approached and knelt before him. "The necklaces may be worn over clothing, but they're more radiant, like Lia's necklace, when resting upon bare skin," Drok said.

A guard handed the choker necklaces individually to Pauline, who cinched them in place on each man. She bestowed a glowing smile upon each subject.

"Splendid," Drok said, when the deed was done. "Accept these small tokens as thanks for the hospitality I've received on your planet."

The men rose, bowed, and turned to face the crowd. Wild applause rocked the slow moving boat. Dylan signaled the band to start the next number, and everyone resumed dancing and drinking.

Bea stumbled between the departing Dylan and the ambassador, nearly falling on Drok. Pauline intercepted the foolish woman, knocking her down. "Drok is untouchable," Pauline announced loudly to the too-quiet room.

"So you say," Bea hollered from the floor as she sat up on her knees. "My sister was right. You dumped Connor for a little green man."

"Drok's not little." It felt like steam shot out of her ears. Pauline's temper flared. She kicked the singer as hard as she could. Electricity arced through the air. The smell of burning flesh rent the air, along with Bea's screams.

Two dowdy women knelt and helped Bea to her feet. Drok placed his hand on Pauline's shoulder. Pauline's thoughts were instantly overlaid by his. "I apologize for Lia's outburst," Drok said through Pauline. "Her actions were not of my will, and I did not sanction them. I will discipline Lia by removing her from the party and taking away her necklace."

When he moved his hand from her shoulder, Pauline tried to block him from taking the necklace, but he didn't falter. As soon as it left her neck, the trembling began. Nightmare energy whispered in the dark shadows of her consciousness.

Pauline gasped, trying to hold it together, trying to appear contrite. "I didn't mean it. I'm sorry. Don't take the necklace. I love it. I love you."

Drok handed the necklace to a guard who fondled her necklace like a lost kitten through his gloved hand. Drok touched her shoulder again. His mind-words roared into her head. *You will take the punishment, Lia. It will make you strong, strong enough to see your future place at my side. You will become very powerful. You will be revered among our people.*

His guards moved in lockstep and muscled Pauline down a deserted corridor. They shoved her in a small, dimly-lit cabin.

Her hands shook. Her stomach hurt. The room spun. Nightmare shadows lengthened. She headed to the bathroom to throw up, but nothing surged up from her empty stomach. She blotted her face with cold water from the tap.

Okay.

She'd learned her lesson.

Drok was top dog. She wouldn't challenge his authority again. With that, she strode back into the main room. She tried the door. Locked.

Shit.

She'd been in this humiliating position before.

She kicked the plastec door as hard as she could. Pain reverberated up her leg like she'd never felt before. Sobbing, she limped to the bed, intent on taking off her shoe and examining her injury.

The shoe wouldn't come off.

It seemed welded to her foot.

She tugged at her leather pants leg. It wouldn't move so much as an inch, so she grabbed hold of the hem and pulled with all her might. The pain was instantaneous and horrible. Glancing down, she saw she'd ripped off her skin.

The raw flesh of her ankle oozed blood.

She touched the wound, then drew her bloody fingers to her face, hoping this was a bad dream or a mistake, but it was real. Nightmare real. She couldn't breathe, couldn't think. All she could do was feel the godawful pain of skinning herself.

Panting, she tried to think as her nightmares loomed. Her clothes had fused to her skin.

The scent of burning flesh hadn't been her roasting Bea alive.

Her own flesh had cooked.

She gagged on the bile rising in her throat. Dark shadows moved from her mind to line the walls. They slithered and roiled like a scary movie.

What had she done?

What had she done?

Chapter 35

Zeke plunged beneath the water's surface. He'd rather die than be controlled by the Maleem, but the alien's musty presence remained locked in his head, paralyzing his limbs preventing him from swimming. What was the Maleem trying to prove?

No answers came to mind, only more questions.

Had the Maleem tired of Zeke?

Was his fate to drown in this foreign sea?

Jessie's worried face flitted before his. She tugged on his rigid arms, trying to raise him to the surface. He made a quick mental calculation. With his unyielding, sinking mass, his chances of survival were less than ten percent. Any second now, Jessie would have to abandon him to breathe. He'd sink even lower.

How deep was the Sea of Japan? If that's even where they were. He hadn't been consulted about the travel plans. He'd been marched to the wharf along with the alien's other power reservoirs.

Some hero he was. He'd botched Jessie's rescue, gotten Forman dismantled, and been kidnapped by an alien. He was no man of action. He'd be dead in three short minutes.

It was dark under the water. If not for gravity pulling him ever downward, he wouldn't know which way was up. A pale orb appeared before his face again. Jessie. She was still here.

Save yourself, he shouted in his mind. *I'm a lost cause. Swim back to the surface. Swim for your life.*

But she didn't leave.

Air bubbles streamed from her nose. She glowed with a soft light. Strands of hair writhed around her like Medusa's snakes. She blew air into his lungs.

Her breath was unlike anything he'd ever experienced. It held a sweet addictive taint, and he wanted more. Lots more. Somehow he managed to angle closer, keeping their lips pressed together. His hands and feet stirred with life, but he didn't want to go anywhere or do anything. Her arms locked around his shoulders, her legs cinched around his waist.

Her physical closeness added to the fervent insanity of the

moment. He sighed dreamily in his throat. Life or death, he wanted it
– with her.

Needle-and-pin sensations tripped through his nervous system
as Jessie's breath unshackled him from the alien's control. His arms
locked around her, binding her to him, and still they swapped breath.

His.

Hers.

Jessie.

She was his everything, his font of life.

Locked in a passionate embrace, they continued to sink. In the
back of his mind, reason insisted this wasn't possible. No human
could survive this long underwater. The thought tickled him. He
wasn't human.

He was Taman. He had no idea what latent abilities he
possessed. Perhaps his species was formerly aquatic, and his skin
acted like gills, extracting oxygen from the water.

With each passing moment, his thoughts gathered, the
immediate sense of well-being lessened as reality dawned. Even if
he somehow possessed an ability to survive underwater, Jessie
didn't. She was human, and he was drowning her. If, by some slim
chance, he survived this immersion, She wouldn't.

Jessie couldn't die. She'd freed him from the alien's thrall.

He summoned the will to move, flexing his ankles, his knees,
and his hips. Gravity had been pulling them down, so he propelled
them the opposite way. Jessie remained life-locked to his lips. His
hands splayed wide on her supple back, keeping her close, keeping
her safe, keeping them streamlined like a surging rocket.

With each powerful kick, his thoughts cleared. Drok's musty
presence receded. His lungs burned with effort. He kicked harder,
determined to survive. Jessie hadn't given up on him, and he
wouldn't fail her.

He wanted to share the sunrise with her, to see her face light up
in that special way she looked at him. He wanted her tomorrows.

He wanted to live.

He reached deep for strength, driving them through the water
column to their future.

The strange chemical in his bloodstream made him want to
laugh and drift along with the current, but he had to focus. *Not yet.
Just a few more kicks. You're nearly there.*

He broke the water's surface and gasped in air but Jessie lay limp in his arms. She'd given him the means to live. "No. Don't be dead. Live." Covering her nose, he pushed air into her mouth. Again. And again, until she coughed water and breathed on her own.

He tread water, holding her, wanting her. Gentle swells rolled through the sea, raising and lowering them. The smell of brine filled his lungs. Overhead, stars twinkled in the night sky. Relief and adrenaline made him giddy. They were alive. Together they'd broken the alien's hold on him. Together they'd beaten the odds.

Together.

What an important word.

"Zeke," she finally managed. "Is it really you?"

He smoothed hair away from her pale face. "It's me."

"Don't ever do that to me again." She tapped his shoulder. "You scared me to death."

"Trust me, I won't. You saved me. Thank you."

"You saved us, so thank you back atcha," Jessie said. "Where are we?"

"In the ocean," Zeke said. With Jessie in his arms, he felt as if he could swim around the world. "Possibly in the Sea of Japan. The boat with the Maleem is long gone."

"He did something to you," she said. "You couldn't move or talk."

"I remember." Zeke scanned the horizon but the only lights he saw were the stars overhead.

"How did you break free of the thrall?" she asked. "We'd sunk so deep. We should've died."

"I didn't break free. You saved us. You saved me."

"Me? I didn't do anything. I got us thrown overboard and nearly drowned."

"The air you breathed into me underwater – what was it? Did you take something at the party?"

"I didn't eat or drink anything. I was too worried about you. But that bitch Pauline put her jeweled necklace on me, and changed me. I felt like I didn't have a care in the world. When she took the necklace back, I fought her for it."

"The necklace made you combative? It might've had a narcotic property. Perhaps it doses the wearer in some way."

"I don't understand. How?"

"Transdermally would work." At her puzzled look, he added, "Rapid skin absorption would account for the near instantaneous effect."

Jessie stared at him intently. "Pauline said she had two more of those necklaces. Her assignment was to bestow them on two more people tonight. What if she put one on Bea? What will happen to my sister? We have to find that boat."

Her fear broadcast upon the waters. Not good. Fear attracted predators. They didn't need another complication from sharks right now.

Priorities. His sole priority was Jessie. Her sister could look after herself for once. Besides, Jessie was in his arms. She should be thinking of him, not her sister.

To redirect her focus, he kissed her urgently, pouring his need for her into the moment. When she responded, he savored the feeling.

He'd never wanted Jessie more than right this minute. But there were practical concerns. He should wait to make love to her. Their first time should be special.

Digging deep, he found the will to end the kiss. "Easy, Jess. We'll get through this, but we're in the middle of the ocean. We need food, dry clothes, and a bed, not necessarily in that order."

"Now you're sounding like yourself." Her body molded to his length. A wave bumped them, rubbing their charged bodies together. "Making lists, prioritizing. I'm glad to have you back."

Rescue.

They needed a plan.

With the Maleem aware of their identities, they needed to stay off the grid. That meant Zeke couldn't use his name or his credentials once they made shore. He'd be operating in the dark. He required expert assistance to create new identities. "I need Forman."

Jessie blanched. "Forman broke the law. He's gone."

He stared at her. "What?"

"Don't you remember? Forman impersonated a human. His crime and destruction were a public spectacle."

Memories crowded into his head. "It's coming back to me. I must have shoved that image out of my mind. I'm a lousy friend."

"Don't be so harsh." She rubbed his back. "Your robot engineered his own downfall. We have rules for good reason. He thought he was above the law."

"You're wrong. He believed in laws, but he bent them frequently. He excelled at creative solutions."

"An odd quality for an artificial life form."

"We were a good team."

She stroked his face. "He took a huge risk going there in disguise. He died trying to save you."

"He's done that before."

Jessie shuddered. "Don't remind me."

With Forman out of commission, they were truly on their own. Zeke had no way to contact Uncle John without others knowing he was alive. The secure net was about as secure as a kid's vid game. Every firewall and security system could be beat.

Jessie kissed his neck. "Whatever we do, it doesn't matter. The Maleem plan to exterminate the human race, and we can't stop them. Let's forget about the world. I'm in the mood for personal gratification. Let's make love right now."

Potent cocktails hummed in his blood, not all of them alien. A small voice whispered caution. A louder voice said go for it.

He drew her close. She was a ray of sunshine in dark times. Who knew how long they had? "I love how you think."

Chapter 36

Jessie burned from the inside out. Seawater buoyed her physically and added to the unreal sense of finally having Zeke's complete attention. The intense energy radiating from him inflamed her senses even more. She'd known it would be incendiary with him.

Hot damn.

"Faster," she demanded, pulling at his soaked shirt.

"Gotta plan ahead. We'll need our clothes later." He dove down, eased her skintight pants off, and came back up with big grin on his face. "Missing something?"

"Long story."

He paddled away from her, treading water with her pants clutched in his hand. Under the starlight, his eyes seemed especially shadowed. "Are you seeing anyone?" he asked.

Her answer squeaked out. "No."

He waited with patience she didn't have. Didn't he feel the pulse of sexual attraction? She shot an imploring look at the night sky. Why should he be analytical about passion?

She could jump him, but this was Zeke. He required an explanation.

Every sensation coursing through her body felt so intense, so urgent. But even if she was under the influence of some alien chemical, she didn't care. She'd wanted Zeke to make love to her for months now. Any place would do, as long as it was right now.

"My clothes are in Tokyo," she said in a heated rush. "I borrowed an outfit tonight from Bea, but I had underwear lines with my panties on, so I nixed the panties. Satisfied?"

He looped her pants around her waist and knotted them. "Getting there."

To her delight, the edges of his voice roughened as his hands explored her contours, sending the mother of all tingles down her spine. His hands made short work of her stretchy tank top, slipping it down her arms. Her breasts seemed to swell in his firm caresses. For so long she'd wanted him to see her this way, sexy and alluring. It had taken an alien abduction and near drowning to bring the man of science to his senses.

She'd better make one hell of an impression tonight because she wasn't going through that again. This was her one shot to convince him he couldn't live without her. Because she didn't want to live without him.

His kiss kindled the simmering fire in her core. Flames of desire shattered her self-control, and she rode the burn, touching him, wanting him. Zeke made a sound deep in his throat, or maybe she made it. She couldn't tell. If they didn't make love now, she'd explode.

She ran her hands under his pink shirt, marveling at the strong feel of his muscled chest. A shudder of anticipation ripped through her as he stroked her body intimately. "I can't wait."

"No waiting required." He grinned wolfishly at her and adjusted his trousers.

His moon-bright eyes gleamed with heat. Impatiently, she rubbed against him, and a wave broke over her head. She surfaced, coughing water and gasping for air.

He smoothed the wash of hair back from her face. "Easy, Jess. I've got you."

She dug her nails into his back. "I can't go slowly. I've wanted this for so long. And now you're here, and I'm afraid it's a dream and I'll wake up any minute now. I have to go fast, understand?"

"We'll go how we go. Do you trust me?"

"Yes, of course."

"Remember that." With that, he surged inside. She felt full. Whole. She'd traveled around the world, but in doing so, she'd come home. Making love to Zeke felt right, more right than anything she'd done in her entire life.

His name sighed from her lips. Alternately rising and sinking in the ocean, they fought each other for the embrace, for breath, for completion. "Oh, God, Zeke," she murmured into his neck. "I've never felt so desperate before."

"Hold your breath." He covered her mouth with his and drove them under in a slow spiral. The water closed around them, and an incredible sense of privacy engulfed her. In this dark, silent world, sensation reigned supreme. Every square inch of her craved his touch. Every point of contact snapped with anticipation. She was lost in a sea of passion.

Tension inside her built like a rogue wave, cresting higher and higher as they surfaced and dove repeatedly until the tension shattered in a glorious burst of pleasure.

She arched and trembled and shuddered. Brilliant rainbows of color flashed beneath her shuttered eyelids. She heard a giant roar. Zeke. Or her. She didn't know. She didn't care. She'd never felt like this before. Soaring and falling. Free.

Anchored to him at the mouth and hip, she drifted bonelessly with the current. Once her heart rate slowed, she opened her eyes and saw nothing. Her breath hitched in her throat as another wave washed over them. Her lungs burned, and she thrashed against the tight bond holding her. Where was she?

Was she dead?

Zeke kissed her again, slowly, reverently, centering her wild thoughts. His hands stroked down her back, calming her, but try as she might, she couldn't get back to that nirvana sensation of a few moments ago. Her breathing quickened.

She tried to take stock of the situation. Her head was above water, so she hadn't drowned. Cold air wafted over her head and bare backside, so she was naked and in the ocean.

Zeke made long, powerful kicks, and she clung to him like a burr. She shivered against the chilly night air and the ocean, but Zeke's body heat warmed her. He'd asked her to trust him, but his swim-like-a-fish lovemaking style had pushed trust to the limit.

Cold fingers of dread brushed against the back of her neck. Her intellect wasn't in the same league as Zeke's, but she was no dummy. Human beings couldn't survive underwater. They required air to breathe. When they'd been thrown overboard, they'd been under for a long time.

How were they still alive?

Jessie's insides quaked as she considered the possibilities. Either Zeke could hold his breath for a very long time, or the Maleem necklace had done something to her and by transference, to him.

Think positive. He was a strong swimmer. He probably *could* hold his breath forever.

She loved Zeke.

She wanted to marry him and have his children.

But, the Maleem had landed and changed the course of Earth's history. If Jessie and Zeke survived this dunking, would the Maleem come after them?

She wanted to weep her frustration. With this trip to Japan, her life had taken a very sharp turn from the straight and narrow. She'd finally gotten what she wanted – intimacy with Zeke, and it was more than wonderful – but she couldn't make sense of the chain of events leading up to their watery tryst.

Damn.

She'd gotten exactly what she asked for, but it wasn't what she wanted, not by a long shot. Worse, she didn't have any explanation for what the necklace did to her. To them.

Something moved in the water nearby. In the pale starlight, she blinked rapidly, straining to see. There it was again. Oh no. A triangular shape. Several of them.

Fins.

Chapter 37

"Ouch," Forman said as a metallic tool clattered on the tiled floor. The thud echoed throughout the workshop. "That hurt."

"You might have Zeke fooled into thinking you're quasi-human, but I'm a realist," Angie said in a bracing tone. "You're lucky I even hooked up your speech and auditory centers before I finished the installation. By all rights you should be crushed in a Japanese recycling center."

"My humble apologies, madam," Forman said to Zeke's cousin. Memories of his ignominious end in front of thousands of concert-goers flashed to the forefront of his thoughts. He inwardly cringed at the humiliation he'd endured. "What are you doing to me?"

"Saving your sorry ass. What kind of idiotic knucklehead stunt was it to go to the concert in disguise without your ID necklace and talk smack about the Maleem?"

More of Forman's memories came online. He'd picked up something useful during the electrical exchange with Pauline. Luckily, the information shunted to his auxiliary module before he'd been ripped asunder. "The Maleem plan to exterminate the people on Earth."

"Where's your proof? Mr. Drok seems pleasant enough."

He managed the equivalent of a human snort. Angie had no idea what they were up against. "Drok somehow amassed enough electrical energy to fry all my circuits without touching me. Don't lower your guard. The Maleem don't have our best interests at heart. They are in this for themselves. He did something to Zeke, some sort of living paralysis. Did you rescue Zeke?"

"We have people looking for him."

"He's in danger." With effort, Forman wiggled his fingers. They felt shorter, thicker. What kind of robot shell was this? Didn't feel like the Gary shell he'd had before. "Where's the Maleem?"

"Taking a midnight cruise with Dylan James."

"Is Bea with them?"

"I believe so."

It was frustrating not being able to see or take action. Is this how

133

Zeke felt? A prisoner in his own skin? "Hurry up. I have to save them."

"You're going nowhere. I'm installing your processors in a Jethro unit."

He groaned aloud. "Say it isn't so."

"I'm afraid so. You can't be Forman again. The international robotic association condemned you and your heinous crime of human impersonation. For that crime, you were decommissioned, and your limited issue model name wiped from the robotic database. Thankfully, I'd placed a tracking chip in your housing before you left Georgia. Our team located you and removed your backup processors before you were flattened, so to speak."

"Ugh. You're heartless making me a Jethro. How can I get my girl back when I'm the shape of a retro garbage can?"

"I don't give a flying fig about your love life. If it was up to me, I'd let them mince you into bits. You're supposed to protect Zeke. You failed, and he's missing. Tell me what happened."

Her censure rankled. "Zeke came up with the idea of disguises for the concert. He thought we could get closer to the Stemfords and sweet talk them into coming home with us if they didn't see us coming." He mentally crossed his fingers. "Zeke didn't know I'd removed my ID collar. Those things aren't sexy. Whoever designed them should be horsewhipped. A simple ID pendant would be enough."

Angie tapped a metal implement on his housing. "Stay focused here. You two went to the concert. How'd you lose my cousin?"

"We were rocking out in the fan pit. I tried to get Zeke to loosen up and dance but he wouldn't. I didn't want him to blow our cover, so I started dancing. Next thing I know he's gone. I scoured the ground floor of the stadium. He wasn't there. The Maleem skybox had everyone's attention, so I figured he went there."

Sorrow blanketed his thoughts. "My assumption was one hundred percent accurate. I found him in the back of the skybox, conscious but nonresponsive."

"Did they drug him?" Angie asked.

"Not that I could tell. His pupils appeared normal; his respirations shallow but stable. It was as if he'd been turned off, if such a thing is possible."

"Interesting." Angie tightened another part and Forman was able to move his head. "Hold still and keep talking. Rumor has it that there was another man in the skybox. A man dressed in rags."

"I recall a man dressed in a dirty robe on the floor, but my focus was Dr. Z. I tried to awaken him. When I failed, I called the Maleem a bully and a liar to his face. You know the rest."

"The entire world knows the rest." Her voice hardened. "The press spun the tale into an international incident of epic proportions. Ambassador Wagner is seeking to ban A.I.s from future meetings with extraterrestrials. Heads of state around the world are concurring, each wanting to be favorably treated in the upcoming galactic trade negotiations."

"It always comes back to money, doesn't it?" Forman said. Light flickered and hummed as his optic sensors came online. Glancing down he noticed that his mud-brown rounded exterior had seen better days. Besides dirt, mud, and rust, there were numerous round holes in his recycled shell. "Where'd you find this Jethro shell?"

"Same place I found you. The junkyard. Cool how that worked out, huh?"

Great. He was buried alive in a robot shell gleaned from the scrap heap. Each hand had three fat fingers and a thumb. He glanced past his childlike hands and gasped. "My feet! They're gone."

"This Jethro had been adapted to work at an outdoor facility with uneven terrain, hence the treads. Look at the bright side. No one will ever suspect you're in a Jethro shell."

Forman threw his arm up to cover his optic sensors. He sighed and slumped forward, his voice trembling with emotion. "No one ever sees a Jethro. I might as well be invisible."

"Precisely," Angie said. "This is the perfect disguise. Find the other man from the skybox. He got zapped, same as you. We know he didn't accompany the group on the boat ride."

"Who am I looking for?"

"Not sure. We believe he's someone from Pauline's former life. We want intel about the Maleem from this man. Think you can find him without screwing up?"

"I can. But I'd rather be searching for Zeke."

"That's my mission right now. Meanwhile, avoid water as you search the streets of Hiroshima. I don't have time to patch up all the micro holes in your shell."

Forman wanted to carp some more about his downgraded appearance, but he'd screwed up. By flaunting the rules, he'd brought unwanted attention to himself. He understood that he had to pay for his mistake.

"Roger that. How will I contact you when I find this other man?"

Angie scooped up her tools and rose with a fluid grace. "I'll find you."

Chapter 38

The first dolphin bumped Zeke's leg. The second splashed his face. The third one leaped beside Zeke and Jessie, who still clung to him.

His thoughts kicked into high gear, edging out the mellow sated feeling he'd been savoring. Not knowing what response was expected, he patted the water beside him. A large female rolled under his hand, the white of her underside bright in the starry night. He rubbed her belly.

Cool. Did I summon you? He projected his thoughts toward them as he did at home. He listened for a response but Jessie shrieked. He caressed her back. "Easy, Jess. They're dolphins, and they mean no harm."

"Dolphins? You sure?"

"You're safe."

"I saw fins." Her teeth chattered. "I thought sure they were sharks."

He hugged her closer, and she shivered. Though his core temperature had held fast, her temp had dropped too low. He needed to get her out of the water.

He studied the smaller male who kept surfacing next to him. No way were these his dolphins from Georgia. But they had the same bottlenose shape. Could he communicate with the Tamans through them? He dared to hope in the possibility.

But how could he explain a transmission trance to Jessie? She'd go out of her mind if he relaxed to the point of unconsciousness while they were floating. He had to convince her to go along with a plan that was sketchy at best.

"The dolphins will help us," he began simply.

"How? How do they know what we need?"

"I'm not certain how they know my thoughts, but I'm certain they understand our situation. Trust me."

"I don't understand anything, but I'm tired and cold. I want to wake up in a warm bed. I don't like drifting along in the open sea like this. Who knows what monsters are lurking beneath us?"

Who knew what kind of monster he'd become? But he couldn't

say that. He smoothed wet hair away from her face. "We've been through a lot tonight, but we're not safe yet. The dolphins will get us to land, but we have to follow their lead. Do you have any energy left? Can you swim?"

She sniffed in a breath. "Of course I can swim. I learned how when I was a child."

"We'll follow them."

"The dolphins? Are they going our way?"

"Crazy as it sounds, they are." She trembled in his arms. "I can't explain my rationale. I trust them, and I'm asking you to trust in my belief."

Jessie looked around. "We don't know where we are. There are no lights on the horizon. We could be miles from shore."

"Perhaps, but we need to make an effort. Swimming will help warm you up."

"Point taken. I'd rather swim than freeze to death."

"That's the spirit."

She unhooked her limbs from her Zeke-raft, adjusted her top to cover her breasts, and began treading water. "I should put those pants on before we go anywhere."

"Allow me." He dove and worked the pants up over her toes, slender ankles, shapely calves, all the way to her magnificent thighs. If not for the dolphins, he'd take her again and damn the consequences.

"Which way?" she asked.

"The dolphins will tell us if we're headed the wrong way. You start. I'll swim beside you."

He watched her for a few strokes then swam quickly to catch up with her. The dolphin tapped his leg and nudged him into Jessie. She sputtered and came up for air. "What?"

"Head more to the right."

"They told you that?"

"They showed me that." Indecision flickered across her face, and his resolve strengthened. Their survival depended on her cooperation. "Trust me on this, Jess. I can get us to safety."

"I don't understand, but I'm too tired to balk. Let's go." She dove underwater to the right as directed, and he followed, matching her stroke for stroke. The pod of dolphins circled them at a respectful distance. As time progressed, Jessie slowed. She started breathing on every stroke. More waves splashed in her face. A big wave knocked her under, and she didn't come up.

Zeke dove to get her. She surfaced coughing and sputtering in his arms. "It's no use," she said. "I'm spent. I don't have anything more to give."

"I believe you." The dolphins circled closer. He tried to gauge their surroundings. Were the swells smaller? Could the shore be close?

"Here's what I want you to do. Climb on me as before."

"But then you can't swim. This is my mess. You swim to safety. You shouldn't have to sacrifice your life for me. Let me go."

"No one's sacrificing anything." He drew her close and lay supine in the water. The dolphins continued to circle. Jessie kept raising her head from his chest to watch them. He rubbed her back. "Relax, let the water carry us. I've got you."

"I'm so sleepy. I feel like I could sleep for a hundred years. But if I fall asleep, I'll drown."

"A little sleep would be fine. I've got you. The dolphins are watching over us. We're safe."

She yawned. "You can't expect me to sleep. We're adrift at sea."

He sculled his hands to keep them floating high. "What better time to take a nap?"

She talked a bit more, each phrase sounding drowsier and drowsier, until she fell fast asleep. Zeke tried "beaming" his thoughts to the dolphins, but they didn't make a flotilla to ferry him and Jessie to shore. They continued to circle, splashing and nudging him as if he were a new member of their pod.

Like Jessie, he was exhausted, but he had two priorities. Get them to shore. Contact the Tamans. He'd ask her to trust him and his dolphin brigade. Now he had no choice but to trust in the dolphins completely.

It went against his survival instinct to relinquish control. He kept treading water until his eyes became too heavy to hold open. His thoughts drifted on the gently rocking water. In the distance, he heard voices. He strained toward the sound. Gradually, the voices became distinct. They were calling his name. He hurried toward them.

I'm here, he said, recognizing the mindlink limbo of Tween. He hastened to the moving shadows.

We thought you'd transmit once you were in the sea, his father said. *What took you so long?*

It's complicated.

Uncomplicate it. This is important.

So's this. Jessie's here. She's with me.

The voices began murmuring, and he occasionally heard Jessie's name. Finally a different, deeper voice cut through the noise. *Is she your mate?*

That's private, Zeke said. He wasn't about to transmit his sex life across the universe.

Your choice affects all of us, son, his father said. *The future of our race depends upon your making a good choice.*

I care about this woman, Zeke conceded. *As to whether she's my mate, I don't know. But I have important news. The Maleem arrived. Drok landed on the planet with bodyguards and latched onto a newswoman as a translator. He visited countries around the globe.*

Did you stay far away from him?

I kept my distance, but he found me. Across a crowded venue, he enslaved my mind. It was terrible.

The murmuring began again. It grew louder and louder, giving Zeke a terrible headache. *Enough!* he shouted. *Tell me how he did this and how I can beat it next time.*

You survived, a deep voice said in a hushed tone. *No one from our race has ever emerged from a Maleem mind lock. Tell us how you defeated him.*

I didn't do anything. The Maleem lock shut down movement, speech, and auditory sensation. But I could still think. Jessie saved me. We were thrown overboard in the Sea of Japan. Her kiss freed me from Drok's thrall.

A kiss saved you?

The skepticism in his father's voice rankled, but to be fair, the edited version of the story sounded like a fairy tale. *She briefly wore a jeweled Maleem necklace before we went in the sea. Through physical contact, the alien chemicals in her body were in turn absorbed by my body. That's when I regained control.*

The link shuddered. Zeke couldn't make out the words they murmured this time. But the overall tone sounded upbeat. That gave him hope.

Did this Drok know of your survival? deep voice asked.

He didn't come after me if that's what you're asking. But I'm going after him once we're rescued. Tell me how I can beat this piece of alien garbage.

Your female wore the Subjugator and recovered?

The necklace? Yeah, but she didn't wear it very long, half a minute at most.

The Subjugator is instant death for our race. If you'd been forced to wear it, you would be dead.

I've made a mental note to self – don't wear the stupid necklace. But the chemicals in it, in trace amounts, are what saved me. I'm certain of that.

We must discuss this, deep voice said. *No one has ever reported this finding to the collective.*

How can I beat the Maleem?

The link quieted. His father whispered, *No one has ever beaten the Maleem.*

Chapter 39

Pauline lifted her newly returned necklace off her collarbone and cradled it with shaking hands. Within an instant, her sense of euphoria faded. Excruciating pain lanced her mind. Her damned leg. The Maleem hadn't done that. He hadn't touched her.

She'd done it to herself.

It felt like a thousand fire ants were biting her leg. She panted in gulps of air and stared at the gaunt stranger reflected in the hotel dresser mirror. For her career, she'd slogged through swamps and battle zones to do her job. She'd slept her way to the top. Those inconveniences had been easily dismissed.

But she'd fallen in the tar pit now.

She'd sought the pinnacle of success.

She'd found the hell of alien addiction.

Face it, Pauline. You need the frickin' necklace.

Hastily, she settled the jeweled collar on her bare skin. Moments later, her sense of well-being returned. So what if her skin was stuck to the leather clothing? At least her body was covered. As long as she wore the necklace, pain wasn't an issue.

She brushed her hair and touched up her makeup. No point in looking like a druggie. Presentation was everything in her business. Scent, too. She dampened a washcloth and blotted her armpits. The stinging sensation stole her breath away. Angry, she hurled the offending washcloth on the floor.

What the hell was happening to her?

Her clothes were glued to her skin, and now she couldn't even rinse her sweaty armpits? She tried smelling herself to see if she stunk, but she couldn't smell anything.

Huh?

She crossed the room to the stunning vase of red roses the ambassador had sent her. Leaning her face close a crimson flower, she inhaled deeply.

They had no scent.

That wasn't right.

This necklace was screwing up her senses.

Good thing she hadn't consumed any food or drink. She couldn't use the bathroom with her clothes glued to her body.

Another thought occurred to her. The spacesuited guards never went to the bathroom either. Mostly they stood still and only moved when Drok commanded them to do something.

She glanced across the hotel room to where a Maleem guard stood in a self-contained spacesuit. The man's eyes tracked her progress around the room, but he stood ramrod straight.

"You guys spend a lot of time on your feet," she said, patting the wide bed. She thrust out her breasts, hoping to get a rise out of this guy. Nothing. Crap. "Sit down and take a load off. I won't bite."

The guard didn't respond. Her previous guard hadn't responded when she'd been able to change her clothes a few days ago. She'd delighted in parading naked in her hotel room that day.

Were they eunuchs? Had they lost their sense of hearing as well as their tongues? Or did the airflow in the containment suit serve as white noise?

All her life, she'd hated being ignored. She marched across the plush red carpet and stopped a few feet away from him. "Can you hear me?" she asked. When he showed no recognition, she repeated her question as loud as she could shout. Damn. Still nothing.

Did the man even speak English? She moved closer so that he couldn't help looking at her. His eyes rounded as if in fear. Interesting. She backed up a step, and his gaze returned to soldier solemn.

He was afraid of her? What could she do to an armed man?

She could tear his suit. That's what happened with the other guard. She'd ripped his suit, and the vapor inside had messed her up. Nightmares such as she'd never known had consumed her days and nights. Only the necklace had stopped the phantoms from tormenting her.

She never wanted to breathe that noxious gas again. No way would she touch his silly spacesuit. He was safe from the likes of her.

Inspiration struck. She hurried across the room, opened the desk drawer, and wrote on the notepad: Can you read this? She carried the message across to the guard and pushed it in front of his face.

He nodded his head the slightest bit. If she hadn't been looking, she'd have missed it.

Yes!

She tried another message. Can you write?

He shook his head, again only the tiniest of movements.

Hmm. She tapped her fingernails on the notepad. He understood written English, but he couldn't speak and apparently couldn't hear her. But he had answers about the Maleem, answers she needed to know.

He blinked his eyes at her.

Blinking. She'd noticed they could blink.

She wrote: one blink yes, two blinks no.

He blinked once.

Adrenaline surged into her bloodstream. They could communicate. What should she ask him? As a reporter, she often led off by asking where her interviewees were from. She wrote: Are you human?

Two blinks. No.

Are you Maleem?

No.

What was he? If she didn't know what race he was, how would she ever ask the right question? His gaze shifted to her necklace. She wrote: my necklace?

Yes.

He wanted to tell her about the necklace? She wrote: you want my necklace?

Three blinks. Yes and no.

Should I take it off?

Yes.

Did you have a necklace once?

Yes.

Pauline danced away from him, her nerves rioting. Was it her fate to wind up in a poison suit like his? He couldn't move of his own accord, couldn't talk, couldn't hear. She had to know more.

She circled back and dashed off another query. Were you always mute?

No.

The Maleem did this to him. That certainty clunked through her. She touched her face with quivering hands. Oh, God. This wasn't good. She asked – just to be sure, and he confirmed her ugly suspicions.

Are you a slave?

Yes.

144

Her breath stuttered. He was a slave. He'd worn a necklace. He was property of the Maleem. She'd suffer the same fate unless a miracle happened.

She'd already thrown her miracle away. Connor had come for her, and she'd channeled electrical current into him. His innocent blood stained her hands. Would the Maleem make her do worse? She'd rather die.

Would this guard? She scribbled the words: do you want to die? No.

Why would he want to live like this? It was beyond her wildest imaginings. What would possibly make living in such restricted circumstances attractive? She flipped the paper over and wrote on the back: do you expect to live a long life?

Yes.

His answer brought more questions to mind, but number one was her safety. She wrote: will the Maleem kill me?

His eyes stayed open. She wrote: You don't know?

Yes.

She might live. She might die. She might become a Maleem slave if she kept wearing the necklace, but slaves had a long life expectancy. The future was exhausting to contemplate.

The door to the adjoining suite swished open, and Drok entered. He wasn't wearing the space suit he wore in public. Pauline startled away from the mute guard. "Yes?" she asked.

His stern face alarmed her. She retreated to the corner of the room, knowing Drok had the power to incinerate her on the spot. He held out his green hand for the paper.

"I'm a reporter," Pauline said, cupping her fingers around the notepad. The flame of guilt seared her cheeks. "It's my nature to ask questions."

Drok flicked a wrist toward the guard, who obediently exited the room. The alien held out his hand and waited.

Out of options and fearful of dying, Pauline handed him the notepad. "How do you understand my language? Who taught you to read English?" Realizing even as she spoke that she ought to have asked these questions of the guard when she had the chance.

Drok didn't answer as he scanned the words on the pages. When he finished, the pad dropped to the floor. Pauline pressed back into the wall, but Drok had her in his sights. Her throat tightened with terror as the powerful alien raised his hand.

Current arced from his extended arm into her body. Every nerve in her body throbbed and burned. She screamed at the excruciating pain, wishing it would end, hoping she survived. The torn skin on her leg seemed to be on fire. She slapped at the injury, but that made her hand and her leg hurt more.

Her eyes rolled up in her head, and the world darkened. She couldn't stand it. She wanted to die. Then the pain intensified. She jerked and twitched and convulsed until she passed out.

Sometime later, Pauline awakened face-up on the carpet. Everything hurt. She groaned aloud, forcing her dry lips apart. Her tongue felt too thick. She must have bit it. Damn. She didn't need more injuries.

Drok's impassive face moved into focus. His jagged teeth no longer looked friendly. They looked downright menacing. Would he lean down and take a bite of her belly?

She shuddered and waited, dread pounding in her ears as each second of her life ticked past. The alien's heavy hand rested on her shoulder. His musty thoughts flooded into her, and she winced at the sharp barbs of energy.

You have displeased me.

"I'm sorry," Pauline said, fighting the throbbing wall of pain for her breath. A new panic coursed through her. She couldn't move her limbs. "I wanted answers."

You forget your place. You are not worthy.

His hands moved to her neck. The weight on her neck lessened. Oh, God, no. He was taking the necklace again. She couldn't go through that withdrawal again. It was too much. It was too soon.

"Please," she begged. "I'll do better. I won't ask questions."

He dismissed her plea with a fierce glare. Her paralysis ebbed, and agonizing sensation flowed into her limbs. Much as she wanted to punish him for hurting her, she was afraid to move.

Her hands fisted in the plush carpet. Tufts of fuzz came up in her fingers. "I need the necklace. Don't take it. I need it. I'll give you anything. I'll do anything." She sobbed loudly. "Please. I want the necklace."

The door snicked shut, and the nightmare visions from the gas she'd inhaled days ago began anew. Phantoms slithered from the dream world into the rose-scented hotel room. A scream welled in her throat, but she knew no one would come. They never did.

She huddled in a corner and wept.

Chapter 40

Zeke drifted along in that wakeful place not quite asleep but not awake either, feeling at peace, feeling relaxed. Water splashed. A bird called. The ocean-fresh air invigorated his senses. Brightness intensified on his eyelids, on his face. Did he forget to close the blinds before he went to bed?

What time was it anyway?

He opened an eye to check his bedside com link and startled the rest of the way awake. He wasn't in his bedroom. Far from it. He blinked and stared up at a giant vault of blue. Fluffy white clouds sailed across the sky. Movement to the right caught his eye. A shorebird wheeled, banked, and plunged into the sea. A giant ship rode the horizon near the rising sun. A fishing boat idled to the west.

What the—?

A growl rose in his throat as he attempted to orient himself by standing, but his sudden movement dumped Jessie off his chest and into the sea. She slid under the water without as much as a sound. *Jessie!*

He dove down, caught her in his arms, and propelled them upward with strong flutter kicks. Panicked, she fought him all the way to the surface. Wide-eyed, she coughed and tried to push away from him.

"Easy," he soothed. "I've got you."

"You tried to drown me," she accused between coughs.

Though she still struggled to get away, he supported her until her breathing stabilized. "It's my fault you went under. My apologies."

She glanced around, her eyes glassy. "What? How? Where?"

Her disorientation worried him. His Taman physiology had kept them both warm during the night at sea, but his energy reserves were low. The sea felt cold to him, so it must feel downright freezing to Jessie. She was in trouble.

"I don't know where we are," he said. "There's a fishing boat off to the right. Let's get rescued. Can you make it to the boat?"

Jessie's chin came up. "You asked that question last night. I swam just fine."

She sounded like her usual self. Reluctantly, he released her, watching closely as she tread water. When she maintained position, he drew in a shaky breath. "And we spent all night in the water," he stated in a level, non-accusing voice. "That's why I asked again. I'm tired and cold, too. But if you're spent, I'll get us over there."

"I can do it," she insisted, slogging through the water toward the small craft.

A few strokes later, she stopped moving. "I was wrong. My arms are too heavy, and my feet don't work right. I can't make it. You go ahead. I'll wait here."

"No way am I leaving you behind. I'll swim for the both of us." He reached for her, tucking her up close, absorbing her tiny shivers. "Hang on."

As he side-stroked, he scanned the horizon for friendly dolphins, but he didn't see them, which meant he had no backup. His strength was nearly gone, but he'd be damned if he'd give up and sink in this ocean. Jessie's life meant something. So did his. He had important work to do.

Like saving the world.

First, he'd save the two of them.

He set out on an intersect vector with the fishing boat. To distract himself from the distance he needed to cover, he made a list of priorities. Get them on dry land. Find out where the Maleem were. Obtain a Subjugator necklace to study it. Figure out how to beat the Maleem once and for all. Live happily ever after with Jessie on Tama Island.

He'd give anything to be home, sitting on his beach, watching his ocean. Stroke, stroke, stroke.

Her shivers deepened into shudders. He felt the coolness of her skin pressed against his. Hypothermia was setting in. "Hang on, Jessie. We're almost there."

He heard a shout, and the unmistakable rumble of an engine. Holding Jessie tight with one arm, he dropped his legs under water, churning his feet like eggbeaters to stay vertical, and waving his other arm. "Over here!"

The fishing boat pulled up beside them and cut the engine. Weathered Asian faces stared down at him. The four black-haired men spoke rapidly in a language he didn't understand.

Zeke had never felt like such an ugly American before. He

shook his head. "I don't understand. Please help us."

A looped rope sailed over the side, splashing in the water next to them. Zeke sat in the loop and cradled Jessie in his arms. The coarse rope shredded his trousers and bit into his legs, but he didn't care. Jessie shuddered against him, her fingers and lips blue.

"Hang on, Jess." His voice cracked with emotion. "We're almost there."

The winch squealed as they were hoisted from the water, swung over onto the boat's stern, and lowered onto the fishy-smelling deck. The solid feel of the boat was like nothing Zeke had ever experienced, even though he still rocked as if in the sea.

His breath hitched in his throat. His arms and legs trembled of their own accord. Tears blurred his vision. They'd made it to safety.

He'd done it. No, they'd done it. Without Jessie diving under and refusing to let him drown last night, they wouldn't have had a chance.

"Thank you," he managed as coarse blankets appeared. He wrapped Jessie in one then wrapped the other blanket around the two of them. She shivered and shuddered in his arms until their combined warmth lulled her into sleep.

Zeke must have dozed too, but when the engine stopped, the lack of vibration awakened him. Men with drawn weapons and official-looking uniforms swarmed the vessel, surrounding them. They jabbered at him, quick and hard. He didn't understand a word.

He raised his hands in surrender. The irony of the situation struck him. Had they survived drowning to be gunned down on land? "I don't understand you. Does anyone speak English? I'm American."

His words spurred another round of buzzing speech and gun waving. He didn't know what they wanted of him. With his rubbery legs, he couldn't stand if he tried. Jessie needed medical attention. So did he.

"Is there a doctor?" he asked. "Please. Help us."

The officials parted, and a solid looking woman approached. She wore the same dark uniform as the men, only her version included a severe suited skirt and heels. Her short hair stirred in the slight breeze. He finally recognized the colorful yin/yang flag patch on the uniforms.

South Korean.

They'd crossed the Sea of Japan overnight?

"I am Officer Kim," the woman said. "Who are you? What is your business in Busan?"

The thought of attaining false identities fled. The only way out of this mess of red tape was to tell the truth. If the Maleem came after them, he'd have to take that risk. He lowered his arms slowly. "We're Americans. I'm Zeke Landry, and this is Jessie Stemford. Last night we fell off a boat in the Sea of Japan."

"The East Sea," Kim said, her almond-shaped eyes narrowing. "We do not use that other name here. Where is your passport?"

Zeke shrugged. "I don't know if it's still in my pants pocket. We spent all night in the ocean. Please. My friend needs medical attention. She's in shock. We both need fluids. We just want to go home."

Officer Kim turned to speak to a tall associate. The drawn weapons pointed at Zeke and Jessie didn't waver. Zeke glanced down and saw four red light spots clustered in a one-inch square over his heart. Snipers? Weren't the dozen guns onboard ship enough firepower for two shipwrecked people?

Not good. They'd come so far only to be denied entry to dry land? What happened to good old-fashioned hospitality?

"Contact my boss," Zeke offered. "John Demery will vouch for us. We mean you no harm."

"Give me his contact information," Officer Kim barked.

Zeke shared his uncle's private com number.

She nodded tersely. "We will check your story. Meanwhile, you and the woman will remain under guard in our secure facility."

"Thank you." Zeke drew in a shaky breath. His uncle would pull strings and get them out of this fix.

The crowd of uniforms parted, and paramedics surged forward with gurneys. Just as he thought to relax, out came the tranquilizer gun.

Damn.

But instead of the twilight sleep he normally experienced upon tranquilization, little dark bits of matter swam in and out of focus in his subconscious. They tugged at his peace of mind, whirling him around in tight circles. The bits joined and solidified, and he smashed into them. Ouch. The cycle repeated again and again. Darkness interspersed with light. The dark wall. The pain of slamming into it.

What did it mean?

Chapter 41

Forman started his search for the man in rags outside the concert venue stadium. He circled the place twice using the cleaning props Angie'd thrust in his chubby hands to complete his disguise. As per his prediction, not one human so much as glanced his way. Jethro units were viewed in the same vein as furniture. He was virtually invisible.

He checked the trash compacters.

Nothing.

This wasn't cutting it. He needed to be more proactive, or he'd never find raggedy man or Zeke. With that thought humming through his circuits, he swiped in the service entrance as if he were on the shift to clean the stadium interior. He mopped his way to the security room. A guard stared resolutely at the flickering vid screens on the wall.

He didn't acknowledge Forman's presence or his emptying the trash can.

Angie was right. This disguise was perfect.

He circled around to the feed output at the end of the hall. The guard never stirred. Forman opened the access casement and plugged in. He found the skybox segment, viewed it at top speed, and then accessed the other cams until he saw the raggedy man stumble out of the stadium.

He groomed the other side of the corridor as he rolled to the exit. His target was still alive. He'd left on his own two feet. Forman's next stop was at a portable banking unit on the next block. He spritzed cleaning solution over the numbered panel as he surreptitiously reviewed recent images. There. Raggedy man. Heading south.

Forman repeated the sequence at four more cam locations until he found another image of raggedy man. This time, the camera snapped a glimpse of the man's bearded face. Forman triangulated the eyes, nose and mouth and plugged the shape into a batch of the Pauline's known associates. The result came through a block later as dawn streaked across the night sky.

Connor Bronsen.

Pauline's co-anchor on Entertainment News.

My, how the mighty had fallen. Gone were the expertly tousled locks, the glowing skin, the glittering gold jewelry. Only one thing would drive a man to such extremes – emotion. With his own unrequited love for Bea burning in his heart, Forman made the mental leap that Connor had it bad for his vid screen costar.

He must've come to rescue Pauline.

The Maleem had booked rooms at the Plaza. Assuming the aliens returned to the rooms after the cruise, Connor would lurk there until he had another chance to grab Pauline.

Yesterday, Forman could have walked into the Plaza and passed for a human guest. Today was a different story. In his junkyard shell, he couldn't pass for anything but a has-been robot. He circled the hotel, seeking the custodial entrance. It was flanked by a bevy of refuse bins. He rolled into the five star accommodation as if he owned the place.

"No, you don't," a woman said, authority ringing in her voice. "Stop right there, rusty Jethro. You do not have authorization to enter the Plaza."

Forman stilled. He turned slowly by rotating one track forward and the other backward. A hatchet-faced female glared at him, disapproval etched into her harsh features.

"I don't know where you came from, but you're not on my access list. You don't belong here," she said, pointing toward the exit. "Out. Get out of my hotel and don't come back, or I'll report you to Supply Central."

Hanging his head, Forman complied. Behind him, he heard the woman mumbling about the nerve of some robots. She didn't know a thing about his nerve. Once she was out of sight, he hitchhiked on the wall-side of a maintenance cart. Moments later, he was inside the swanky hotel.

He switched to carpet cleaning mode and shampooed a swath to the admin offices. In the manager's office, he palmed a master key, which he secreted in his hollow core. Four offices later, he found an unguarded com portal. He accessed the system, learning the Maleem's rooms were on the top floor. That's where Connor would be. That's where Forman didn't want to be.

Wishing for the best, he joined a bevy of human-like robots in the service elevator. He kept his optical sensors on the floor and refrained from communal data streaming. To his relief, the other bots left him alone.

One by one, his uptown associates exited to go about their authorized business. Only Forman rode the elevator to the top. He rolled the length of the hall, not seeing Connor, not seeing another soul. There were four suites up here. The news anchor had to be hiding in one of them. Conversely, the Maleem were ensconced in another suite.

Nothing like a little Russian roulette.

If he opened the right door, he got the man. If he opened the wrong door, all hell would break loose.

Much as he hated getting his circuits fried, he'd complete his mission because it stood in the way of him helping Zeke. Once he found Connor, he could help Angie locate Zeke.

On his next pass down the corridor, Forman examined the locks of each suite. With the master key, he could open each door and look inside but if the security latch was on, he would draw unwanted attention. He needed a reason to access the rooms, so he opened the floor's linen closet and grabbed a prop from the bedding inventory. Pillow in hand, he knocked on doors. "Housekeeping."

A grumpy man in 3060 denied needing another pillow. A thin woman in 3040 took the pillow anyway. Two down, two to go. He had a fifty-fifty chance of opening the right door. The next door had a do-not-disturb card wedged in the cardkey slot. Too bad. Forman grabbed another pillow and knocked on 3010. "Housekeeping."

No answer.

He paused to gather himself. Unlocking the door, he rolled soundlessly inside and flipped on the light. The pristine room appeared to be unoccupied. No visible luggage. No discarded garments. No waste in the trash. And yet, large sprays of fresh flowers adorned the two tables. A giant fruit basket remained untouched.

A dull circlet lay on the sink counter. Forman studied it with growing excitement. Was this Pauline's necklace? It must belong to the Maleem.

He circled the lair of his enemy. There were two closed doors. He opened the first. Bathroom. A dark shape in the tub caught his eye. He rolled closer, not knowing what to expect. He called softly, "Connor?"

The shape didn't respond. It couldn't. The green-skinned body in the busted spacesuit stared at him with sightless eyes. Dead. Forman felt a spurt of hope. It was possible to kill them. That was good to know.

He retreated without touching it.

Before he could open the other door to check for occupants, he received an urgent transmission from Angie. She'd found Zeke. Time to go.

But not before he helped himself to a souvenir. He wrapped the necklace in a pillowcase and stuffed the purloined item in his hollow core. The Maleem had taken his identity from him. Time for a little payback.

Chapter 42

People said a person's perspective changed after a near-death experience. Jessie knew that to be true via firsthand experience. Months ago, a secret society had done their best to kill her, and now she'd had a close call with the sea.

And an alien encounter. She couldn't forget Drok or Pauline, his human puppet.

Shivering, she tucked the covers tighter around her. The chill in her marrow wouldn't ease. She'd been so cold in the water, she didn't think she'd survive. Zeke had saved her … them. Zeke didn't let her drown.

He was a living, breathing hero.

She glanced at the other gurney where he slept. What would he do if she crawled in bed with him? She wanted to rest her head on his chest, to feel his strong arms holding her close. She wanted him to make love to her again. To reassure her that they were fully, gloriously alive.

But there was the small matter of the armed guards in the room.

Not that she had the energy for all of that romping, but still, a girl could dream.

She slid back into a restless sleep, waking to feel muscled arms enfolding her. "Mmm," she sighed dreamily, nestling closer to his amazing body heat.

"You're okay," Zeke murmured in her ear. "I've got you."

"About time," she managed as warmth crept through her body. Sleep dulled her mind, and she drifted on the happy current of her love. She loved Zeke. She'd known it for weeks, but now she didn't have to hide her feelings. She would to shout it from the rooftops, but first she needed to sleep.

***

Jessie ate breakfast for supper, alone. While she slept, Angie arrived and dispatched the armed guards. Zeke had awakened before Jessie and was working in the next room. She flexed her hand. Her fingers felt normal again, no more wrinkled fingertips. She still felt exhausted, but she was alive.

After eating, she showered and dressed in a white bathrobe which had been hanging in the bathroom. Not exactly sex kitten apparel, but it was better than naked which was a poor choice for mixed company. She stared at the pale-faced woman in the mirror. She wasn't eye-catching or sexy like her sister, but Zeke cared about her.

She finger-combed her damp hair, pulling and tugging at the snarls.

How should she approach Zeke? Technically, this was the morning after they'd made love for the first time, and she didn't want any awkwardness between them. Should she kiss him on the mouth? Would he open his arms to her so she could jump on his lap? Would he propose?

Stop that, she lectured herself. You made love with him once. In the ocean. That has nothing to do with a marriage proposal. He likes you. Maybe even loves you. Chances are he doesn't know it yet.

"Ready or not, here I come," she said softly. "Lights off."

The blue-tinted air in the next room took her breath away. She'd heard of data streaming, but she'd never actually seen it before. A fat, rusty robot sat in a dense data cloud.

"You're sure?" Zeke said.

"Sure about what?" Jessie asked.

He waved in acknowledgment and turned back to the Jethro. "The dead guy."

Her romantic hopes faded. No open arms. No kiss. No glance at the shadowed cleavage revealed by the thick robe. She was back where they started. She shook her head to clear the cobwebs. So much for her powers of seduction.

"What dead guy?" she asked, moving forward.

"Forman saw a dead guy. In the Maleem's room."

"Forman?" She stared at the rust bucket beside Zeke. Was it possible? "I thought he committed robot hari-kari."

Zeke grinned, and her heart raced at his disarming smile. "He did. But Angie stuffed him into this Jethro suit, so there you go."

Confused, she glanced from Angie to Zeke to the robot. All nodded. She rubbed her eyes and then her temples. "Would someone please stop the world for a minute while I catch up?"

"You're doing fine," Angie said. "After what you've been through, you're better than fine."

Jessie's blood heated. She didn't expect to be patronized. Zeke had been through the same experience, and yet he looked like he could take on a fleet of Maleem. Where was the justice in that?

"I lost nearly twelve hours. A lot can happen in twelve hours." Another thought occurred to her, a chilling thought. She grabbed the back of a chair. "Does anyone know what happened to my sister? Where is she?"

The room quieted. Data stopped streaming. Forman turned to her. "Bea and Dylan James jetted to the Riviera early this morning."

Her heartbeat roared in her ears. White light temporarily blinded her. "No. That can't be. She wouldn't leave without me."

The air snapped with energy, then the vid screen illuminated. Bea wore a sheer nightie with all of her attributes on full display as she walked barefoot beside Dylan toward his plane. She preceded him up the ramp, pausing at the top to kiss Dylan full on the mouth, before disappearing inside.

Jessie gripped her belly as her breakfast turned to stone. "I'm stunned."

"She broke my heart," Forman said.

Her sister's impulsive behavior showed a lack of respect and immaturity. Cavorting with Dylan James of all people. She wanted to be sick. And poor Forman. He'd worshiped Bea.

If Zeke did that to her, she'd die from heartache.

Angie cleared her throat and killed the image. "Ambassador Wagner appears to be the Maleem's new interpreter. No one is sure what happened to news anchor Pauline Curran, but she hasn't appeared all day. The new guy, Wagner, held two press conferences. The Maleem negotiated landing sites on all continents. In the next week, they'll install their representatives on our planet to referee trade agreements."

"Did they say what they want?" Jessie asked, taking the hint that no one wanted to discuss her sister's love life. Forman and Zeke talked in hushed tones she couldn't hear, which added to her irritation.

Angie cued up the image of the Maleem spaceships again. "Minerals."

The skin on the back of her neck got all itchy and crawly. "Not gold or gems?"

"Nope. They want minerals."

"That doesn't make any sense," Jessie said. "There are a kazillion uninhabited planets out there with minerals. Why come here and pay for ours when they can get them for free?"

"She's sharp," Angie said. "Jessie sees what heads of state and entrepreneurs fail to realize. These invaders are here for us. We're what Earth has in abundance. People. Billions of them."

"We have to tell someone. Why would anyone let them get a foothold here?"

"Something is being done. I'm telling you this in the strictest confidence. The unified military is planning an assault from the new Space Station. Officially, we're welcoming them. Unofficially, we're going to kick butt."

"Seriously?" Air snorted from Jessie's nostrils. "They travel across galaxies, zap folks with electric current from their fingertips, and we're going to outgun them? I don't think so."

"Right again." Angie beamed." Zeke's going to come up with a Plan B scenario."

Jessie turned to Zeke. "What's Plan B?"

"Working on it," he said.

Chapter 43

Thoughts careened through Zeke's head at the speed of light as he winged home in his uncle's private transpo. He'd known pressure before, but responsibility had never weighed so heavily on his shoulders. Despite the clear sunny day, Zeke's outlook soured.

After being in life and death mode, he finally had time to catch his breath and study the horizon. He didn't like the danger he saw there.

His fingers dug into the leather armrests. So much had happened in the last few days. Between the Maleem enslaving him, nearly drowning, and making love with Jessie, his head ached with unfinished business. The Maleem. Death. Jessie. He couldn't focus.

Pull it together, he told himself.

Much as he wanted to go after Drok, he had to respect his special vulnerability to the Maleem. But he'd find a way to stop the alien. He wouldn't give up as long as he had breath in his body.

Nearly drowning had taken him to the brink and exposed latent Taman abilities. He could survive underwater longer than a human. He could channel his energy into maintaining his core temperature under adverse circumstances. Each discovery was a wonderment and a mystery. What other talents might he still have? How many other ways would he be different from humans? If only he could ask his father.

The scientist in him needed to run experiments on himself, but other matters were urgent.

And Jessie.

He cared for her. Making love with her topped any experience he'd ever imagined. Was she his mate? Was that why he felt so bereft without her? Her name thrummed in his veins. Softly. Insistently.

"You're awake," Forman said, rolling into sight from the rear of the plane.

Startled, Zeke released the armrest and clenched his hands in his lap. "Couldn't sleep."

"Figured as much."

"Completed your sweep?"

The robot circled and stopped across from Zeke. "No active listening devices detected on this flying bus. But no need to report in. Angie installed a sub electron com link in my circuits and she can read me whenever she wants."

Zeke let out a slow breath. "We wouldn't be here if not for my cousin's foresight. She's on our side, so we'll let the security breach stand." For now, he added silently. He didn't like the idea of anyone spying on him.

"You're missing Jessie?"

The robot had misinterpreted his scowl. Better to go with that train of thought anyway. "I am. She saved my life."

"From her account, you saved hers." Forman glanced out the window before he met Zeke's gaze. "You slept with her."

Why did everyone have such a fascination about his love life? "I don't discuss private matters."

Forman clapped his chubby hands and rocked on his rollers. "Great! I'm thrilled you two finally hooked up."

"I didn't say that."

"You didn't have to. I thought you'd blow a gasket when she refused to come home with us. I knew something major had happened. About time you two became a couple."

"It's complicated," Zeke admitted.

"Yes. It is. But a man of your talents can do complicated. You were a child prodigy and could have a dozen degrees right now instead of one PhD. Why didn't you do that?"

Where was this going? Tension knotted his shoulders. "My father taught me to keep a low profile."

"Did he teach you how to keep a girl?"

"We didn't talk about that, but I have his example to follow. He loved my mother. Even when they argued, their accord glittered like a prized trophy."

"You didn't agree with Jessie about her sister. Have a heart, bro. She's been both mother and sister to Bea. If you want to stay in her good graces, you should consider her feelings."

"She didn't consider mine." The words slipped out uncensored. All the emotion he'd been throttling back roared to life. He rose and paced the cabin, articulating his thoughts with hand gestures. "I wanted her with me, where I can keep her safe. The Maleem is out there. He knows her identity. Jessie is a target because of me, but she won't listen, not where her sister is concerned. Bea is an adult. She's responsible for her own actions. I know you have a thing for Bea, but I'm not a fan of her behavior. She's out of control and that's dangerous."

"You could have gone with Jessie," Forman pointed out.

Zeke stopped pacing to massage his throbbing temples. "The entire planet is about to be enslaved. I have work to do, and the only place on the entire planet where I have total clarity is Tama Island. I promised Uncle John I'd work on the alien problem once we got Jessie out of Japan. Time for me to uphold my end of the bargain."

"Which is why we're winging home. If it's any consolation, your idea to send Angie with Jessie was positively inspired. Angie is one tough chick."

Zeke shot the robot a sharp look. "You've switch your allegiance from Bea to Angie?"

"Bea's the love of my life, but Angie gave me life. She's like my mom or something."

What would Forman do with a mom? Not long ago he wanted to sleep with Angie. Zeke shuddered. Not a good image. "We should call you Lazarus instead of Forman. Do you remember each death?"

"I do."

The robot's steely tone sliced into Zeke's heart. He leaned against the bulkhead, feeling the slight engine vibration through his entire body. "Sorry. I thought they nuked those files when they rebooted you."

"They didn't. Would you like me to describe death for you?"

"Some other time." Zeke's near brush with death hovered in his mind. "Let's switch gears. The Maleem will strike back when Earth fires on their ships. We need more information about them, about their technology."

"I hoped you'd say that." Forman rubbed his metal abdomen as if it would bring him good luck. "I have a surprise."

With that, he opened his core. Zeke knelt to see inside. Amidst the cleaning solutions, greasy rags, and stinky refuse, sat a bulging pillowcase. "What is it?"

"Take it out," Forman urged. "See for yourself. The Maleem hurt me, so I hurt him by lifting this."

Zeke rocked back on his heels and scrambled away like a crab. "The necklace?"

"Yep."

"I can't touch it. Not here. We'll study it in the lab."

Forman cocked his head in interest. "Don't you want to see it?"

"You have no idea how much I want to study it. We need to take precautions with the Subjugator. It's dangerous."

Forman re-sealed his core. "The device enslaves people? How do you know?"

He couldn't admit his mindlink with the Tamans, but he had enough data to make a strong case. He queued up the vids of the skybox incident. "The whole world saw Pauline Curran change before their eyes. She allowed Drok to control her mind and body. After she wore the necklace, she became violent and mean hearted. If that's not proof enough, consider this. Pauline attacked her co-worker, not Drok. The energy came from her."

Forman clicked off the vid. "If the device enslaves people, the ambassador is compromised. Dylan James, too. Good thing we sent Angie with Jessie. If Dylan wants to keep Bea, he won't play fair."

Zeke swore. "I should've gone with them."

"We could turn around."

It would be wonderful to swoop in and save Jessie again. Logically, there was no reason for Dylan to thwart Jessie. She should be safe enough. And there was the matter of saving the world. "Angie will keep them safe. Without Maleem training, Dylan might not know how to siphon energy from others."

"Huh?"

Zeke slid into his seat, happy with his linear thinking. "I felt Drok draining me before current arced out of him. The Maleem draws energy and life force from his slaves."

"His slaves," Forman repeated slowly. "So his alleged bodyguards aren't there to protect him? They're energy reservoirs?"

"After being under his mental control, that's my working theory."

"Drok likes to fry people and machines. He must go through a lot of slaves."

Zeke sat forward in his chair. "Lots of potential human slaves here to serve his every whim."

"We have to stop him, but how?"

"I'm hoping the secret is in that necklace. I'll contact Uncle John."

Zeke made the com call to his uncle. After a few pleasantries, he informed his uncle of Forman's prize and stated his needs. "I need at least a dozen young pigs, the latest sample analysis machine, and an astrophysicist."

"Are you planning a luau? We don't have time for a party."

"The pigs and the sampler are for research purposes, to test the necklace."

"And the astrophysicist?"

"I need someone who understands the realm of space. Someone who won't question our line of inquiry and will be helpful. Can you find someone and get them to the island immediately?"

"I can."

Zeke exhaled a breath of relief. "What happened with your inquiry into missing persons?"

"The baseline for missing persons in Vegas is wildly divergent, so we couldn't tell there. We hit pay dirt with their next stop. Paris had twenty percent more missing persons during the time of the Maleem's visit."

"I was afraid of that."

"Reports from Cairo tell of two people deep in conversation on the city street and one vanishing in thin air. One minute she was standing there, the next she was gone. At least a dozen eyewitnesses confirm this account."

"Damn and double-damn! They're culling us, using humans to fuel their bodies during their sneaky people-snatching maneuvers. We've got to hurry. No telling who will be taken next."

"I'll have those items you requested on the island when you land. I have someone in mind for your astrophysicist request. I believe she's available."

"Do whatever you have to do to convince her. I need help, and I need it fast. Keep me informed on world news. I tend to become so focused I don't notice what's happening."

"I don't know if this is relevant."

"What?"

"We've had more meteorites burn up in our atmosphere since the aliens ships arrived."

"You think they're causing this?"

"I think we should keep an eye on it."

Chapter 44

From a safe distance, Zeke studied the mellow pig wearing the Maleem necklace. Without Jessie's intervention in Japan, this alien artifact would've been the instrument of his own death. Strange how the world turned. Strange and necessary. He'd do his level best to unravel the necklace's power.

"Ten more seconds on subject P5." He counted the numeric sequence aloud.

On cue, Forman removed the glowing necklace from the piglet's neck. The bright crystals faded in hue as he waited before the next test pig. Meanwhile, P5 fought its restraints, squealed and bashed into the gate. Then it lay down, shivering uncontrollably. Zeke made a note of the pig's odd behavior. He'd started the necklace trial at thirty seconds of dermal contact. With each successive test subject, he added thirty more seconds to the trial.

It didn't look good for P6.

Both P6 and P7 displayed similar self-destructive reactions upon necklace removal. Zeke nodded to Forman who waited before subject P8. "I'm calling an audible here. Leave the necklace on for an hour. I'm going to load the blood samples into the SuperMax. Keep an eye on P8 and don't touch anything in the lab. Your gloves are contaminated with the chemicals."

"Roger," Forman said.

Zeke snipped the sample tubes from each pig's autosampler line and loaded them in the analyzer. Blood samples had been collected every ten minutes and sealed in the tubing, and they'd continue to be collected as long as the experiment ran. He'd established a baseline for each pig first thing this morning when he set up the monitoring station.

Uncle John had moved mountains to get the pigs and the prototype machine on the island by the time they returned from the Far East. The astrophysicist was harder to come by, but Dr. Sidra McIntyre would arrive in the next twenty-four hours.

His com link beeped. Annoyed at the interruption, he glanced at the caller's ID.

Jessie! His mood lightened. The room seemed brighter.

He tapped the com twice, and her drawn face filled his vid screen. "Zeke, you're there. Thank God."

Her hushed tone alarmed him. He stepped out of the lab. "What's wrong?"

"It's Bea. She's collapsed." Jessie's voice rose higher with each word. "Best we can figure she got into a scuffle with Dylan. Angie threatened the manager who finally let us in her room. The place is trashed. She's huddled on the floor, shivering, sweating, and crying. I can't wake her. I'm so scared for her."

Zeke's heart stilled. Bea's symptoms matched those of his test subjects. "Did she wear the Maleem necklace?"

"I don't know. What am I going to do? What's wrong with her?" Tears streamed down Jessie's face. "She's never been like this, even when she overdosed. I don't know what to do."

Remembering Forman's relationship advice, Zeke gentled his voice. "Easy, Jess. You don't have to deal with this alone. I'm here. Sounds like your sister was exposed to something that shut her down. Find Dylan or someone who traveled with them and ask them what happened. The med team can help her faster if they know what they're up against."

Jessie sniffed and wiped the tears from her pale face. "Okay. I can do that."

"Good. Getting information is the best way to help your sister. I wish I was there with you."

"Me, too."

"You're strong. You can ask those hard questions. Don't let them stonewall you." She nodded, and Zeke cleared his throat. "May I speak with Angie? I want to work out the details of your transportation back to the island."

"She's right here."

Angie looked grim but under control. "Yes?"

"Don't touch the Maleem necklace. And make damned sure Jessie doesn't either! It dispenses chemicals transdermally. Find out if Bea wore that necklace and for how long. Put both sisters on a plane with a med team as soon as possible. If it's the necklace that caused Bea's mental withdrawal, I'm working on a cure. If it's drugs, the med team will be able to detox her en route. We need to keep a lid on this for Bea and Jessie's sake."

Angie nodded, her beaded braids clicking with the motion. "Got it. Our transpo is on standby. I'll ask John to put an Institute med team on board. What's in the necklace?"

"Highly addictive chemicals. I repeat. Don't touch it. Don't wear it. Don't let Jessie anywhere near it. I'm analyzing the metabolites now."

"What about Dylan James?"

By Zeke's calculation, Dylan had worn the necklace for two days. Chances were he was past the point of recovery. He chose his words carefully. "I don't know the full extent of our employer's reach, but it would be good to have that alien artifact and Dylan out of circulation. We don't need anyone else getting hooked on this stuff. Do whatever is necessary, but keep Jessie and Bea out of the fray. They've been through enough already."

"No problem. I'll arrange a separate extraction team for Dylan."

"Be forewarned. He won't relinquish the necklace. He will exhibit classic addiction behaviors."

"We can handle the situation."

The screen went dark before Zeke could ask to speak to Jessie again. He stared at the SuperMax analyzer. So much depended on this instrumentation. Would it decode compounds of alien origin? Could he save Bea?

As he studied the real-time analysis screen, a pig squealed painfully in the other room. Alarmed by the high levels he saw, Zeke hurried to the testing area. "Stop the test," he told Forman as he paused on the threshold. "Remove the necklace and store it in the shielded fume hood. Dispose of all three sets of gloves as radioactive waste."

"The exposure timeline is incomplete on P8," Forman began.

"I'm seeing chemicals in the first blood draw. We don't need additional samples at this point. With our limited sample population, this trial won't withstand scientific scrutiny. But eight pigs are enough for our purposes. We'll focus on what we have. Keep the pigs isolated in their test chambers. I need to step out for a bit."

"You're leaving?"

"I need to stretch my legs and think. You're in charge of the sample analysis. The situation is critical. I believe Bea wore the necklace. She is very ill and needs our help."

Forman rolled back into a cabinet, turning his head from side to side. "Dear God. Say it isn't so."

"God had nothing to do with it. Unless we identify the

unknowns in the samples and figure out how to eliminate them, Bea may not survive. Remove the necklace from P8. We must focus on the next phase of the test. We must devise a successful detox protocol."

"On it, boss." When Forman tried to remove the glowing necklace, P8 lunged forward to keep its head in the circlet. It snapped sharp teeth at the robot. Forman delivered a karate chop to the pig's snout, freeing the necklace. The pig squealed as Forman lifted the necklace out of the pen.

"Figure this out, Z. I'm counting on you to save my girl."

"Will do." Zeke hoped he could live up to Forman's expectations.

He ran flat out to the lighthouse, his shadow stretching before him on the sandy lane. The sun was setting for the day. Would it set on the human race as well? Not one bird or insect stirred. Not one person ventured out in the late afternoon heat. Only Zeke.

The entire planet waited with hushed breath.

He unlocked the transmission room with the keystone and hurried to the chair. His pulse raced as he reclined in the leather-like seat and his thoughts hurled through space. The familiar disorientation and darkness of Tween's thought plane settled upon him like a heavy cloak. He sent out a mental probe to his ancestors.

"Dad?"

"We're here, son."

Zeke's relief at finding his late father available dimmed at the reason for the visit. *"I'm running experiments with the Subjugator, but time is short. More people are wearing the necklaces and getting sick. What do you know of the illness?"*

The link hummed with angry voices.

Dad! I need answers. Jessie's sister wore the necklace. She's shuddering and unresponsive.

A sepulchral voice separated itself from the loud din. *Death will follow. We saw it time and again.*

I don't accept that answer. Surely, something you tried helped. I need to buy some time.

Zeke mentally cringed at the volume of outcry his comment drew. How many Tamans were on the link? He'd assumed a dozen but it seemed like so much more. The roar was as loud as the crowd at the concert.

One thin voice repeated the same thing over and over. Zeke

strained to filter out the rest of the voices and to listen. *Salt!* the man shouted. *Give the female salt.*

Salt.

The ocean was salty. Had it detoxed Jessie? She'd been immersed in it and swallowed plenty of it when they were in the Sea of Japan.

The ease and practicality of the solution appealed to him. He replied and the others quieted to hear him. *Thanks. I'll try salt. Next question. Will more ships come or can three Maleem ships enslave a planet?*

A strong voice spoke. *One Maleem warrior can conquer an entire galaxy.*

Not the best of news, but it wasn't the end of the world. Three ships would be fewer targets to neutralize than an entire fleet.

Tell him, a new voice commanded. This speaker hung onto the last syllables of each word as if he were in a contest to see how long he could drag them out.

Tell me what?

The Maleem knows what you are, the dramatic voice continued. *He will come for you.*

He thinks I'm dead.

Your woman was seen alive. The Maleem are relentless. You are in grave danger.

Why? I've done nothing to him. What does he want from me?

Your mind. He wants your mind. With you under his control, he will activate the Taman mindlink and destroy us.

He can't have my mind or any other part of me.

Give the Taman keystone to your mate and leave instructions for its use with your unborn child. Destroy yourself. It's your only way to escape eternal torment.

First, Jessie isn't my mate. Second, she isn't pregnant.

The Maleem will imprison her to obtain your son. You must hide her away.

Forget it. I won't kill myself or kidnap Jessie. We need another solution. Work with me here. I've been dreaming about shards of dark light. In my dream, the dark pieces come together and break apart. It's like nothing here on Earth. The only thing I can figure is its dark matter in space. Can Tamans do more than send their thoughts through space?

The link dissolved in vocal chaos. He heard the undercurrent of a chant but he couldn't make out the word. It became louder and louder and still he didn't understand the word.

Zydmoq? What the heck was that?

Finally, his father's voice distinguished itself from the fray. He sounded ecstatic. *You have made us all proud. We've been waiting for you for untold generations. You are our salvation. The hope of all our people.*

What? How? I'm one person. A man.

You're Taman.

I don't understand.

You already have the answers you seek.

With that, the link faded.

Chapter 45

"Leave me alone," Bea growled, slapping Jessie's hands away. "I want to die."

"You're not going to die." Jessie gave Bea's lifejacket a little shake. The cameras in this private facility recording her every movement didn't faze her. Bea's wellbeing trumped the need for privacy. "You'll beat this and be a better person because of it."

Bea's head lolled back to the rim of the seawater tank. "I'm turning into a giant prune. My fingers are wrinkled beyond repair. Let me out of this hellhole."

"Soon."

"Why are you doing this to me?" Bea smacked the water with her hands, spraying water out of the tank and soaking Jessie. "Why can't you just let me be?"

If her sister didn't see Jessie's intervention as caring, she was wasting her time.

Abruptly Bea pushed away from the wall of the tank, twirling in tight circles until she retched. Jessie caught the vomit in a shallow basin. "You're all right. Get that poison out of your system."

Bea shuddered violently. "I hate you. I hate my life. I hate everything."

Drug addicts said things they didn't mean, Jessie rationalized through the slashing pain of the words. Bea was withdrawing from several powerful drugs, some alien, some recreational. None of this would have happened if they'd stayed put in their Japanese apartment.

"Not much longer," Jessie said in an encouraging tone. "The seawater helped me detox from the necklace. It will help you if you give it a chance."

"I have to pee. All those saline fluids you guys pumped into me have to come out. Get me out of here."

Even if that were true, Jessie had no sympathy. Zeke said Bea needed to stay in the seawater overnight as they'd done, so Jessie would make sure she stayed put. "Pee in the tank."

"You're mean," Bea howled. "You've always been mean to me.

Everything has to be your way."

Jessie had bent over backward to help her sister time and again. Bea's reckless behavior and bad decisions had landed them in harm's way. This time, both of them had nearly died.

Bea slid into a troubled sleep, crying out, and jerking. The heated seawater whirled around her as Jessie maintained a solitary vigil. A nurse came in an hour later and offered to relieve her. Jessie shook her head, hugging her arms to her middle. "I'm staying until she turns the corner."

She prayed.

She bargained with God.

She missed Zeke.

With thoughts of love on her mind, the warm moist chamber, and the hum of the tank whirlpool motor, she dozed. In her dream, she walked on a sparkling shore, sand crunching under her bare feet. Gentle waves lapped the sun-kissed beach, and a breeze blew her hair away from her face. Holding her hand was a curly-headed young boy clutching a toy tugboat. Someone walked toward them on the beach. A tall man with a big smile. The boy called "Daddy!" and ran to him.

A nearby movement awakened her. The nurse. She'd leaned over the med tank to monitor Bea's vital signs. "She's better," the nurse said in heavily accented English. "Her pulse has finally slowed, and her heartbeat is normal. Her color's better, too. She has only one more hour in the tank. I will stay with her. Why don't you get some rest?"

Jessie leaned down to see for herself. Sure enough, Bea looked like her normal self. Remembering her own ordeal after wearing the necklace, she knew Bea still had a ways to go to continue detoxing the alien compounds. She thanked God and Zeke for the miracle of bringing her sister back from the edge. "I'll do that."

Angie waited for her in the antiseptic corridor. Dressed in navy scrubs, she looked like one of the medical team at Belle Harbor. "I hear Bea's improving. Zeke's immersion therapy worked."

Emotion tightened Jessie's throat. She nodded.

"You need rest, but since you're also Bea's manager, I need to tell you the news. Someone leaked a video of her going bonkers in that Riviera hotel."

Anger colored Jessie's thoughts. "Crap. When did that happen?"

"Don't know. The vid shows Bea and Dylan fighting over that

damned necklace. She takes it from him, preens around the room. He orders her to give it back. She tells him no. They race around the room. He catches her, smacks her around, and grabs the necklace. After he leaves, she crumples to the floor, same spot we found her. We blocked the vid soon as it came to our attention, but others could have bootlegged the feed. These things take on a life of their own once they hit the net."

"As her manager, I need to see it, just not tonight. I need sleep and a clear head."

"Do you want to make a statement on her behalf?"

She could call a press conference and make everything right for Bea. The public tolerated a lot from an entertainer, especially if a rationale explained their bad behavior. Another Bea mess for her to clean up. Resentment tasted bitter in her mouth. Her sympathy reservoir was empty. She'd pulled Bea's career back from the brink too many times. Bea needed to step up and take responsibility. Jessie was done being her fulltime babysitter.

"There will be no statement. As soon as Bea's out of the woods from the alien necklace chemicals, we'll move her to a secure detox facility. She needs counseling and a chance to stand on her own two feet."

Angie jerked a thumb toward the exit. "I can put you on a plane right now to take you home to the island."

"Thanks. Much as I'd love to go home," and to Zeke, she thought privately, "my place is still here with Bea."

"As you wish," Angie said.

"I need to crash. Do you know where I'm supposed to go?"

Angie gestured down a side corridor. "This way."

The Spartan room held a cot, a chair, a bedside table and nothing else. "It's perfect," Jessie said, sinking down on the mattress. "Thank you for all you've done."

Angie nodded and left.

Jessie yawned and pulled the covers around her. Sleep came, and with it, dreams of the tall man and the little boy. Her son.

Chapter 46

Forman needed a break from the thick, brooding atmosphere of the lab. "I'm headed out to check on the survivors."

Over at the containment vessel, Zeke grunted in acknowledgment.

His boss had been studying the Maleem necklace for hours. Forman wished Zeke would forget the intellectual puzzle of how the thing worked and focus more on diminishing the effect of the toxins on necklace wearers.

Lights illuminated the grassy path to the outdoor holding area as Forman rolled outside. Of the nine pigs exposed, the four who wore the necklace for two minutes or less exhibited normal behavior. Three of the five who wore the necklace longer were dead.

Two minutes.

Not long at all.

He halted beside the two active salt tanks, each with a recovering pig immersed in the water. This test hit too close to home. Emotion welled up, and he let out a dry sob. Bea wore the Maleem necklace. She never did anything part way. Chances were good she'd worn it for more than two minutes. Their data suggested she had less than a fifty-fifty chance of surviving the detox process.

Why, Bea?

Why wasn't I enough for you?

Though pale fingers of dawn edged the eastern horizon, Forman had no interest in the daily event. He couldn't enjoy anything as long as Bea was in danger. He ached for her. For him. For what she'd thrown away.

She was flawed. If she were a robot, he'd reprogram her, but that wasn't an option. Humans were autonomous. They exercised free will.

Bea had done this to herself.

Would she survive like P6 and P8 who drowsed in their respective salt tanks? He hoped so. Even if she didn't want him, he still wanted the best for her.

He turned from the pigs to study the brightly illuminated lab.

His brilliant boss had worked through the night on the necklace. With the wisdom of hindsight, he realized his infatuation with the singer had put Zeke's life at risk. He'd messed up big time.

But now he had himself in hand. He would never put his feelings before his responsibilities, no matter the personal cost. This wasn't about him. This was about supporting Zeke.

Forman wheeled inside to find Zeke still examining the dark necklace. Unless the necklace was on a living being, the jewel tones weren't visible. The SuperMax had been working on the synthesis of the chemicals for hours. But the chemicals were only one aspect of the necklace. The structure somehow dispensed a nonlethal dose to wearers. An hour ago, Zeke had discovered a handful of black crystals at each compass direction in the necklace framework.

"Interesting," Zeke said.

"What's that?" Forman rolled next to him, cursing his shortness and his temporary Jethro shell. When this alien threat was over, assuming they survived, he required a new robot shell. Or at least one that his entire wardrobe of aloha shirts would fit. He hated the drab rust-colored exterior of his current habitat.

"The crystals function as a switch. Watch." Inside the containment vessel, robotic hands moved a heat source under the necklace. The colored areas brightened. "Warming the crystals releases micro amounts of narcotic, which is transdermally adsorbed by the wearer. The higher the heat, the higher the dose released."

His statement made sense. Despite his intent to stop thinking about Bea's fate, Forman hoped her chances had improved. "You figured that out in the five minutes I was outside?"

"I figured it out an hour ago. I proved it in the last five minutes."

"Okay. We know how it works. What now? How will this save the world?"

"I have a theory. The only Maleem we've seen are Drok and his bodyguards."

"You said the bodyguards aren't Maleem. They've slaves."

"I remember. See if you follow my reasoning. Drok's worn a spacesuit the entire time on Earth; his action suggests he requires different atmospheric composition, but I believe that's a ruse."

"Why?"

"The Maleem have slaves from different races, different planets. Their slaves and the Maleem themselves have remarkably human

174

appearances. Stands to reason they'd need the same air as us."

"I'm not following. Even the slaves wear suits."

"Humor me. The necklace is a chemical delivery system. Addicts develop tolerance for chemicals. The Maleem necklace enslaves subjects, but at some point a higher dosage should be needed to ensure continued compliance. The suits must be the next step in the dosing system."

"The slave I saw," Forman said. "His suit was broken. That killed him?"

"It's a good theory."

Forman considered the ramifications. An offense move surfaced. "We could prepare a batch of spacesuits, fill them with soldiers or robots, and sneak them onto the Maleem ships to decommission them from inside."

"Like a Trojan horse."

Forman savored the approval in Zeke's eyes. "With the Maleem gaining footholds on the planet, there will be routine transports to their ships. We have opportunities to infiltrate their ranks."

"They know each other. Won't they recognize us as intruders?"

"Not if we replace an entire unit. The substitution wouldn't be noticed until they were on the mother ships, if that."

"What about security codes?"

"We'll leave that to the spies. Unless you've got a better idea."

The Maleem had hurt Bea. Forman wanted retribution. "I like the idea of blowing the ships to pieces. Send them a strong message about our hospitality."

"That stratagem has holes, too. We don't know their firepower capability. We need a nontraditional approach, which is why I requested an astrophysicist."

"What about hiding folks under the transpo corridors?"

"Uncle John said the idea met extreme resistance. The higher ups refused to consider it. The strategy is sound, but I can't implement it from here."

"Fools. If the Maleem come to coastal Georgia, I'll hide beneath our mainland transpo tunnel. We wouldn't have the benefit of water to shield us, but we'd be safer in the tunnel than here on the island."

Zeke grinned. "Uncle John said the same thing. Rations are being stored there as we speak. The planet may fall to the Maleem, but we'll have a local pocket of resistance."

The com link buzzed. Speak of the devil, Forman thought as he activated the secure call from Zeke's uncle. He diverted the incoming image to the large six-foot wall screen.

"What do you have for me?" John Demery growled.

"Good morning to you, too," Zeke said. "Miss your morning coffee?"

"I need more than coffee at this point. Tell me you've got something for us."

"I do."

Forman puffed with pride as Zeke relayed his idea to infiltrate the alien ships.

"Risky, but it might work," Demery said. "I'll pass it along. Maybe the world leaders have the sense to implement this strategy. Sorry about your water in the tunnels idea. It was brilliant."

"I'd like to be on the advance team boarding the Maleem ships," Zeke said.

"Not happening. I won't risk losing you that way. Besides, Dr. McIntyre is arriving today on the afternoon ferry. You must work cooperatively on ways to defeat the Maleem. The wider-based our attack strategy, the more likely we are to be successful."

Zeke sighed. "I need to recharge before I do anything else. We were up all night studying the Maleem necklace. The dosing mechanism is ingenious."

"Be that as it may, we need to broaden our scope to stop the Maleem. Give me another solution besides hiding people."

Zeke's uncle leaned forward as if he were switching off the link. Forman quickly asked the question he'd been holding in. "Sir, any word from France?"

"Bea is still alive and responding to salt therapy. Her vitals are strong, and she's conscious, which is an improvement."

A beam of sunshine bathed his dark thoughts. He dared to hope for her recovery. "No self-destructive tendencies seen?"

"Not that I'm aware of."

"Is she coming home soon, sir?"

"One moment."

Forman waited for what seemed like eons.

Thirty seconds later, Demery spoke again. "She's slated to enter a rehab place stateside once she can travel. Her sister will accompany her."

"Thank God," Forman said.

"Thank your boss. Without the salt immersion therapy, we'd

have lost her."

Zeke moved in front of Forman. "Uncle Zeke, any more people missing? Do you have the Cairo totals yet?"

"They had a marked increase in missing people at the time of Drok's visit to their city. Cairo officials detained the husband of the woman who was taken in broad daylight. Religious groups are claiming it's the rapture. Egyptians are trying to hold the comments under wraps because they want to be a trade partner with the Maleem."

"What does our government think about the coincidences?"

His uncle shook his head. "They blew me off. Our leaders have their eyes on the trade agreement prize. Unless there's solid proof the Maleem are behind this 'rapture,' we're the only ones who realize the imminent danger of attack."

The link clicked off. Joy overwhelmed Forman. If he had tears in this version of himself, he would have wept pure gratitude. "Thank you, thank you, thank you for saving Bea."

Zeke was glad about Bea's recovery, sad about his tunnels-as-hiding-places theory getting no respect. Saving the world was hard work. "I didn't do it alone. You helped." He yawned. "I need three hours of shut-eye. Can you manage for a bit?"

Forman nodded and followed his hero out of the lab to the sleep room. "Sure. Anything. Tell me what you want."

"Weaponize those dark crystals. Construct a barrier in space around our planet. Figure out how to kill a salt tolerant, electricity-shooting alien. Stop the human abductions. Bone up on astrophysics."

Forman snorted. "Is that all?"

Chapter 47

Pauline gazed at the wintry scene with wonder. All around her, snowflakes flurried in a delightful array. Beyond were snow-kissed trees, a park with benches, and a snowy church steeple. The scene seemed so familiar, and yet she couldn't quite place it.

Wait. Snow should be cold, but when she put her hands out the flakes weren't cold. They weren't flakes at all. They had form and substance. She brought one to her mouth. It crunched in her teeth like beach sand.

What was this place?

She walked and she walked, but the scene never changed. Out of ideas, she sat on the park bench. *This is a helluva mess, Pauline. You're lost, and you don't know the way home. Think. Stop trying to make it on your looks and use your brain.*

Her internal voice sounded a lot like her mother chiding her to pick up the clothes on her bedroom floor. God, what she wouldn't do to feel her mother's arms around her once again. To know that degree of comfort and unconditional love.

Connor loved her. But she'd thrown him away. She'd killed him with a force she'd never possessed before, an alien force.

Those damn aliens. They'd done this to her. *You did it to yourself,* a sly voice whispered. *You schemed and plotted and stabbed people in the back to get to the top. And look what it got you. Crazy.*

"I'm not crazy," Pauline yelled into the snowy world. "I've seen crazy, and it doesn't look like this. Crazy is clothes draped on sticky bushes. Crazy is washing your hands ten times in a row with butterscotch pudding. Crazy is running off to Mexico and leaving your kids with monsters. I'm not crazy."

The voice laughed and laughed. Pauline covered her ears and closed her eyes but she couldn't block the creepy cackling sound. The brightness beyond her eyelids faded, and she tumbled into a dark world, flailing and falling. A scream ripped from her lips.

Something caught her, and she jarred to a teeth-clattering stop. Shivers and shudders shook her frame, and she couldn't catch her breath. A faint noise sounded in the void. Hide. Whatever it is, it can't be good. Hide. But something had her. And the voice was louder. She struggled to get free.

But there was nowhere to go.

Nowhere to run.

"Pauline!"

She cocked her head in the darkness. That voice. She knew it.

"Pauline! Wake up. We've got to get you out of here."

She focused on the voice and soared through the void to the grayness. As she did, pain intensified. Oh, she hurt. A sob escaped her dry mouth.

"Pauline. Come on, baby. Come back to me."

She searched the familiar eyes in the bearded face. "Connor?"

"It's me, babe. Wake up. We've got to get out of here."

"Am I dead too?"

"Neither of us is dead, though if anyone finds us here, we might wish we were dead."

Connor. He'd come for her. She cried dry tears. "I'm sorry," she managed.

"So am I. Can you walk?"

She blinked through the pain, through the slowly spinning room. "Not yet. Coming around. How did you find me?"

"I came for you. I wasn't going home without you."

"But I, I, I did terrible things to you."

"That alien did those things. My sweet Pauline wouldn't hurt me."

Her head dropped. "I'm not a nice person. Save yourself, Connor."

"I'm saving us both."

"I'm a mess. Look at my burnt skin, my poor hair. I'm sick to my stomach. I don't know what all they did to me. I might be crazy. I see things, hear voices."

"Doesn't matter. You're my girl. I love you no matter what happened to you."

"I don't deserve you."

"You deserve to be loved. Everyone deserves that."

"Huh." Pauline pushed up to a sitting position, gasping at the sharp pain movement caused, and tried to take stock. Judging by the impersonal bed, dresser and vid screen, she was in a hotel. The hotel room Drok locked her up in after he removed her necklace. Damn him.

She needed the jeweled collar to manage the pain. "Did you see a necklace in the other room?"

"It isn't there, but you don't need any jewelry from them. You have me."

"The necklace is valuable," she lied. "We need it to get home."

"I found us a ride."

"You did? How? Who?"

Connor pulled a business card out of his dirty robe. She tried to focus on the small print and failed. She pushed the card away. "Who is it?"

"Said he was a friend of a friend. I ran into him outside the hotel. He said if I got you out of here, to use this money to get to the airport. He said this card would be our air ticket home."

"Sounds too good to be true, but I don't care anymore. What about the Maleem? Where are they?"

"Last I heard they were headed to Sydney, Australia."

Betrayal knifed through her. "They left me behind."

"Ambassador Wagner is the alien's new translator."

That got her blood going. "Wagner? How?"

"Don't know. I'm glad you're free. They were killing you, babe. Did you eat? I've got a water bottle here. Are you thirsty?"

"I was hungry at first, but then I couldn't eat. I can't drink either. Liquids burn my throat."

"Can't survive without water."

"The Maleem can. They never ate or drank."

"You're not a Maleem. You need to eat."

"Not yet." She eyed the voluminous robes he wore. "You got any zoners in there? I need a pain blocker."

"Sorry. I didn't think about that. Maybe we can score something on the way to the airport. Think you can walk now?"

She glanced down at her leather-clad body, at the monster high heels heat-welded to her feet. "Ready as I'll ever be."

With effort, she staggered up and made it to the reception area of the suite. "What day is it?"

He told her as they strolled toward the elevator.

"You see anyone else going in this suite?"

"No people came in here. Only person on this floor last night was a junkyard robot."

How odd. "You'd think a nice place like this would have decent staff."

"This one was a mess. I saw him through the peephole of the room I was hiding in. The Jethro had bulldozer tracks for feet and his rust-colored shell had seen better days. He tried to give everyone on the floor a pillow."

"Did he bring a pillow in this suite?"

"He did, and that must be it over there. He didn't leave with it."

She glanced at the lump of white fluff. "No. Where's the pillowcase?"

"Maybe the Maleem swiped it."

Her eyes narrowed with speculation. "Or maybe that thieving Jethro stole my necklace."

Chapter 48

Zeke ignored the whop-whop sound of the arriving chopper. He was no pathologist, but he'd dissected animals in college biology classes. And with a limited data set, he had no room for error.

Uncle John thumped his new cane on the laboratory floor. Pigs squealed and ran to the other end of their test cages. "Looks like you made the right call with the salt detox therapy for the necklace."

Zeke looked up from test subject P3 and shrugged. "I got lucky. It was an inspired guess based on our prolonged swim in the Sea of Japan."

Uncle John peered over Zeke's shoulder. "Some of the best field work has come from inspired guesses. There's often not a lot of time in developing situations to explore options."

Ignoring his uncle, he teased the fascia away from the spleen, excised the cylindrical organ, and placed it in the tissue cassette Forman held. "We don't know if there are long-term effects from the necklace but on a short-term basis, bloodwork of the components and their metabolites dropped significantly once exposure stopped."

"Everything look all right?"

Zeke nodded and handed Forman a liver sample. Instead of burdening the tissue pathology laboratory with too many rush samples, he'd elected to only examine brain tissue, liver tissue, and the spleen. In addition, he'd collected spinal fluid and blood from all subjects at euthanasia.

"Did you identify the dosing agent?"

"It's a blend of three novel compounds, new to us, that is," he qualified.

"And?"

Zeke signaled Forman, who slid the pig off the exam table into a large bin. While Forman hauled the pig away, Zeke began cleaning up his work area. The too-sharp smell of fixative hung heavily in the air. His remaining test subjects eyed him warily.

"One is an addictive narcotic, similar to function and composition to morphine, and it induces a false euphoria," he said as he sprayed the stainless steel counter with disinfectant. "Another element functions in much the same way as an aggressive antipsychotic by eliminating self-initiation and self-will. We're not exactly sure of the third compound's function. On a cellular level, it seems to rewire the neural pathways. From what I witnessed in Japan, I theorize the third compound insulates the recipient for the vast amount of energy which the Maleem push and pull through them."

Uncle John clapped him on the back. "Excellent work. You've made great strides in the past twenty-four hours. We need to wind up this investigation and focus on the next problem."

Forman returned, hovering in the doorway, hands worrying together in front of his rusty barrel chest. "Any word on Bea and Jessie? Where are they?"

Uncle John grinned. "Can't find them, can you?"

Forman shook his head.

"Good deal. Jessie requested privacy, and I made sure they got it. If you can't find them with your superior search skills, Bea can recover without fearing visits from the Maleem, Dylan James, or rabid fans."

Zeke couldn't miss the earnest "do-something" glance Forman shot him. He cleared his throat. "We appreciate your efforts on their behalf, but if it's possible, we'd like to talk with them by com."

Uncle John stood a bit taller. "That's up to the Stemfords."

"Sounds like it might be up to you," Zeke said.

"You've got me pegged." Uncle John waggled his bushy eyebrows. "I might have encouraged the high level secrecy, but Jessie wants privacy. Even more, I need for the two of you to be wholly focused on saving Earth, the same way you figured out the Maleem necklace. I need two hundred percent from you guys, and I need it in a hurry.

"Oh, and there's another matter you should know about." Uncle John's smile was grim. "The daughter of the Chief Minister in Mumbai vanished. He has torn the city apart looking for her. He's come right out and blamed the aliens, but no one is taking him seriously because once again there is no proof."

"No proof ought to be a clue that it couldn't possibly be a human-induced effect. People always leave evidence behind. How long's the girl been missing?"

"Close to twenty-four hours now. Two of her female friends also vanished."

"They should have listened to us. They should have given Drok the boot."

"We have an Institute representative in Mumbai sharing your idea about hiding people. But it comes too late for the Chief Minister. Do you think the girl is dead?"

"I don't know. If she wasn't taken for her spleen—"

"What's this about a spleen?" Uncle John's bushy eyebrows arched.

Uh-oh. He had no proof for his knowledge of this either, only his conversation with the survivor of Drigil Eight. Nothing to do but tough it out. "I believe that an organ such as the spleen is what they seek from humans. The spleen helps remove old red blood cells and contributes to the immune response."

"This is the first I've heard of this theory."

"I don't have proof to back it up. Heck, now that I think about it, I wonder if the people are being raptured up to the spaceships, harvested, and dumped into space. That would certainly explain the extra space junk currently burning up in our atmosphere."

"They dump the bodies in space?"

"Why not? They wouldn't want to take them anywhere."

"That's an even better reason to move quickly, before we all become space junk. What do you have for me?"

Still sitting, Zeke crabbed his chair away from the counter to put distance between him and the fixative. "The best offense is a good defense. Any chance the higher-ups will revisit my hiding the important people strategy? The Maleem are making themselves at home. Once they go on the offensive, it will be too late."

Uncle John leaned against the counter. "Folks at the very top have private bunkers for protection. The consensus is that the alleged Maleem attack may not occur, and nobody wants to sit underground indefinitely." He pointed his cane at Zeke. "Would you do consider doing it?"

"My place is here, trying to figure out how to stop the Maleem. I wouldn't go."

"Exactly. It's a great idea for later. Meanwhile, what kind of offense have you come up with?"

"We have to disable their ships, but they're out of range of our conventional weapons. None of our shuttles or rockets can get there undetected, and we don't have the technology to hit them with a missile from Earth. You have any luck getting a friendly on that

184

diplomatic envoy that visited the Maleem ship?"

"Too risky to send one of ours. We planned to appropriate the delegation's photos, but none of their electronic devices worked. They returned empty-handed. Even the listening devices planted in their trouser cuffs were disabled."

"We already know from Forman's Maleem encounter that electrical systems fare poorly in their vicinity. I need input on their power system and weapons capability. Without that, I'm making uneducated guesses."

"Sketch artists are working with two diplomats to create a rendition of what they saw. The bad news is that two more diplomats came home wearing those necklaces. They have no idea what they're getting themselves into."

Zeke scrubbed his face with his hands. Saving the world was hard work. Doing it with no information was like shooting a toy gun into the dark. Chances of neutralizing a Maleem threat were minimal. He needed to up his odds, and for that he kept coming back to the necklace.

"What about Dylan James?" he asked.

"I've got Angie following him," Uncle John said. "Looks like he's a regular party fixture these days. He's never seen without the necklace."

"Because he can't take it off without serious withdrawal problems," Zeke said. "He's a lost cause, and so is Ambassador Wagner. I doubt if either of them could survive the rehab process at this point."

Uncle John vibrated with energy.

"What?" Zeke said, leaning forward. "What do you know?"

"We've been following Pauline Curran and Connor Bronsen. It was her necklace that you decommissioned. She survived the detox process, but her mental acuity isn't what it once was. She's alive."

"I didn't expect that, not from what we've seen with tiered dosing subjects in our range-finding experiment. How many days did she wear the necklace?"

"We're not sure. Two days, maybe three. But that's not her only effect. Her physical appearance changed as well. The integrity of her skin is different. It's gummy and adheres to her clothing."

That finding sparked Zeke's curiosity. "May I examine her?"

"In good time. For now, I need you to focus on stopping the Maleem."

"You're hampering my investigation, and it isn't the first time you've directed my focus. I don't like being so constrained."

"We all take orders from someone."

"Yeah? Who's your boss?"

Uncle John headed toward his waiting chopper. "A higher power."

Chapter 49

Taking apart the Maleem necklace had been a snap compared to the complexity of astrophysics. As Zeke watched the passengers unloading from the last ferry, nodding at friends he'd known his entire life, he hoped he was up to the intellectual challenge of absorbing a new scientific discipline in a matter of hours.

Had Dr. Sidra McIntyre missed the boat?

"Where is she?" he asked Forman, who lurked beside him at the other end of the dock. Palmetto fronds rustled in the gentle breeze. "You sure she boarded the ferry on the mainland?"

"Very sure," Forman said. "The younger of these two women talking on the gangplank matches her photo ID."

"She's a kid?"

"She's a brilliant astrophysicist. Didn't you read the info packet?"

Sidra McIntyre looked to be every bit of sixteen. Nothing about her retro electric blue striped long hair, her sparkling orange top, denim skirt, or high heeled boots screamed brilliance. She resembled every other teenager in the world.

He was ready to dismiss her altogether when another feeling broadsided him. He'd never met Dr. McIntyre but she felt familiar to him. That realization kept him from moving forward to greet her. What was it about her that he recognized?

He didn't know her professionally. He'd never met her personally. That left the other stuff. The weird intangible stuff that defied logic. Huh. How did he know her? Was she Taman?

"Ya gonna go get her? Or shall I go?" Forman asked.

"I'm going." Zeke strode down the dock to where she stood, but her back was to him and she kept talking to her companion about what an idiot someone named Christian was.

He waited for a few seconds, but she didn't turn to acknowledge him. He cleared his throat. Nothing. So he tapped her on the shoulder.

Zeke heard a slight intake of breath, then there was a blinding flash of orange as she whirled in a tight circle, catching his face with her pointy-heeled boot.

"Never sneak up on me!" she yelled. "Have you lost your mind?"

He blinked from the pavement where he lay. His hand inched up to touch his moist face. Blood. This woman was crazy. He should have nothing to do with her.

Forman rolled in front of him. "Dr. McIntyre?"

"Who are you?" she asked.

"Dr. Landry's assistant, ma'am. Are you going to power kick me, too?"

"Oh, dear," the older woman said. "Sidra, you have to exert more self-control."

"It's not my fault, Ronni. He touched me."

Ronni bustled over and helped Zeke to his feet. "Sorry, gov," she said, handing him a wad of tissues. "Looks like you need a stitch or two. Didn't you read the briefing documents?"

"I didn't read anything. I've been too busy," Zeke grumbled, pressing the cloths into the open wound.

"Sorry," Sidra quipped, smacking a wad of gum. "I have issues."

"You're a kid."

"Bite me. I am."

He struggled not to reach across and throttle the imp. Forman interceded. "This way to the transpo, ladies. We'll stop at the med unit to get Dr. Landry stitched on the way to the lab."

Forman kept up a tour guide banter with the women as Zeke got his face numbed and stitched. The whole time Zeke kept thinking, *I don't have time for this.* If he'd had a moment alone, he'd have called Uncle John and blistered his ears.

Finally, they pulled up at the lab. Forman shot him a quizzical look. "Conference room," Zeke said. Putting a table between him and the kid might not be enough, but it was the best he could do for now.

"Cool digs you got here," Sidra said, bounding around the room like a puppy. "I like."

"So do I. Why did Uncle John select you over your colleagues?"

"Me first. Why is a backwoods hydrologist working on an astrophysics problem?"

"Because I am." He inwardly groaned at his tone. Now he sounded like a playground kid.

"I checked up on you," she said. "You should have read up on me. I read all your journal articles on the way out here. Your computer models have a higher accuracy than any others. You find things others don't. In other words, you're bloody brilliant."

He tried to ignore the warm feeling her compliment invoked. "My uncle said he was sending an astrophysicist. You must be exceptional, or you wouldn't be on his radar."

"I am exceptional, but I have issues which keep me out of the mainstream."

Zeke touched his face. *Issues* barely scratched the surface of this crazy chick. "Enough with the chitchat. How are we going to destroy the Maleem ships?"

"How about we build our own spaceship and blast them out of the sky?"

"Fine. You've got twenty-four hours. Maybe a week if we're lucky."

"Making it a challenge? I'm game."

"You'd better be more than that. The Maleem plan to kill every human on this planet."

"And you know this how?"

"I *know*."

She tapped her fingers together. "Secretive and brilliant. I love that in a man."

"We need to think outside the box here."

"What I wouldn't give for a speeding asteroid or a black hole," Sidra quipped. "I'd even settle for a gamma-ray burst from a death star galaxy."

"We've got stone age tools to deal with a problem from the future. Stay grounded on what we have and make it work for us."

"We could steal one of their short range ships and use it to blast the mother ships. If we used an A.I., we wouldn't risk any loss of lives."

"Not a bad plan, except these Maleem aren't people at all. They channel untold amounts of power through their fingertips. Anything electrical shorts out around them. An A.I wouldn't work."

"Yeah, I saw that other robot get fried on the vids. Not a pretty picture. That why you have this crappy Jethro helping you now?"

Forman startled, and Zeke laughed. "Indeed." He leaned forward. "Now tell me why my uncle selected you from all the other astrophysicists in the world."

"WIMPs," she said, dead-faced. "They're my specialty."

At his puzzled expression, she continued. "Galactic dark matter, also known as weakly interacting massive particles. They're dispersed everywhere. On this planet. In outer space. If we could somehow manipulate the WIMPs to come together and create a physical barrier, the Maleem couldn't break through it."

Zeke nodded to Forman. "Check it out."

Forman left the room. Zeke attempted to hold his own in an astrophysics conversation. "What basis do you have for your theory?"

"Space is a vacuum. We can't travel through it fast enough to vanquish our enemy. I know the WIMPs are out there. What I don't know is how to bring them together."

"What do they look like?"

"You need special imaging equipment to see them. They are invisible to the naked eye. They respond to gravity but not electromagnetic forces. It's theorized they're like neutrinos, only slower and bigger and colder. We've seen evidence of them under special conditions in the Soudan Mine and in other experiments."

An invisible particle that took special conditions to detect? His confidence in this idea wavered. "Has anyone manipulated them before?"

"Not on this scale. Pretty much all we've done is detect them. These are primordial particles. If you think of them like cells inside a developing baby, you can see how dark matter has unlimited potential."

Dark matter rang a bell. In his dreams, he'd seen dark crystalline shapes fitting together from a primordial mass. Could saving the world be as simple as piecing together a puzzle? How did one move the stuff, particularly if one couldn't see it?

"Say I buy into your theory," he began slowly. "What would we need to do? Blast photons into space? What attracts these WIMPs?"

She glanced everywhere but at his eyes. "This is where my theory goes off-road."

Didn't she feel the ticking clock of alien invasion? No matter how preposterous her theory was, he needed to hear it. He couldn't evaluate a secret idea. "Go on."

"No one takes me seriously because my ideas are so out there. But I feel the rightness deep in my bones." She met his gaze. Her eyes glowed amber bright. "I know it has to be true."

Intrigued by her unusual eyes, he could only stammer. "What?"

She held perfectly still. "Mind over matter."

He drew in a long, slow breath. His pulse sounded loud in his ears. She walked on treacherous ground for a scientist. "What about it?"

"With the right person, we can will the WIMPs to do what we want."

Zeke reeled back in his chair. She was a whack job. A complete crazy. What was his uncle thinking to send a child to help him with such a serious problem? The sooner he got shed of her the better.

"Mind over matter?" he scoffed. "That's it? That's your brilliant out of the box strategy?"

She nodded.

The room heated with expectation. Steam seemed to blast from his ears. White noise trumpeted in his head. He had to get out of here. He needed to think clearly, and this gum-smacking kid was messing with his head. What she was asking was beyond the realm of possible. It was seriously out there. Fully improbable. How could anyone manipulate unseen matter using thoughts?

Contemplating it made his head hurt.

He stood. "I'm going for a swim."

She did a fist pump. "Great idea. I'm in."

So much for getting away from her. "I've got to do something else first. Forman will escort you to your quarters so you can stow your gear and change." He edged toward the door. "Give me an hour."

Sidra grinned. "It's a date."

Chapter 50

Encouraged by Bea's recovery, Jessie finally had something positive to report. She'd put off calling Zeke, not sure what to say, not sure how to face him after their tryst. She wanted their relationship to be balanced, but she couldn't gauge his level of commitment. No telling what he thought of her. They'd finally been intimate and she'd chosen to help her sister instead of staying with him.

With privacy in mind, she strolled amongst the gardens, stopping under the shade of an old oak tree. She took a deep breath, smoothed her hair back from her face, and made the com call. No answer.

Rats.

Was he screening his calls?

Should she leave a message?

No. If he wasn't speaking to her, she didn't want to appear clingy and desperate. Plus, who knew how secure links were these days. The Maleem could be monitoring every transmission. It was best to talk with someone than to leave a message that might be misconstrued. She called Forman.

He answered immediately, his rigid android face filling the com screen. "J-girl! How are you? How's your sister?"

"Good. Good. We're both good. Getting better every day." Oh, God. She was blowing this. She had to do better. "How are things on the island?"

Forman's answering growl made her laugh. "Dish," she said, trying to contain her grin. "Tell me. Does he miss me?"

"Things are not good."

In the rusty Jethro shell, Forman's expression was hard to read, but the concern in his voice came through clarion clear. Something was wrong. Her levity faded. "Do I need to come home and straighten you fellows out? What's going on?"

"Oh, we'll muddle through," Forman said. "A new scientist is here. She's not what we expected."

Who was this woman? Worse, was Zeke romantically interested in someone who could meet him on a higher intellectual level? Had

Jessie lost her chance with him by staying with Bea? Her stomach clenched. She tried to keep her voice breezy. "She disrupting the good ole boys club you guys have going on down there?"

"You're funny." Forman choked out a laugh. "Far from it, this gal came in with a bang, literally, and knocked Dr. Geek off his feet. He needed stitches, so we got him sewn together. They exchanged ideas and Zee needed a break, but the woman won't leave him alone. She's invited herself along on his evening swim. You know he likes to swim alone."

It was worse than she thought. This woman was muscling her way into every layer of Zeke's life. Worse, she was *swimming* with Zeke. Don't go there, she told herself. Though Forman didn't mention the Maleem invasion problem, Jessie was sure that's what the scientists were working on. Planetary defenses couldn't wait.

She glanced away from the vid cam to blink back tears. If she'd lost Zeke, it was her fault. The fate of the free world was more important than a fledgling romance.

"You keep them in line, Jethro." She paused to gather her thoughts. "We'll be home soon. Tell your boss I called."

She ended the link and plunked down on a wrought iron bench. The deep shade under the trees felt less welcoming, more sinister. This anxiety was her fault. She'd placed her sister's welfare above her happiness.

She could've made a different choice, but she'd yielded to duty and fear. She'd used Bea's immaturity as a crutch.

The revelation startled her. All this time, she thought she'd been the strong sister, but she was afraid of rejection. Did Zeke care for her? By fostering their separation, she could live the fantasy life she wanted, the one with him as her husband, a home, and children.

"Miss Stemford?"

Jessie glared at the uniformed attendant. Her thoughts of a rosy future faded to the cold light of day. "Yes? Is my sister okay?"

"Your sister's in art therapy. This package came for you."

Her name was printed in bold letters on the manila envelope. Despite her rocky emotions, the familiar sight brought forth memories of working happily with her sister.

Their anonymous benefactor had found them again.

Chapter 51

Zeke accessed the private Taman lair with a profound sigh of relief. His new home away from home. After running all-out to the lighthouse from the lab, his heart slammed against his ribs in protest. He glanced around the simple room with jaded eyes. The rickety wooden desk. His father's notebooks. The transmission chair. The sand on the floor.

Nothing about this hidden room bespoke excellence and certainly not alien intelligence. And yet, this room endured for hundreds of years, maybe longer. His ancestors had met their obligation to communicate earth's technological status. Had they faced such dire consequences as an alien invasion?

If he failed, the Maleem would exterminate mankind. Chances were high he wouldn't survive, or if he did, he'd be enslaved. His back teeth ground together. All it took was a glance across a sea of people for Drok to turn him into an automaton. Him, and no one else. How was that possible? He looked like everyone else. Did Tamans emit a distinctive brainwave signature? Were they more susceptible to Maleem domination?

Hell, how was any of this possible?

As a scientist, he believed in facts. He collected and analyzed data. He used his intellect to connect the dots, to form hypotheses. The dots in this situation were few and far between. Worse, all data indicated he had a pivotal role to play.

What if he couldn't meet expectations?

What if he failed?

His hands shook. *Pull it together. If you focus on the big picture, you'll get overwhelmed. Break down a problem to the building block stage. Focus on one step at a time. That's doable.*

He took a few deep breaths as he eyed the leather chair. Each time he communicated with his father and the other Tamans, he came away with more questions. This time he wouldn't be denied. He needed answers.

Firmly resolved, he strode across the dimly-lit space and reclined in the chair. His eyes were barely closed before the disorientation sensation started. He imagined himself in a Superman pose, hurtling through the cosmos faster than the speed of light.

We've been waiting, his father began. *How are you, Son?*

I need answers, Zeke said. *Our situation is dire. The Maleem established outposts on each continent. The number of humans wearing a Subjugator necklace increases daily. People are disappearing at an alarming rate. We don't know how to fight them.*

Did you save your friend's sister?

Yes. The salt therapy and hydration flushed the necklace cocktail from her body.

A miracle!. You've made history twice now.

I want more than that on my tombstone. I want to beat the Maleem. How do we get them to pack up and fly away?

Your planet's resources are too attractive. They will not retreat.

Then he'd make them go. *I identified the necklace chemicals. Tell me about the black crystals inside the necklace. They appear to be faceted gems. At first, I thought they were tourmaline, but their composition doesn't register on our detectors. What are they? What is their function?*

The stones are their energy source. When the large stones are damaged, the Maleem break them into smaller stones for routine functions like the Subjugator necklace.

Where do the stones come from?

The Maleem.

The answer made no sense. Conscious of having to meet the astrophysicist for a swim soon, he had to push harder for answers he could use. *I don't understand. Do they mine them from a planet? Do they occur naturally? Are they formed in some process?*

He waited as his father conferred with the others on the mindlink. Why were they so hesitant to dole out information? It felt like he was the one supplying most of the information, and this should be a two-way street. Finally, the buzz on the link quieted, signaling his father would soon speak to him.

They are Maleem, his father said. *The "stones" are interconnected inside this race, much like your skeletal system. Each Maleem is a power conductor. The stones store energy and discharge it.*

I witnessed the discharging part. It wasn't pretty. How do we drain the energy from a Maleem?

No one has ever done that.

What blocks the energy?

Adult Maleem must take energy from others. If you isolated individual Maleem, they would eventually run out of energy, but that would never happen. We believe there's only the one true Maleem in your invasion party. All the rest are energy reservoirs, and they depend on this Drok for their very lives. Without the chemicals Drok produces, they'll die, so they fight to their last breath to protect their Maleem leader. It's a symbiotic system, which makes the Maleem race invincible.

His thoughts churned as doubt blossomed. He quickly silenced those negative thoughts. *No one is invincible. I'll study the crystals and figure out a way to drain them or die trying. As for stopping them, a colleague suggests we manipulate dark matter to thwart the Maleem. What do you know of this?*

A new, reverent voice emerged from the Taman collective. *It is as the prophets said.* A general muttering increased to a mild roar in Zeke's head, with random phrasing standing out.

He is the Messiah!

He will save our people!

He will defeat the Maleem!

Stop. Please, Zeke said. *I need concrete help. Time is short here. We must act at once. But how? Do you have any idea how to do this?*

You are the Guardian, Son. And you are more than that. The Guardian draws from his strengths. Find what makes you strong. Use it to shatter the crystals and stop the Maleem. You must believe in your abilities and surround yourself with people who believe in you.

I'm supposed to beat the Maleem through positive thinking? Get real. I need weapons of mass destruction and armed spaceships. I need King Kong ripping through outer space and tearing the head off the Maleem.

Set aside your human strictures. Expand your conscious and apply it to the problem at hand.

I'm a scientist, Dad. I have to do things a certain way. I can't abandon everything I know and float off into a touchy-feely realm of good vibrations.

Then we are all doomed.

Chapter 52

Sidra's laughter caught the wind as she splashed in the shallows. "I love the ocean. Isn't this grand?"

"Sure." Zeke tried to sound upbeat. His peaceful evening swim had been transformed into a spectator event with Forman and Sidra's companion Ronni settled on the beach to watch the action. Before he plunged through the breaking waves, he gazed out to the horizon.

A few months ago, he stood here and felt bereft. Work couldn't fill the gap left by the death of his parents. He'd been alone. Or so he thought. Since then, he'd assumed his father's role of Guardian, and each day brought new challenges. He didn't have time to be lonely anymore.

Now, with the Maleem elbowing their way into Earth's society, his responsibilities increased exponentially. His job was to save the planet.

His best offense didn't rely on time-tested technologies. This slip of a girl, a child almost, expected him to manipulate space with his mind.

Like he knew how to do that.

Like that was even possible.

He dove through the waves, ignoring Sidra and the onlookers. He swam and dove and got far away from everyone. And felt his worries recede. Just him and the sea. The shore was a distant white ribbon and that was how he liked it.

He lay back, studied the sky, and gently rocked on the ocean swells. Beyond that blue was the cold and dark of outer space. And threaded throughout his world and the hostile world of space were these WIMPs. Sure, he'd dreamed of them, but how did one bridge the gap between dreams and action?

His dolphin pals swam to greet him. Nicola, the female with the nicked fin, bumped him first. Then little Boz, still a bit smaller than the others, and, he suspected, Nicola's offspring. The other two surfaced nearby, splashing and spraying each other, accented by clicks and whistling. He smiled at their antics, relishing the fact that he was momentarily included in their pod.

"It's good to see you guys," he said aloud. Did dolphins understand human speech? Just in case they didn't, he repeated the sentiment as a thought. *It's good to see you guys.*

Boz levered his dolphin nose in and out of the water, causing a spray of saltwater to drench Zeke's face. The cut on his face burned a bit more. He splashed back, enjoying the play and the relaxation.

With their pokes and shoves, they seemed to be urging him back toward shore. He glanced toward the beach and saw Sidra trying to swim out to where he was. Damn. Couldn't she leave him alone for a moment? Then he worried she wasn't a strong swimmer and hurried to intercept her.

Boz swam ahead, flanked by the other bottlenose dolphins. Zeke's arms and legs churned through the water. The burn felt good. It felt damned good. *Gotta save Sidra,* he thought as he sped through the waves.

A few minutes later, he reached her. "You all right?" he asked.

"Dolphins!" she squealed as she spun in a circle. "I love them. I love this place. It's so flurking real."

He thought about steadying her but he didn't want to get kicked in the face again. "Of course it's real. Did you think it was make-believe?"

She stopped spinning and studied him. "Sometimes I get so caught up in my thoughts that the line between real and imagined blurs. Sometimes my mind takes me far away."

Uh-oh. This sounded vaguely familiar. His heart rate sped up. Was she Taman? Were there others like him on the planet?

He tried to keep the wild hope out of his voice. "It does?"

"I'm not like other people. That's the best explanation I have."

Tell her or play it safe? The question stormed through his head. "I'm a bit different, too," he allowed.

"You're part dolphin?"

Boz sprayed him again. "Not quite. But this guy is special. This is Boz."

"I got that. Hi, Boz. That's his mom over there, Nicola, right?"

A wave knocked into him. He struggled to reorient himself. "How'd you know that?"

Sidra shrugged. "I just know."

"Huh."

She pointed to the other dolphins. "The one with a big smile is Klickie and the shy one is Tunis."

Their names felt right. He sounded them out in his head, Klickie and Tunis. Definitely right. He cocked his head toward Sidra, his interest keen. "Have you done this before?"

"Never." She turned to stare at the most distant dolphin. "Tunis says thanks for rescuing her little brother."

Zeke tread water and tried to think logically. She wasn't reading his mind because he didn't know the names of the other dolphins. "How do you know these things? Did someone tell you about it?"

"Yeah. Tunis. She said he was stuck in the cage for two suns, and they were scared he would drown."

Made sense, he grudgingly admitted. This bottlenose pod was quite perceptive. "They herded me out to the platform a few days ago. I didn't know what to expect, but I believed their actions had a purpose."

"We all have a purpose, Zeke. Don't you know that?"

"I'm beginning to get that impression."

"They say you'll save the world."

Had she been talking to Uncle John? "They who?"

"Your podmates here."

The casual way she tossed that out there worried him. "How do you communicate with them?"

"I can't explain it. They tell me it's okay for you to touch me. That you won't harm me."

"Of course I wouldn't harm you. You didn't have to swim out here to learn that."

"But I wanted to see you in your element. You're at home in the ocean. You are a merman. And I'm a mermaid."

That didn't sound good. "Now you've veered way off track. I'm as much a human being as you are."

Sidra laughed. And laughed some more. "Good one."

Zeke glanced at the nearby beach where Ronni and Forman paced the shore. "We should return."

"Only if you promise we can come out here again tomorrow."

"I don't make promises I can't keep. This Maleem problem could have us on the other side of the world tomorrow."

She stuck her tongue out at him. "Be that way. Klickie says she'll give me a ride back to shore."

With that, Sidra grabbed hold of Klickie, and they disappeared beneath the sea. Dang. That wasn't good. He couldn't see her at all. Tunis swam beside him and whistled.

Given Sidra's exit, was he being offered the same courtesy? Why not?

He grabbed hold and plunged under the surface with the dolphin. Water streamed by quickly, and he found it difficult to focus his eyes. Should he help kick? He tried it and got rolled and dislodged. Sputtering, he surfaced. Okay. That was a bad idea. He swam toward her, thinking the word *sorry*. The dolphin whistled and clicked at him, but he didn't understand.

"I won't help this time." Tunis swam by him, slowing and allowing him to catch her fin. Instead of skimming the surface as Klickie and Sidra were doing, Tunis dove again. Good thing he could hold his breath for a very long time.

As they bulleted through the water, he wanted to shout for joy at the sheer thrill of water sluicing past his body. What a rush! Tunis slowed abruptly and the sandy ocean bottom came into focus. Zeke glanced up, and the light of day shone right above him. They'd reached the shallows. Tunis rolled him off, and they surfaced for air. Then she circled around for a belly rub. He obliged.

Sidra and Klickie splashed up. "That was awesome," Sidra said as she released Klickie, who splashed circles around them before returning for a belly rub. "You are my favorite dolphin in the whole world."

"Know that many dolphins, do you?" Zeke asked.

"Can't say as I do." She narrowed her eyes at him. "How'd you beat us? Are you part dolphin?"

He snorted at the biological impossibility. "I'm just a guy. You're the one who speaks dolphin."

They waded into the shallows where Forman and Ronni fussed over both of them, but Zeke couldn't stop turning Sidra's question over in his mind.

Was he part dolphin? He'd held his breath for a very long time on that dolphin ride. Longer than most humans could hold their breath. And he seemed to be communicating with them on a rudimentary level. One thing he knew for sure. Dolphins were important to his mission on Earth. He just needed to figure out how.

Chapter 53

The next day, Forman handed John Demery an encrypted file of the whacky astrophysics solution Zeke and Sidra had pieced together. Because the information might save the planet, Zeke insisted it had to be hand-delivered to the mainland.

Before he left Demery's house, Forman probed Demery's super computer for information about Bea. In less than five minutes, he had an address of her rehab place in Charleston. If he took an express pod, he could get there and back before the afternoon ferry to the island.

He rolled into the transpo station and boarded an express pod. While he hated for Bea to see him in this crappy Jethro shell, he needed to see that she was recovering.

Thirty minutes later, he arrived, purchased candy, and headed to the rehab center. The guard at the gate stopped him.

"Service bots use the rear entrance," the rent-a-cop said.

Crap. He didn't think of that. A few weeks back he could pass for human. Now he was certifiably a bucket of bolts. "I'm short on time, and my master sent this candy for his girlfriend," he improvised.

The guard reached for the box. "I'll see that she gets it."

Forman didn't come all this way to be turned away at the gate. "I have to see her face when I give her the candy and the message. To record her expression for my master."

"We don't allow guests in the facility. Our residents are guaranteed privacy."

"Jessie isn't a resident. Her sister is the guest here. Jessie's her moral support. She's pining away for my master, and he misses her so much the big lug can hardly work. Surely, you wouldn't be so cruel as to turn me away."

"Wait here," the guard said, disappearing into the shack. He returned ninety-eight seconds later and motioned Forman inside. "You are to wait on the grounds. Miss Stemford will meet you outside."

Forman nodded and rolled into the flowered courtyard. The

beautiful flowers and peaceful setting couldn't quell his nerves. Would Jessie bring Bea out with her? Would she believe Zeke sent her candy? For that matter, would Bea even know it was him?

Did he want her to know?

Love sucked.

Damn this emotion chip.

He needed to get past this fascination he had with the pop singer. She wasn't in love with him. She looked out for herself. A one-way affection invited heartbreak.

When he was about to resort to plucking petals from flowers, he heard the whirl of an old-fashioned wheelchair. He turned, and there she was. Dressed all in white, like an angel. Dark circles rimmed her eyes. Her cheeks were sunk in. Her hair looked dull and lifeless.

But Bea was alive.

He'd never thought anyone looked so good in his life.

Before he could speak, Jessie called out to him. "Are you the Jethro that requested an audience with me?"

She knew he was stuck in this crappy Jethro shell. Why the subterfuge? Unless she gave him a signal, he would maintain the ruse.

"Yes. I have a message from Dr. Zeke Landry. He sends his regards and this box of chocolates." He handed Jessie the box of candy.

"I want one," Bea said in a cross voice. "They feed me high protein shakes and nothing sweet. Please Jessie, I want one."

Jessie clutched the box to her breast, starry-eyed. "They said no sugar. The shakes help detox the rest of the chemicals from your system."

"But they don't know, do they? I'm the first one ever to recover from the necklace thingy. They could be wrong, and I'd be missing out on chocolate and sugar for nothing."

"I'll think about it." Jessie turned back to Forman. "Tell me the news. How is Zeke?"

He studied her face and noted how wan she looked. "Have a seat, if you like." She sat, placing the box on the park bench beside her, and he continued. "My boss is fine. He has a new helper, an astrophysicist."

She nodded. "I remember you mentioning her before."

"She's brilliant, like Dr. Z, but they're forever arguing about things. I'm glad to have an afternoon away from that noisy pair.

How are you two holding up?"

"I hate it here," Bea said, wheeling herself along the courtyard perimeter. "They won't let me leave, won't let me have my music stuff. I'm in a prison."

"You're not in a prison, Bea," Jessie stated in a parental tone. "You're in rehab. Big difference."

"Easy for you to say, sis. You can walk out any minute. Why don't you? Why don't you leave me the hell alone?"

Forman flinched. His lovely Bea didn't sound like herself at all. How was that possible that she could've changed so much? Was her surliness a function of the residual necklace chemicals?

"The therapist said you'd feel this way," Jessie soothed. "It's part of your recovery."

"This sucks." On Bea's next lap around the courtyard, she snagged the box of chocolates wheeled away, squealing for joy. "These are mine. Pirate's plunder."

He'd intended for Bea to enjoy the candy, too, so her newfound happiness eased the ache inside. The smile on her face was his doing. Though she didn't recognize him, didn't seem to care about anyone, not even her sister, his Bea was still somewhere inside the bitter person before him, still had a chance of being herself again.

"You shouldn't have those," Jessie said, rising from the bench. "Give them back."

"Can't stop me." Bea pushed piece after piece into her trembling mouth.

Forman trailed Jessie over to Bea's wheelchair.

"I said that's enough." Jessie reached for the candy box.

Bea shot energy out her fingertips, knocking Jessie off her feet. Forman caught her as she fell.

"Enough!" Forman said. He placed Jessie behind him on the nearest bench. "You hurt your sister, the one person who has stood beside you this entire time."

Bea rose and wobbled, her skin tinged green. "Thought I'd lost my super power, but I still got it, baby. Get in my way, crappy robot, and I'll zap you to hell and back."

Forman retreated behind a tree with Jessie. What had he done? His Bea didn't act like this. His Bea may have been self-centered, but she was no killer. This didn't make sense. He sent out a subsonic pulse to the facility's main computer. *Trouble in the courtyard. Send help.*

Alarms rang. The gates clanged shut.

Bea shot energy out of her fingertips and toasted the flowers. The acrid smell of smoke perfumed the air. She shot pure bolts of energy overhead. She threw a lightning bolt at the gate, knocking it down.

"I am all powerful," Bea shouted as she leapt from the flowerbed retaining wall to the park bench. "I am the Queen of the Universe."

"You're the queen of crazy," Jessie muttered beside Forman. "How is this possible? How can she do that?"

"Stay close. One of the drugs in the Maleem necklace rewires human physiology into an electrical discharging system. It seems the effects are more long lasting than we predicted."

"She was getting better until she ate the chocolate."

Her observation added to his growing remorse. "It certainly seems to be an agonist. I will contact Dr. Z immediately."

Zeke answered his com at once. "What are you doing in Charleston? I thought you were with Uncle John."

"Long story," Forman said in hushed tones. "The short version is I came to see Bea. She was okay until she tasted the chocolate I brought. Then, she started shooting energy out of her fingertips. She shocked her sister."

"Is everyone okay?"

"Jessie's conscious again. We're hiding behind a big tree. Security is maintaining a healthy perimeter as Bea scorches the earth. What should we do?"

"Remove the chocolate."

"Too late. She ate the whole box."

"When I observed this electrical phenomenon before, the Maleem bodyguards were energy reservoirs. Without an auxiliary host there for her to draw from, Bea will run out of juice soon. Since she's drawing on her own reserves, expect her to suddenly pass out. Keep me informed."

The screen went blank. "You get all that?" Forman asked Jessie.

She nodded in tight-lipped silence. Then she prodded him with her elbow. "Look."

Weapons drawn, security guards approached Bea from all four directions. "Those are tranquilizer guns. To sedate her," Forman said to ease Jessie's fears.

The guard in front took his shot. Bea roared with outrage and pulled the dart out. She pointed her hand at the guard and sent a blast of energy his way. Each time she hurled energy from her fingertips, her skin tone became darker green. If Forman didn't know better, he could easily mistake her for a Maleem.

The other guards opened fire. It appeared initially that Bea was immune to the tranquilizer, but then, as Zeke had predicted, she crumpled and toppled off the bench face-first. Forman rolled toward her and barely caught her head before she struck the paved surface.

He cradled her green, unconscious body. "What have I done?"

Chapter 54

Zeke ended the recording of Bea's horrific display and turned from the guest com station in his uncle's office. The long shadows concealed Uncle John's face. "What did you think?"

"That poor girl." Uncle John shook his head. "She was making such progress. I thought she could be saved."

His uncle thought Bea was a loss? That wasn't good. "I'm not giving up on Bea yet, but we're remiss if we don't take advantage of this new information."

Uncle John shifted in his chair. Now that he'd gained some of his weight back from his stint as a captive, the leather creaked a bit. It was a good sound. Zeke waited in the painful silence, mentally kicking himself for not stating the sugar problem more strongly. He'd posed his caution about sugar as a suggestion because he had no physical proof. Now Jessie's sister had to pay the price.

"How so?" his uncle asked.

"Right now, the public knows nothing about the enslaving power of the necklace. They view them as harmless trinkets. If we discredit these necklace wearers publicly, then we can isolate them and weaken the Maleem presence on the planet. And it will stop others from wearing the necklaces. We could leak information to the media that the necklaces make people dangerous. Chocolate wouldn't be suspected in any way."

Uncle John's bushy white eyebrows rose and fell. "We'd lose the benefit of having spies in their midst."

"We don't have spies in their midst. No human who went aboard their ships reported useful information in the way of space propulsion or weapons systems. None of your snoopers or drones survived the trip. What about the necklace mockups? How's that coming along?"

"We have mockups made," Uncle John said. "But the scientists on the project believe the dark crystals are essential to passing the fakes off as real. That's the hold up. We only have one set of crystals. Angie will wear a mockup with the crystals in the next batch of folks who ferry out to the ship. She will get us the intel we need."

Zeke winced. "Does it have to be Angie?"

"We've added a contact barrier to the necklace to protect her. Don't worry about Angie. She's tougher than she looks."

"I can't help but worry. She's family. I don't have much of that left."

"She'll be fine. Now, let me bring you up to speed on the planetary defenses. The Soviets have armed the Space Station to detonate remotely. They'll sacrifice it if the Maleem ships get within the blast radius."

He'd been wondering about the military's plan of attack. Trust the people with guns and bombs to think those were the answer. "It might help, or it might just make them mad. Until we know the full extent of their weapons capability, I urge caution in launching a first strike."

"We hope to have other options by then. How are you and Sidra coming on the astrophysics solution?"

"We agree WIMPs are the answer. Implementation is the answer."

"Damn it, Zeke. I need progress. Make this happen. We don't have much time."

"I'm aware of that, sir, but this has never been attempted before. I can't even give you a percent probability of effectiveness."

The leather chair creaked as Uncle John leaned forward out of the shadows, an intent expression etched on his craggy features. "Tell me more."

"Sidra's stuck on this mind over matter idea. She believes we can create a barrier out of nearly invisible particles she calls WIMPs. I accept her proposal as a theory, but I can't do much more than that with it. That's the good news. The bad news is that we have nothing else, short of blowing ourselves up so the Maleem can't have us or our planet. But that sucks for humanity, and the aliens'd only go elsewhere and continue their rampage. We need a better way to destroy them, once and for all."

"When you've exhausted all the possible ideas, whatever's left, however improbable, is the solution."

"Now you're sounding all Zen-y like my dad."

"Winston could be vague on occasion, but he was right more times than wrong. Don't consider Sidra's solution as impossible. See it as a challenge. If you were going to make it work, how would you best accomplish it?"

"The problem is too big for one mind. It would take many minds working in conjunction."

His uncle shrugged, his dark eyes glittering. "So you'd need a laboratory with brain connectivity capability. I can make that happen."

Zeke pondered the puzzle again. "Not a lab. The ocean. For me to orchestrate this, we need to be in the ocean. Near Tama Island. With a team of like-minded people."

"In a boat?"

"In the water. Maybe on rafts that are partially deflated so we're in contact with the seawater. And connected. We have to be physically touching each other."

"Sounds doable so far."

"I don't know how many people I need, but they have to trust me."

"Native islanders?"

"That might do it. Six or twelve sounds manageable but I don't know if that's enough."

"If it's all we've got, we have to try."

Uncle John's com alarmed. He flicked on the large screen and swore. Three large domes cast shadows on the moon. "The Maleem aren't waiting in deep space any longer. They're here."

Zeke's stomach dropped to his knees. "Time's run out."

"Not yet. We're moving forward on all fronts. Take my chopper back to the island. Set up your mind-trust flotilla. Meanwhile, I'll orchestrate Operation Chocolate to remove the compromised citizens of Earth from the global stage. We don't need insiders under Maleem control. We need to fight the Maleem, not our own people."

"Understood."

His uncle's link buzzed again. He glanced at the message and over at Zeke. "Forman has returned. He'll meet you at the helipad."

"Got it. And, Uncle John?"

His uncle paused in his sending out messages. "Yes?"

Zeke's throat went dry, and he couldn't get a word out. There was so much he wanted to tell his uncle, so much he couldn't tell him. He coughed to clear his throat. "If we don't make it, I want you to know it's been a pleasure to know you and work with you. I can't guarantee this mind over matter experiment will work, but I'll give it two hundred percent."

"Good deal. Now get hopping. Time's a-wasting."

Chapter 55

Pauline knotted the silky fabric under her chin. Between the scarf and the dark glasses, she was sure no one would recognize her. "Why the hell does Zeke Landry have to live on an island?"

"I don't know, love," Connor Bronsen said as the hovercraft ferry powered over the water. He shooed away a mosquito. "But we'll be there soon and you won't have to worry about anything ever again. I'll make this right for you."

He'd been saying that a lot lately. Connor wanted to take care of her. She didn't give a hoot about him. All she wanted, all she needed to survive was the necklace. "My life depends on getting that necklace back. I have to have it. We can't leave here without that necklace."

"We'll get it. I promise you. Then everything will be all right." The sappy look in his eyes nearly made her laugh out loud. "It'll be like old times."

Promises. She knew all about broken promises. "Of course. But the necklace helps my leg. It hurts so much. You have no idea."

"I want you to feel good about yourself. About us. If I have to fight this Landry fellow, I will. Don't worry your pretty head about it. Connor will get your necklace, and you will be yourself again."

And then she'd fry his ass and anyone else's who got in her way. She'd had a taste of the Promised Land, and she aimed to have it back.

Another couple on the ferry walked by. Pauline instinctively turned away to face the marsh-lined banks of the river. They'd come so far on this quest. They'd sold Connor's blood. He'd slept with women for credits. She'd gone down on fat hairy men for credits. And they'd stolen ration cards and valuables from every trick. All to get to this nowhere place on the Georgia coast.

"I don't know what I'll do if the necklace isn't here. Ow!" She glanced down at the mosquito that bit her hand. Just before she fake smacked it, she had the satisfaction of seeing the insect die from her altered blood. One bite and it keeled over immediately. Lovely. She brushed the nuisance aside.

Connor rose and glanced longingly at the vending machines in the center of the vessel. "I'm hungry. We have enough for a snack. You want a soda or something sweet to eat?"

She shook her head. "Nothing for me."

"You have to eat."

His patronizing tone irritated the hell out of her. If only she could zap him right now and be done with this charade. "I will. Once I have the necklace again."

He sat beside her again. "Okay. I'll pass too then. That way we'll share a meal together and celebrate our success." He reached over and patted her hand. "You're so beautiful. I want to spend the rest of my life with you."

"You're sweet," she murmured. When she got the necklace, she'd kill Connor and take his credits. She'd resume her rightful place at Drok's side. Together they'd roam the stars. This puny rock of a planet couldn't hold her. She was destined for greater things.

The necklace.

Everything hinged on that necklace.

Chapter 56

Zeke glanced out the helicopter window at the hovercraft ferry en route to the island. To his island. If his plan to save the planet didn't work, the Maleem would have free reign over all the earth. He didn't want that.

He turned to Forman. "I'm sorry about Bea."

"She's not well. I brought those chocolates into her proximity. She would've been released by now if not for me."

"She wasn't ready. Imagine if she'd freaked like that at her house. She might have hurt herself and Jessie. As it was, only a few flowers got torched."

"I dunno. The necklace changed her. It brought to the surface her most selfish desires. She's not the sweet woman I fell in love with. I'm not sure I love her anymore."

"You have the right to focus your attention on someone else. But I wouldn't write Bea off yet. The Stemfords have been resilient to date." He glanced to the western horizon and beheld the shining glory of the sun. It was too bright. Too raw. Too elemental. Like his feelings for Bea's sister. He shot Forman a sideways glance. "How was Jessie?"

"She survived the shockwave blast with no apparent ill effects. Other than that, she looked tired. Her eyes glowed when I told her I'd brought her a box of chocolates from you. Dude, why didn't you send her a present? That woman nearly cried when she took the box from me. She pressed it close to her heart. Why didn't you call her or talk to her?"

"I didn't know if she'd take my calls. She could've come home with me but she chose her sister instead."

"Time to grow up, boss man. Her sister is in a world of hurt and trouble. Bea is her only family. If you can't see that family comes first, you don't deserve to have one."

"I want a family." The words popped out of Zeke's mouth before he could recall them. "I've been a little busy saving the world since Jessie and I parted."

"There's always time for a call."

When Zeke didn't answer, Forman kept digging. "Oh my God. You're afraid she'll reject you. She won't, bro. She had other obligations. Surely, you understand divided loyalties. Surely, you understand that duty and responsibility are hard-wired into Jessie's soul."

He was an idiot. Forman had pegged him accurately from the get-go. Relationships were messy, and Zeke sucked at them. He wanted Jessie to be with him. He wanted to build something special with her. Had his cautious approach cost him her love?

He nodded his head. "Thanks for thinking of the chocolate. I'm sorry about Bea, but you helped my case with Jessie. I owe you."

The whir of chopper blades filled the gap in the conversation. Zeke wished he didn't have duties and obligations right now. He'd like nothing better than to go to Jessie and start fresh. The idea glimmered with startling appeal. He could be a regular guy, going to see his girlfriend.

But the Maleem wouldn't step aside from their agenda. They were up there, orbiting with the moon, waiting for a signal to begin the bloodbath. Thanks to the Tamans, he'd viewed Maleem carnage firsthand. They'd rape the planet, plunder all its resources, and drain it of life. When they were done, Earth would be a wasteland.

Jessie would have to wait.

His destiny lay before him. On the island. If all went well and he stopped the Maleem, he might have a future with Jessie. If he didn't stop them, there'd be no future at all – for him and Jessie, for his uncle, for the entire planet. His priorities were clear.

"We need to tell the islanders to bring flotation devices and meet me at the lighthouse tonight a little before midnight. There's a new moon, so the sky will be at its darkest. We'll move forward on Sidra's plan tonight. The Maleem have given us no choice."

"You believe Sidra's plan has a chance?"

"I believe we have no other viable options. If we fail, Earth will fall to our enemy."

"We cannot fail."

"Right. You've got those power tracks for legs, so I know you can go anywhere on the island. That's your primary mission once we get to the island. I'll go to the lab and coordinate with Sidra. You tell everyone who was born on this spit of sand that the Guardian needs them. Give them the time and place and nothing else. Got that?"

"Got it."

Chapter 57

Jessie couldn't stop shaking. After Bea was drugged and restrained by armed guards, she'd wandered the halls of the rehab facility and ended up in the vacant respite room. She turned on the vid screen to stop thinking about her sister. Out of habit, she tuned the channel to Entertainment News, but Connor and Pauline weren't the ones expressing shock and horror over world events and the recent abductions.

Some other dumb schmuck in a bad suit and shiny tie was making a hash of it. Disgusted by his ineptitude, she switched to a mainstream network. The female newscaster showed more cleavage than teeth, but the edgy tremor in her voice was real.

"Ambassador Wagner, Dylan James, and many more around the world are considered armed and dangerous. People who wear the Maleem necklace are said to be a danger to themselves and others," the not-so-perky woman reported.

"No joke," Jessie muttered. She watched in shock as the station replayed when newscaster-turned-Maleem interpreter, Pauline Curran, fried her former lover in Japan. Next, Forman became a hero trying to stop the Maleem. Tears flooded her eyes at his destruction. What was happening? The world had gone crazy.

Images of people wearing Maleem necklaces flashed across the screen. Important people. Heads of state. Military leaders. Rock stars. Government flunkies. Fortunately, Bea's picture wasn't in that list of the afflicted. But she was. Afflicted.

And it broke Jessie's heart.

"These people are considered armed and dangerous," the talking head continued. "Call the police if you spot one of them. For our protection, they must be taken to a secure facility now that the Maleem ships are so close."

"What's that?" The newscaster gazed at her notes and cupped her hand over her ear com.

Jessie stepped closer to the screen, her arms hugging her middle. She'd failed her sister. She'd failed to live up to her responsibilities. She'd ignored the advance knowledge of the imminent danger from the Maleem that her anonymous benefactor sent. She'd failed everyone.

She'd acted to protect her family.

To hide from danger.

But the danger mounted.

She'd turned away from the one thing she wanted. Zeke. She couldn't believe how much his gift of chocolates meant to her. He cared. Sending a woman chocolates was the universal language for caring. Everyone knew that.

"Breaking news," the female reporter said. "We've received confirmation that our Space Station blew up. No one is sure if the destruction is related to the Maleem ships orbiting our planet. But the Space Station is no more and the three ships are fine."

"Holy cow," Jessie whispered. "It's happening. People are disappearing. The ships are coming. The destruction is starting." She could no longer afford to sit on the sidelines. She had to do something with her insider knowledge from Anon. She silenced the vid screen and jabbed her com link for the emergency number.

"Please state the nature of your emergency," the dispatcher said.

"My emergency is planet-wide," Jessie said. "The Maleem will fire on the planet and destroy us. Tell people to get out of the cities. Tell them to hide underground. This is a real emergency."

"One moment."

Jessie heard a few clicks before the man came back on the line.

"Ma'am, are you calling from a psychiatric facility?" he asked.

Her irritation fed into her voice. "I'm calling from my vid link, and yes, I happen to be at the facility because my sister is a guest here. I saw the news. Once the Space Station blew up, we're on a doomsday countdown. The Maleem will retaliate. Get the people out of cities. Do it now."

"How do you know this? What proof do you have of Maleem ill will? We are establishing trade agreements with them. We can't jeopardize that with a call from a funny farm."

"Nothing about this call is funny," Jessie insisted. "I'm no crackpot. My name is Jessie Stemford, and the Maleem tried to kill me in Japan. I won't be silenced. I will be heard."

Jessie heard a laugh from the operator's end of the line. Right before the connection cut off she heard someone ask, "Another doomsday crackpot?"

"I'm not one of them," she yelled at her wrist link.

She rubbed her throbbing temples. Staying here was pointless. If her information was accurate, the Maleem were about to attack. In her doped up state, Bea wouldn't know Jessie was gone.

In less than five minutes, she'd packed her meager belongings and placed a call to John Demery. "You were right. I'm not needed here. What can I do to help?"

Chapter 58

After parting ways with Forman at the helipad, Zeke headed straight for his lab. The chopper pilot relayed the news about the Space Station blowing up. Only a matter of time until the Maleem blasted Earth. People would die.

People he knew and loved. The Earth would be no more.

A glance at his lab silhouetted by the setting sun caused him to stutter-step. Something was wrong. He never left the lab door wide open. Worse, his research pigs milled around the building, uncontained.

His pace quickened. What was Sidra doing? He didn't give her permission to release his study animals or to access his files either. Those were private.

They were also encrypted.

But a genius like Sidra could decode the best encryption he and Forman had to offer.

Had he inadvertently let an enemy into his inner sanctum?

Of all times not to have Forman with him. He was no match for Sidra's martial arts skills.

But he wouldn't give up without a fight. "Sidra!"

No answer.

The hair on the back of his neck electrified, and his pace unconsciously slowed. Something evil waited in his lab. Something much more terrible than a quirky genius with boundary issues.

He crossed the threshold. Inside, two bloody strangers stood looking down at a squirming imp. Sidra. Both the male and female of the pair displayed bloody faces. Sidra hadn't gone down without a fight. But the man had a gun. Zeke's tranquilizer gun. A blast from it wasn't lethal.

Good to know it wasn't a real gun with bullets.

"Who are you people?" Zeke asked. "What happened to my colleague?"

The woman closed the containment chamber and lifted the necklace in triumph. "Kill them both. I have the necklace."

"No!" Zeke said, rushing in.

The man shot Sidra. She passed out in one point four seconds. He trained the gun on Zeke.

Zeke raised his hands. "I surrender. Don't shoot."

When the necklace didn't light up, the woman screamed with rage. "Don't murder the bastard. He tricked me."

"Who are you people?" Zeke repeated. The scratch on the woman's thin face looked odd. Dark even. "What do you want?"

"What did you do to my necklace. It doesn't work," the woman said.

"I'm studying the necklace. It's still intact. It isn't in pieces."

"Lies. The panels aren't lighting up. It feels different. Empty." She extended her fingers toward his mass spectrometer. "There's no juice in the necklace, and I demand to know what you did with it."

Her voice sounded familiar. Information clicked. "You're Pauline Curran, aren't you? The newscaster who accompanied the Maleem. Is that you, Connor Bronsen? I never thought I'd meet such a famous couple. We watch your newscasts all the time. I mean we watched your newscasts all the time. Before the aliens came."

He stopped talking because Pauline's face got darker and darker with each word he uttered.

"Yeah, it's us, dude." Connor kept the gun trained on Zeke. "Fix the necklace, and we'll leave."

Zeke kept his hands in the air. He needed a plan, but nothing viable came to mind. He'd never felt so dumb in his life. "I can't. This one is empty. The chemicals were used up in testing. You'll have to acquire another necklace."

"Can't do that." Pauline picked up a lab stool and smashed an electron microscope. "All the chosen were rounded up like vermin. Special ops got them. The Maleem are gonna be royally pissed at losing their protégés."

"The Maleem will exterminate the human race. Don't you get it?" Zeke asked. "That's what they do. They galaxy hop and plunder at will. They destroy everything in their path."

"They're powerful," Pauline said. "I've tasted their power, and I want it back. Fix the necklace, or I'll wreck everything in this place."

"I can't do that, ma'am," Zeke said. Out of the corner of his eye, he saw Sidra begin to stir. He had to warn her to stay still. They could both communicate with dolphins telepathically, so maybe he could communicate with her that way as well. He beamed thoughts her way. *Don't move, Sidra. These people are whacked out but harmless. I'll get them out of here, but you play possum. Hear me?*

I hear you. I don't like it, but I hear you.

It worked! Much as he'd like to figure out how it worked, he had to act as if telepathy was a normal occurrence. *As long as they think they can kill me with the tranq gun, I've got a chance. If you come back to life, my chances go right out the window.*

Back to playing dead, boss.

He tried to remain expressionless during the exchange, but he must have slipped.

Connor jabbed the gun into his ribs as if it were a knife. "What's so funny, pretty boy?"

"You. Me. This situation. You want something I can't give. I don't want to die. I can't believe you shot my friend."

Pauline raged around the lab, bashing and smashing anything that would break. Zeke winced at the carnage. Uncle John wouldn't like this one bit. Hell, he didn't like it either. There was a baseball bat behind the door. Perhaps he could angle over and pick it up.

"Don't move," Connor said when he attempted to sidestep.

Pauline came over and pressed her hand over his face. The action blinded him. His mind writhed in agony. No. Couldn't be. She wasn't a Maleem. But as he gazed at her facial wound he saw under her skin. Her blood was no longer bright red. Her exposed cheekbone looked decidedly dark. Like a Maleem necklace crystal.

His thoughts whirled. Maleems were made not born? Was that possible?

You will do as I say, she silently commanded.

He cursed inwardly as she shackled his thoughts, much as Drok had done. Her tactile method was cruder, but effective. He couldn't move a muscle without her permission.

"Speak to me of the necklace," Pauline said when she removed her hand.

"It is empty."

"Where are the contents?"

"In the pigs, outside."

She slapped his face. "Pigs? You gave my precious elixir to rutting farm animals?"

His cheek stung. "I did."

"And the generator?"

"The dark crystals are gone."

"Who has them?"

"I don't know."

"Who did you give them to?"

"My uncle."

If only he could lie to her. If only her command didn't hold him spellbound.

"What will happen if I don't get more of the chemicals?"

"I don't know."

She slapped him harder, and pain lanced his thoughts.

"The full truth," she demanded, her sour breath blasting in his face. "What happened in your experiments?"

"The subjects with the highest doses displayed increased aggression and disregard for their well-being. One pig killed himself by bashing his head repeatedly against the side of the pen."

Pauline swore viciously. She gut-punched him. "You miserable worm. Do you have any idea what you've done? You've killed me."

He stared mutely ahead, moisture welling in his eyes. She hit hard for a girl.

"You have the pretty necklace, Paulie," Connor said in a placating tone. "He can't fix it. Maybe someone else can. We'll keep looking."

Pauline grabbed Zeke's arm and aimed her index finger at Connor. An electrical charge shot out her fingertips. At the same time, Zeke felt his energy being drained. But the effect was short-lived.

"Ouch!" Connor backed up into a lab counter. Broken glassware crunched under his feet. "That hurt. Why'd you zap me?"

Her sinister laugh rang throughout the ruined lab. "Because I could be so much more, don't you see? This guy ruined it for me."

"He can't fix the necklace. Come on, Paulie, let's go home. I'll take care of you."

Pauline snorted. "How the hell are we going anywhere? The damned ferry doesn't leave for another two hours."

"Maybe he knows a way," Connor said.

"How do we leave this place?" she asked.

"There's a canoe nearby," Zeke said.

"Is that a boat?" she asked.

"Yes."

"Excellent. You will lead us to it now. Move."

Zeke exited the lab. Unlike Drok's mind control, Pauline's hold on him was tenuous. If he could get them out in the canoe, he'd flip it once he got offshore. By then maybe her mindlink would have lapsed. He'd swim to safety and leave them to the sharks.

He once again had the ability to think clearly when she directed his movements. Not a soul was in sight. Forman must be still making his rounds. Everyone else must be glued to a vid screen. The blown-up Space Station would be a top story until the Maleem attacked. Then it would all be in vain.

"Put the gun away, Con," Pauline said. "The doctor will do as I say."

"How do you know he won't trick us?"

"He can't. I don't know how to explain it. The necklace changed me. I can do the things the Maleem do."

"That's scary. I want you to be the way you were before."

She zapped him again. "Shut up. I can't take any more of your prattling."

"This isn't right," Connor yelped. "We're supposed to be together."

"Halt," Pauline ordered.

Zeke stopped. He hated being so helpless. He hated the Maleem. He hated Pauline.

"Come here, Connor," she said sweetly. "I want to kiss and make up."

"Now you're talking." Connor hurried to join Pauline at Zeke's side. He pressed his lips to hers.

Zeke wished he couldn't see this, wished the dumb oaf could see that Pauline was playing him.

Pauline broke off the kiss, placing her hand over Connor's face as she'd done with Zeke. "You've been a bad boy. I want you to move only at my command."

Connor shied away from her touch. "I did what you wanted. What's wrong with you? Don't you love me?"

She screamed in rage and shocked him again. "Why won't you do as I say?"

That was a very good question, Zeke thought. How was Connor immune to Pauline's fledgling mind control skills?

"I've always done what you said, but I don't like it when you shock me," Connor said. "Do it again and I'm leaving."

"I'm sorry," she said, sounding petulant. "I don't know what's come over me. I was so disappointed about the necklace that my emotions are all over the place." She touched Zeke's shoulder, zapping him with his own energy. "Move."

He jolted into motion, howling at the fiery pain her touch inflicted. A tide of emotions swamped him but revenge edged his thoughts. He would find a way out of this mess. And when he did, this alien would meet her match.

Chapter 59

Zeke trudged through the honey-suckle scented darkness of Tama Island. He could give in to despair easily enough, but he'd been under another's mind control before and survived. There would be an opportunity to escape. She'd make a mistake, and he'd watch for the opportunity.

"How does he know where to go?" Connor asked. "It's so dark out here."

"He knows," Pauline said. "I can feel his certainty."

What else could she feel? Zeke keep his feet moving toward the sound side of the island. Unlike Drok, Pauline didn't have a firm grasp on his mind, only his motor functions. Even so, she could make him do anything she wanted, and he couldn't deny her commands.

He hoped they didn't encounter any islanders along the night-darkened path. He didn't wish to harm anyone. Except Pauline. He'd like to zap her. Boy, would he.

"I heard that." She zapped him from behind.

Zeke cried out in pain but his feet plodded ahead. Lesson learned. Any thoughts felt with strong emotion spilled into her mind during the link. He'd have to dial the intensity down, keeping his private thoughts on a subroutine status.

"Stop." Pauline ordered. "Look. Up there."

Since she'd commanded it, he lifted his gaze to the night sky. Bright flashes streaked across it. His breath stalled. Oh, no. They were too late.

"Too late for what?" Pauline asked, shoving him forward.

"To stop the attack," Zeke said as he continued walking the sandy path.

"Maleem are firing on the planet?" she asked.

"Yes."

"That isn't right. They wouldn't move forward without me. They need me."

"Don't cry, Paulie," Connor said. "Whatever it is, we can fix it."

Zeke felt the pull of energy. He feared for Connor's life. He waited, his dread increasing with each second that ticked off his life clock. The pull subsided.

"You. Doctor Smarty Pants," Pauline ordered. "Stop. Find out what happened."

Zeke tapped his wrist com link and queried the net through his lab system. He noted the time – thirty minutes to midnight. The islanders should be safely on the other side, by the lighthouse. A few more taps of the screen and he had the requested information.

His horror grew with each burning image he saw, each word he read. "Beijing, Manhattan, and London were targeted. Those cities are on fire."

"Casualties?"

"Sat images of the locations show no movement in those locations. All are feared dead. The spaceship blasts were like nothing seen on this planet before."

Pauline's teeth flashed greenish-white in the darkness. She barked out a harsh laugh. "Of course not. Our weapons are superior in every aspect. The power of the collective is behind our mind blasts."

"Pauline?" Connor asked. "You're talking crazy again."

She shocked Connor again. "Don't you get it, fool? I am crazy. The aliens did things to me. Things I can't change. Things I must complete because I can't go back to being me again. Without the necklace, I'll die halfway through the transformation. My skin will rot off in clumps. My blood will putrefy inside my body. But my pickled brain will survive to my last breath, even beyond, if I enslave enough power sources."

Her statements were nothing more than Zeke suspected, but they sent a tidal wave through his mind. Her transformation had been halted, but she understood the Maleem mindset. Could he use that against her? Against the Maleem?

"Be afraid," Pauline crowed. "Be afraid because this planet is ours. Nothing will stop us. The Maleem are invincible."

"People live on the planet. Families. Children." Connor circled where Pauline and Zeke stood, his voice wavering. "Don't do this, Paulie. Don't be one of them."

She flicked a wrist and shot a mini-pulse of energy at him. "I want you to be by my side. I want you to share in the glory, Con, but you resist me at every turn."

Connor stood his ground. "I don't understand what's happening

224

to you, to us. Our planet is under attack. We have to fight for our homes and lives."

"Open your mind to the new reality. Your individual life is meaningless now, but in the collective you will be valued. If you aren't my slave, you could be my primary protector. I will need bodyguards."

"I love you, but you scare me with this crazy talk."

"You've got nothing to worry about, as long as you do what I say." She zapped Zeke. "Move. Get us off this spit of sand and back to the mainland before I lose patience and fry you both."

Zeke moved forward, powerless to deny her command. He had to get Pauline off the island. No question about that. It was the next step that had him stumped. How would he stop her?

Chapter 60

The crowd milled around the lighthouse. Someone lit a small fire on the beach nearby, and cinders sparked in the air. Jessie stared into the flames for ten minutes, but there were no answers to be found. Only more questions.

She recognized some of the people, but not all of them. She'd followed Forman home from Charleston, ready to stand by her man, ready to let her sister stand on her own. But the edginess in the group jangled her nerves.

Zeke should be here. He issued the request for everyone to gather at the lighthouse and then didn't show up? That wasn't like him. He always acted logically. Unlike her. But she'd changed. She was putting herself first from this moment forward.

She asked Forman her question again. "Where's Zeke?"

"I don't know," he answered in his Jethro voice.

"Something's wrong," she said, careful to keep her voice pitched low.

"I agree. Zeke's in trouble," Sidra said, coming up behind Jessie. "Two people attacked me in the lab and shot me with a tranq gun. When I woke up, they were gone. Zeke, too. I can't reach him." She paused and looked at Jessie. "Hullo. I'm Sidra."

"Jessie. Nice to meet you." Heart in her throat, Jessie studied the teen. To her relief, Sidra looked much too young for Zeke. "What do you mean you can't reach him?"

Sidra chewed her lip. "We connect differently than most."

Wanting to throttle the other woman, Jessie kept her voice calm. "And?"

"I can't sense him. His thoughts have been dampened or something."

Jessie got a sick feeling in her stomach. Despite her disbelief of Sidra's preposterous claim of telepathy, she'd witnessed Zeke's thoughts being controlled before. She had to take the woman seriously. Her voice rose on the wind. "Dampened? Like shut down or turned off?"

"Yeah."

"We're in trouble." Jessie's hands fisted at her side. People were staring at her. She didn't want to be the center of attention, but she had to say what was on her mind. Her knowledge of a similar event could make a difference in how the group responded to this threat.

She had to move outside her comfort zone and do what was right for Zeke. "That's what happened in Japan. Drok turned Zeke into a robot, no offense Forman."

"None taken," he said. "You believe Maleem are here on Tama Island?"

She nodded. "Look at the facts. Zeke called this meeting. Zeke is missing. Sidra believes his mind has been dampened. The Maleem did this to him in Japan. I believe they're here."

"This is an island," Forman said. "How'd they arrive?"

"Maybe they arrived on the evening ferry with me."

"Did you see any green people or spacesuits?" Sidra asked.

"Not funny," Jessie countered. Sidra had a point. As a person who rode the ferry, she had insider knowledge that could be helpful. "There were islanders in their orange robes, and a few people who looked like they were headed to the Institute. And that was it. No, that's not right. There were two people who stayed inside the cabin."

A thin, dark-skinned man stepped forward. Baggy. She remembered he stayed on the island after the fire a few months back. That he owned a four-wheeler.

"Those people in the cabin stunk," Baggy said. "None of us could stomach the musky odor. That's why we sat on the deck for the crossing."

Jessie'd stood in the bow wanting to be the first to see Tama Island. The cabin people had worn robes of some kind and shawl head coverings. She remembered seeing a robe like that recently. In Japan. When she was in the Maleem skybox. The man on the floor wore a robe. The newscaster guy. Did he follow them home?

"I might know who it is," she admitted.

"Tell us," Sidra urged.

"I saw a man dressed like that in the skybox where the Maleem enslaved Zeke's mind. I believe his name was Connor Bronsen."

"The newsie?" Sidra asked.

Jessie nodded. "I know it's a stretch. What are the odds, right?"

"The odds are quite likely," Forman said. "The newscaster traveled to Japan to free his co-anchor, Pauline. We took her necklace to study. They might have come here to retrieve it."

227

"I could run back to the lab and check," Jessie offered.

"No need. I can manipulate the security cams from here."

Jessie chewed on her fist. If she was right, Zeke was in trouble.

"The necklace is gone," Forman said. "I tried to view the tapes backward to see who took it, but there was too much signal interference."

"Assume the newscasters are on the island," Sidra said. "They've got the necklace. They've got Zeke. What would they do next?"

"They'd leave," Jessie said. "But the ferry doesn't run until tomorrow."

"It's too far to swim. What about a boat?" Sidra asked.

"There are several small craft on the island," Baggy offered.

"Zeke and Angie used a canoe before," Jessie remembered. "If they have Zeke, he could paddle the canoe to the mainland."

Baggy bristled with energy. "We can go after them."

Jessie waited for Sidra or Forman to answer, but Sidra said nothing. With Forman's impassive Jethro face it was hard to know what he was thinking.

"Do that." Jessie and Forman said at the same time.

"Sorry," Jessie said. "I wasn't trying to take over. But this is Zeke. We've got to act now. They might kill him if we don't move forward."

"You're right," Forman said. He turned to Baggy. "Take a com with you so that we can keep in touch."

As Baggy and three others sprinted to the woods, Jessie's mind continued to mull the problem. Assuming Zeke was in a boat, he'd be on the water. An idea occurred to her. "What about Zeke's dolphins? Are they offshore now? Can anyone see them?"

Sidra bounced on the sand with childlike enthusiasm. "I can communicate them, but I have to be in the water."

"Go for it," Jessie said. She didn't understand Zeke's closeness to the dolphins, but it was a fact. If Sidra could do the same thing, they needed her help.

When Sidra and two islanders loped down to the water's edge, Jessie turned to Forman. "How can we beat them? What's effective against the Maleem?"

"We haven't studied the Maleem. Only the Subjugator," he replied. At her sharp look, he qualified, "The necklace."

"It keeps coming back to that damn necklace, doesn't it?" Jessie paced around the fire. Folks moved out of her way. Forman trailed after her. "Saltwater detoxs the necklace compounds. Pauline wore the necklace, so we have to get her in the ocean to break her control of Zeke." She snapped her fingers as it came together in her head. "That's what he's doing. Getting her in the ocean. But he might need help upsetting the boat if she's got him in a mind lock. Someone tell Baggy's boat flotilla to turn the canoe over and stay clear of the crazy lady. Bring Zeke back to this side of the island."

A boy ran up from the water. "The lady in the ocean says the dolphins aren't here. They're in the creek behind the island, and they're worried. Should she call them here?"

Surf pounded the beach. Wind rustled Jessie's hair. Zeke's life depended on her making the right decision. "What do you think, Forman?"

He gazed at the water and then back at Jessie. "Zeke needs to be here on the beach. We should try everything within our means to make that happen."

She waited a few painful seconds for Forman to say something. Why didn't he tell the young boy what to do? She believed the dolphins responded to Zeke and obviously to Sidra as well. She had to believe they could help Zeke because she didn't know if Baggy's rescue boats would get there in time.

She knelt in the sand to be on eye level with the child. "No. Don't call the dolphins to the beach. Ask them to turn Zeke's vessel over."

"Say what?" the boy asked.

"You heard me." Jessie pointed at the sea. "Relay the message. Please."

He raced away.

An orange-robed islander stepped in front of Jessie holding her raft. "I'm Micheala, a friend of Angie's. What can I do?"

With Forman uncharacteristically silent, Jessie wracked her brain for another plan of action. "Zeke asked everyone to come here tonight to help fight the Maleem."

People stopped moving and talking. They seemed to hang on her every word. She drew in a deep breath and continued.

"I haven't known Zeke as long as the rest of you, but he's a good man. He's the Guardian. Our planet is under attack from the Maleem. They bombed three cities tonight, and no telling what tomorrow will bring. We have to take action now."

Micheala nodded. "What can we do?"

"We follow his plan. He asked for us to be in the water to help him. Sidra shares Zeke's talent of communicating with the dolphins. She can help us focus until he can join us. Because he will join us. This fight belongs to all of us."

Jessie studied the crowd again. They were young and old, men and women. But they appeared intent on helping Zeke. "Everyone can swim, right?"

"I can swim circles around you," a boy in the crowd taunted.

Jessie laughed. "Good. You may need to." She drew in another breath. "We need a way to stay together, to float on the tide. We need to draw strength from our numbers."

"I brought rope," a woman said. "I will tie the rafts together and run an anchor line to shore."

"Excellent. If you're hungry or thirsty, partake now. I don't know how long we'll be in the water."

"We'll carry water with us," an older man said. "The Guardian will protect us."

Jessie bit back her reply that the Guardian was in trouble. "I want everyone ready to go in the water in ten minutes."

"What about me?" Forman asked. "What can I do?"

"You'll monitor our anchor line."

His wheels rocked in the sand. "I'm not watertight."

"Not literally. I wouldn't put a hole-ridden, rust bucket like you in the sea. You will be our liaison with John Demery. Don't contact him until we've given it our best effort. Understand? We don't need him interfering with our plan, with Zeke's plan."

"Got it." He handed her a protein bar and a water bottle. "Nice job of assuming command, by the way."

Jessie's smile was bittersweet. She'd gotten the ball rolling, but had she done the right thing?

Chapter 61

"I hate islands," Pauline muttered, huddling deeper in the canoe seat. "They're surrounded by water."

"It won't be long, luv," Connor soothed. "We'll be back on the mainland before you know it."

Danger. Her senses relayed the message again and again, but in the inky darkness, she saw no apparent threat. "Paddle faster."

As her slave complied, drips of water slung off the paddle, striking her robes. She quickly lifted the damp fabric away from her undergarment and snarled, "Sling water on me again, and you're a dead man."

"Shh. Easy," Connor said. "We're making progress. We're leaving the creek now."

"Is it over?"

"Not yet, love. Have to cross the sound first."

"More water?"

The vessel shuddered, and Pauline shrieked. "What was that?" She stared at Zeke. "What was that? Answer me."

"I don't know," he answered, stroking for all he was worth.

The wind picked up. The water grew rougher.

"I don't like this." Pauline shot a blast of energy at Connor. "Fix it."

Connor sniffed. "Ouch. You said you wouldn't zap me anymore."

"Did I?" She rubbed her throbbing head and came away with a gooey mass of skin. She shook the offending crud off her fingers. Dry sobs burst from her mouth. "Why is this happening to me? Why?"

The cursed boat shuddered again. It rocked precariously.

"Something's down there." Pauline clung to the seat with both hands. "It's after us. Kill it."

Connor stared over the side. "I don't see anything. Just water. I think it's the wind. Calm down."

Pauline stood, propelled by her outrage. "Calm down? How can I calm down? This is all your doing. If you hadn't been so inept, we'd be at the top of our careers right now. I did this for us. For me and you. I wanted more for us."

"Sit down, Paulie."

She zapped him again, smiling as he twitched in pain. "You will never order me around again. Never. I am your master."

She braced her legs as the small craft cut through the water. Wind billowed her robes, tussled her hair. Despite the danger, she felt wondrously alive under the faint starlight.

The boat rocked a third time.

Too late, Pauline realized her error. Standing tall, her center of gravity was too high. When the boat rocked, so did she, and there was nothing to hold onto.

Her hands clawed at the air.

"No!" she screamed.

Scenes from her life flashed before her eyes. Growing up in squalor. Using sex to earn favors. Landing a network job. Hooking up with Connor.

She reached for her lover, but it was too late.

It was too damned late.

Her head struck first. The water burned acid-strong on her skin, eating away at the loosened flesh. Intense pain attacked her from all sides, stealing her breath. She uncurled her fists intending to shock the water, but she had no juice.

She had nothing.

The heavy robes weighed her down.

The water rocked and bubbled. Pauline screamed anew as arms locked around her. Her head broke the surface.

"I've got you," Connor said.

Her skin was on fire. Her bones burned from the inside out. She spat out her teeth and groaned in agony. Each ragged breath could be her last. A wave slapped her in the face, ripping a throttled scream from her throat.

She was dying.

She had one last chance to do the right thing.

"Let me go," she whispered. "It's too late."

"It's never too late. I love you, Pauline. We're meant to be together."

The fool would die for her?

"No."

He reached for something. The overturned boat. It bobbed in

and out of focus.

"Don't," she managed.

"Shh."

"Kill me."

"No."

Another wave splashed over her. His hand shielded her face, her eyes.

"I love you, Pauline," his whisper-soft voice found her ear once they bobbed on the surface again. "I've always loved you. We were together in life. We'll face death together."

With that, he released the boat, and water closed over their heads.

Chapter 62

Pauline's control over Zeke's mind abruptly ended when he tumbled into the water. One moment he couldn't move independently, and the next he could. The warm sea embraced him like a long-lost friend. Zeke swam for all he was worth, needing to put distance between himself and the fledgling Maleem.

When shapes appeared in the water beside him, adrenaline-laced panic charged into his veins. He kicked harder, fearing Pauline or Connor would grab him. A dolphin rolled under him, propelling him faster. Tunis! He grabbed her fin and held on.

They surfaced after a bit. Zeke caught his breath and reoriented himself. Open water to the left, an island to the right. Near the north point of Tama Island. Far above, stars twinkled in the night sky. A gentle swell of waves rolled in from the Atlantic. Best of all, Pauline and Connor were nowhere in sight.

Zeke heaved in several deep breaths of relief. The rest of the pod circled him, nudging him. They clicked and whistled.

He didn't know what they were saying, but he felt sheer joy at seeing them again. Nicola. Boz. Klickie. Tunis. They were his salvation. Again.

"Thanks, guys." He gave each of them a belly rub.

Boz pushed him in the direction of the beach. "You know about that?" Zeke asked, feeling guilty and tardy. "I'm supposed to be there right now. Can you help me swim back to the beach?'

They shrilled in unison.

Sounded like an acceptance to him. Perfect. He couldn't do this alone.

Moments later, Klickie appeared on his right, Tunis on his left. He reached for Tunis as before but the dolphins swam away without him. They returned in the same formation. "Something different? Okay. I'll try this."

He reached an arm around each dolphin and simultaneously felt pushing against his feet. "Got it," he said, gulping air and becoming the center of a dolphin sandwich. He saw a flash of white as little Boz took the lead, breaking the water. They powered along under the sea. He stayed still as the dolphins propelled him toward shore.

What a night.

His thoughts shuddered. Pauline had meant to kill him. She nearly succeeded. But she failed, and hee was free. Stay focused on the positive, he told himself.

The biggest challenge of the evening still awaited. He didn't have time to analyze what he'd been through. Time enough for that later.

Would the islanders be waiting for him at the beach? Or would they have disbanded when he didn't show up? He allowed himself to hope they were assembled and ready for him.

His lungs burned. He needed air, but he had no idea how far they were from the surface. *Need air*, he thought as hard as he could. The dolphins didn't break stride. What he wouldn't give to speak their language like Sidra. The image of gasping for air like a fish out of water dominated his thoughts.

The dolphins rose as one.

Hmm.

He snatched in quick breaths and pondered the significance of his discovery. He could communicate with dolphins through imagery. They appeared to be waiting his signal. He pictured them swimming underwater again. They mustered into formation.

He hung on as they sliced through the water.

Very cool.

Three more quick stops for air, and they stopped moving. He broke the water surface and searched for landmarks. A darkened lighthouse stood tall in the distant tree line. There seemed to be an odd collection of rafts circling him.

"Stay together," he heard Jessie say. "Whatever you do, don't let go."

Was he dreaming? "Jessie?"

"Zeke," she exclaimed. "We knew you'd come." A head popped up, then another. "Everyone, he's here."

"Yay!" Sidra said. "Good to see you. Ready to kick some Maleem butt?"

Zeke felt an odd mixture of pride and determination. These people risked everything to help him. They'd done it without question. They believed in him.

He sent an image to the dolphins to stay close, and they complied. His lips lingered over Jessie's. He had so much to tell her.

235

Later.

He swam from person to person, thanking them for their help. Once he'd greeted them individually, he couldn't afford to delay any longer.

"We're here to fight the Maleem," he said. "Our weapon is untried, impossible to test without alerting the enemy of our intent. This has never been done before. If successful, we'll rewrite history books. If we fail, the Maleem will win the day, and we're doomed."

He swam to the center of their circle. With all his heart, he hoped they would be up to the task. "I'm asking you to trust me with your thoughts. Through the sea and the power of touch, we will be connected. Sidra understands space in a way that we don't. Our weapon is mind over matter. We're willing particles in space to align and block the Maleem. It's our only chance to defeat them, however improbable it sounds."

Zeke summoned the dolphins close with a mind picture. "I'll be here in the center with the dolphins and will appear to be asleep. I will be safe, just as you are safe on your rafts. Relax as best you can. United we are strong. We can move mountains or WIMPs or whatever it takes to stop this threat to our planet."

"We're with you, Zeke," Jessie said from her raft. Others echoed her sentiments.

"This is it. We'll only get the one chance at this and even then the Maleem may discover our attempt and try to stop us." He paused, his chest heavy with emotion. "I love each and every one of you. Thank you for your gift of self."

It was up to him now.

They were twenty strong. Men, women, and children. And four dolphins.

Was that enough to save the world?

Chapter 63

As ocean swells rocked his floating body, thoughts stormed through Zeke's mind. He had no procedure to follow, no equation to solve. He didn't even know what WIMPs looked like.

Uh-oh. He was breathing too fast again. He stilled his thoughts and steadied his breathing. Time ticked by in slow motion intervals. How could he make something out of nothing? The aggravating question tormented him.

The dolphins took turns supporting him, staying nearby. Their concern lapped at him in waves. Remembering his success in communicating with mental imagery before, he sent them an image of him resting in the water, which decreased the questioning nudges they gave him.

He drew in a few deep breaths. Everything was as he'd envisioned for this important task: the islanders floating with him, the dolphins, Sidra, and even Jessie. He had the best crew possible. There was no time for him to have a panic attack.

If, no, *when* he brought the WIMPs together to form a barrier, it would be impenetrable, like a brick wall. There was a start. Bricks. He knew what they looked like.

With mind over matter, all he had to do was think an object into existence.

He thought hard about bricks, about stacking them up one at a time. To his delight, bricks formed. He stacked them. After a hundred bricks into the mental exercise, he glanced at the far reaches of space. It was huge. Too huge. Time was too short to stack bricks individually. He needed help. His friends. He imagined each of them stacking bricks in space. The wall rose faster but not fast enough to suit him.

It would take years to finish at this rate.

Zeke?

He recognized the faint female voice. *Sidra? How are you in my head?*

I've been trying to reach you this whole time. Thank goodness you realized how to bring us into your mindset. We're doing it.

237

We're building a space barrier with the WIMPs.

Are the others here?

Silence answered his query, then Sidra spoke in his head again. *They're here but they seem mute. Jessie is strongest telepath of the crew, but none are able to vocalize. They're definitely with us though. I feel their number. I see their ghost images stacking bricks beside me.*

Zeke carried more bricks to the wall. As he placed them, he glanced over his shoulder at the ominous alien ships. *If the Maleem notice what we're doing, they'll try to stop us.*

No one's ever done this before. They won't even notice until it's too late.

We need more help.

Couldn't you just imagine us moving something bigger to build the wall?

He tried to picture Jessie moving a boulder. His brick wall began to crack. He focused on bricks again, and the image solidified. *No. It has to be bricks.*

Sidra carried three more armloads of bricks and peered around the heavens. *You're right. At this rate, we'll be here forever. We need lots more people to build this wall. Hundreds. Thousands. More if we can find them. What are we going to do?*

Boz rested his bottlenose on Zeke's chest. He whistled a long low note. Its plaintive tone reminded Zeke of the final bagpiped notes of the hymn "Amazing Grace." It was a popular choice for funerals. He'd included it in his parents' memorial service.

His parents.

His dad.

Was Boz urging Zeke to access the Taman link? Could the Tamans help them fight the Maleem?

There might be another way, he began to Sidra. He didn't like the spark of hope that shot through him. He couldn't afford to make the wrong choice here because so many depended on him.

You've got a thousand people secretly on retainer?

Something like that. He risked a glance over to her raft. *This might get weird.*

She laughed. *What could be weirder than floating in the ocean and building a space wall with invisible particles? Go for it. I'm all in. You should be, too.*

She was right. In order to be all in, he had to relinquish control and trust in the Taman collective. When he'd accessed his ancestors previously, it had been on his terms. He could leave whenever he wanted.

This would be different.

He would be begging for their help.

His survival depended on people he couldn't see, hear, or feel.

Can you keep the wall construction going? he asked.

Bricks tumbled from her arms. *Where are you going?*

To get help. I don't know how long it will take to convince the others to help us. He hesitated. *I won't be conscious. You must assume control of this mind ring.*

You're the key, Zeke. I don't know how to do this without you.

Boz splashed him again. Klickie made dolphin sounds.

The dolphins. Sidra understood dolphin-speak.

Tighten the circle and join me in the center, he instructed. *I'll hold the group focus for a bit longer, but to communicate with my other group, I need this part of my consciousness. You must expand to fill the void my leaving will create.*

The islanders floating beside Sidra murmured softly as she unclasped their hands and rejoined them to each other. She sculled her raft toward him.

He kept up the mind banter, preferring not to alarm the others with the change in plan. Overhead, he noticed a slender belt of the night sky had gone dark.

Look, he said. *It's working.*

We need more, Sidra said. *We need WIMPs to cloak the sky and the Earth. We need to send the Maleem scurrying back into space.*

He took her hand. Klickie floated nearby. *Are you ready?*

Sidra reached for the dolphin with her free hand. *No. I'm not ready. What if I can't do this? I've never focused a mindlink before. I don't know how to do it.*

You think I do? I trusted in the link and made mind pictures. You're the one that initiated the mind over matter concept. We're making progress. Keep it going while I get help. We're all counting on you.

How? I'm afraid.

Easy. Believe.

Chapter 64

Supported by dolphins, Zeke's thoughts arced through space and time, seeking the Taman mindlink. He was tired, his thoughts spattered like buckshot across the universe in diverse directions. Ugly, ugly, but it was all he had. He heard the distant voices of his people and attuned his thoughts to their heading.

Zeke! His father shouted as he neared. *Are you all right? What's happened?*

The darkness was absolute in Tween, the thought plane where they met, but he was used to the sensory deprivation. *I'm here, Dad, but I'm in trouble. I need your help. I need all the Tamans to help me.*

We are helping, a deep voice boomed. *We advised you to avoid a confrontation with the Maleem.*

He doesn't need our help, someone else countered. *He's the Messiah. He will singlehandedly save our race as it was foretold.*

This Messiah reference to deity irritated Zeke the first time around. It made him twice as annoyed tonight. *I can't singlehandedly do anything. The Maleem are attacking Earth. We're building a space barrier out of dark matter with our thoughts, but it is taking too long. We are too few. I need more thought power. I need the Tamans.*

We'll have to call a council meeting to discuss your request, a cultured baritone said.

No time for that. I need you to return with me now. I need your energy and thoughts to beat the Maleem.

No one can beat the Maleem, the baritone continued.

I can. Zeke stated the fact emphatically. *Who's with me?*

I'll go with you, Son.

This is highly irregular, a reedy voice interjected. *Who's to say he's not a Maleem spy? We might get trapped on the wrong side of the cosmos. It's suicide to go with him. What has he shared of his latest Maleem encounter? How will this benefit Tamans?*

He will die without our help, his father said. *We haven't evolved this far to throw away a precious life. Zeke is the future. He will rid the skies of the scourge. We will soon walk in light again.*

I'm not going anywhere, the reedy voice said. *We're safe here in Tween.*

He was losing them. He had to make them see. He had to give them what they wanted. *You want information? I'll give it to you, right now. Maleem are made. They create new Maleem through the Subjugator necklaces. I dealt with a fledgling Maleem earlier this evening. She had been human two weeks ago.*

Made? Not born? the baritone questioned. *Preposterous.*

Seawater is caustic to fledglings. The one with me died in the sea. After her skin fell off.

A murmur swept through the link. This was working. They craved information. He only had a little more to share. He hoped it would be enough to win their support.

The fledgling controlled my mind with her touch, but the lock was different, not as oppressive. She could draw my energy and shock others as well, but again, the draw was smaller than when Drok had me under his control.

No one's ever seen a fledgling, reedy voice said. *Are we to take his word for it?*

The Maleem must keep close track of them, Zeke answered. *They wouldn't want the word getting out that they assimilate other races through the necklace system. Oh, and one man was completely immune to the Maleem mind control.*

We must study this man, baritone insisted. *Tell us more.*

Nothing to tell. He died with the fledgling. I must return before my world is destroyed. I don't know how many Maleem ships are in their fleet, but if we destroy these three, that's a start. You can be part of it. Please. Time is so short.

He doesn't know, a commanding voice said.

You won't tell him, his father said. *Each of us makes our own journey of discovery. I am with you, Zeke. Together we will hold the link open so others may join us.*

The link strengthened immediately. Encouraged, Zeke gathered his thoughts for the trip home. Having his father's support meant so much. They were a team again, and oh, how he'd missed that feeling.

Five Tamans joined them for the trip across the universe. Zeke came out of the darkness into the gray nether world of WIMPs and brick walls. He didn't see Sidra and the islanders, but they'd added three more rows of bricks to the barrier.

How do we help? his father asked.

Zeke glanced at the six orbs of light near his head. *We have to build this barrier to block the Maleem.*

Open your mind further, son. Use the strength of our thoughts to augment your efforts.

Before Zeke could ask how that was possible, the orbs winked out. At the same time, his thoughts became very precise and energetic. WIMPs coalesced into bricks at an amazing speed. The wall soared high overhead.

He heard an excited squeal – Sidra.

You did it! Look at that wall. She bounced around him like a puppy. *We've been working nonstop since you left, but this is amazing. Incredible. How are you doing this? I've never seen anything like this before.*

Keeping his focus on brick-making, he shot a line of thought to Sidra. *There you are. I have help, and I'm connecting your mind ring into the stronger focus I now have.*

Cool, she stated, awe filling her voice. *I'm blown away at the energy you've tapped into. And the WIMPs – they seem to recognize and respond to your suggestion almost before you make it.*

The power of positive thinking, he said.

Mind over matter, she corrected. *Don't forget to shield all the way around our planet.*

Getting to that, he said, bending the wall sideways with a wave of his hand. *Hold the focus and your comments. I need to put everything into this.*

Of course.

With each brick added, his consciousness expanded. He felt his father and the other Tamans in his mind. Sidra, Jessie, the islanders, and even the dolphins were somehow there, too. Working together to save Earth.

Unprecedented and amazing as Sidra had said.

He could spend the rest of his life analyzing how this was possible.

The link rocked. And flickered.

His focus weakened as static filled the connection.

Something big hit the wall.

The bricks cracked, a deafening, gut-wrenching sound.

Chapter 65

Lightning arced through the broken bricks in pulses. The pattern seemed random until current funneled Zeke's way. The jagged streaks intensified. Energy missiles bombarded his position.

He jumped in front of Sidra. *Pull back. Break the mindlink*, he ordered, taking a blast meant for her. Though he wasn't whole on this thought plane, the attacking energy seared his projected image and stole his breath away.

Sidra faded from sight. He hoped she escaped unscathed.

Instinctively, he huddled beside the bricks. Snake-like, the current slithered down the wall heading straight for him. He had no doubt who was behind this attack. Drok. He couldn't let down his guard now. He had to hold it together.

Dad?

We're with you, Son.

What do you recommend?

Fight, retreat, or be captured. Decide quickly. You're on fire.

Zeke glanced down and saw that was true. He quickly diverted WIMPs from the brick wall to form a bubble around him. The current encircled the bubble, snapping and crackling. Other bolts of current arrowed down to the planet.

I don't know how long I can hold this protective focus, Zeke said. *Anyone else have an idea?*

Retreat, Reedy Voice said. *He'll kill us all. If he takes control of your mind now, he'll get all of us in the bargain.*

How does he even know you're here? Reedy Voice asked.

The same way he accessed your mind earlier. He reads us, his father stated.

I don't understand. Zeke reinforced and enlarged the WIMP bubble around his head. To the naked eye, there was only one entity here. His father and the other five Tamans weren't visible. Only their thoughts and energy were here.

Wait. Their energy. Tamans could send it long distances with laser accuracy. Why didn't he think of this before? The Maleem had picked him out of a crowd of thousands in Japan.

It's true, isn't it? Drok is Taman.

The Maleem attacked our planet many times, his father said, as if that explained everything.

Release us, Deep Voice said. *We must escape from this energy-attracting body. We're in danger here. We're all in danger.*

His body. That was the problem. To fight an energy war, he needed to shed his physical body. But doing that would change everything. He'd become like his father, an energy nexus existing only in a place called Tween. He'd no longer walk the Earth.

He'd be dead.

As he hung in thought limbo, broad bands of current raced past him to the planet. There were people down there, people who'd never done anything to the Maleem, and yet they were being ruthlessly exterminated and enslaved.

Earth's defenses were child's toys to Drok's energy blasts. The military had already fired their weapons, blown up the space station, and gotten nowhere. Zeke was the last line of defense. The only thing standing between Earth's existence and its destruction.

Zeke or nothing.

He opened a link to probe Sidra's mind.

Yes? She sounded frail and afraid. He hated that the battle had taken away her natural ebullience. He hated the Maleem.

I must change tactics. The walls won't hold them back as we'd thought. It's only slowing them down. I'm losing the energy war. The only course of action is to become pure energy so that I can fight the Maleem on a level playing field. I can't do it in a human body.

What are you saying? Her voice wavered. *You have to die?*

It's the only way. Submerge my unconscious body. Hold me underwater until I'm dead. Do it quickly. Don't think about it. Just do it.

Omigod, she wailed. *I can't do it. I can't kill you.*

It's our only hope.

I can't. And I won't. There has to be another way.

I've run all the possibilities. This is the only viable option we have. Otherwise, the Maleem will come. They will kill, destroy, and enslave our citizens.

Sidra wept.

Zeke? A faint female voice entered the link.

He heart skipped a beat. *Jessie? That you?*

Yes. Since you returned with the others, the link is stronger and

I'm able to project my thoughts. I understand what you've asked. I don't like it. And I don't want to do it. She paused. *But I will. If you say this is the only way, I believe you.*

Jess, there's so much I want to say to you, but there's no time. Maleem fireballs are streaking past me toward the planet. People are dying right now.

I love you, Zeke.

Zeke hovered in the void of uncertainty. Others were listening. He couldn't blurt out his feelings. But he wanted to. Oh, how he wanted to.

Say it, Boy, his father urged.

He was right, Zeke thought. What did he have to lose? *I love you, Jessie.*

Jessie's sobs filled the link.

Do it now, he said. *I can't hold off Drok's energy any longer. If you wait, all will be lost.*

He felt her palm over his face. The dolphins parted, and she pushed him under, sobbing the whole time. In his unconscious and vulnerable state, he died in a matter of seconds.

He expected pain. Expected a dark tunnel and a bright light. Expected his dying mind to flash through a highlight reel of his life. Expected to lose all physical sensation.

One moment he was weak to the point of exhaustion, his body drowning underwater while his spirit locked in mortal combat with a powerful enemy, the next instant everything changed.

The sense of weight and physical constraints he'd always known weren't there. Instead of feeling adrift, he felt buoyed like the first time he had swum in the ocean. Not hot and not cold. Just right.

But his consciousness. It was more in a way he couldn't describe. Blazing. Vibrant. Each thought a super-charged particle orbiting a nexus of consciousness.

He wasn't, but he was.

He jolted aware, a sensation akin to an awakening, but layers deeper.

The energy shield around him dissolved. Raw current flashed through him. He felt different. Compact. Powerful.

Am I an orb like you? he asked his father who hovered beside him in space. Below him lay the bright blue Earth, beyond that the open universe. Five other entities glowed beside his father. Counting Zeke, they were an army of seven.

You are.

How?

We are thought energy, but you are ... more. You can effect physical change while in this state. You are Zydmoq, the bridge between corporeal and astral. You are neither and both.

That's a lot to take in, and I'd love to hear more about what happened to me, and what I am, but the energy bolts hurtling past us to Earth must be stopped.

Agreed. I've never been more proud of you, Son. Move out.

With urgency propelling him, Zeke thought his way across space to the Maleem ships. The travel happened so fast he couldn't gauge the speed. Faster than light. Faster than anything he knew.

Current snapped and crackled in a tight circuit between the three Maleem ships, but only one ship hurled the energy toward the planet. Drok's ship. He recognized the alien's musty energy signature.

Do it now, his father urged. *While he's bent on destroying the planet. Lives are being lost.*

Understood, Zeke said. He didn't relish destroying anything, but this was war. If he didn't stop the Maleem, they'd take Earth. He wouldn't allow that. Couldn't allow that.

WIMPs existed on the Maleem ship. He nudged the invisible shapes into the control consoles and thought them into solid form. He felt Drok's rage immediately.

The discharge turrets swiveled to Zeke's position. He thought himself and the other Tamans to a new position milliseconds before lethal energy surged to their last location.

Zeke, his father warned. *Take those out.*

He pulled a few WIMPs from the moon and hurled them at the weapons, smashing them. A roar of triumph resounded in his consciousness.

Inside the ship, he sensed movement. Drok. Pounding down an empty corridor, a cadre of his suited guards flanking him. For a moment, their minds met and tangled. He pushed back Drok's mental probe and felt great satisfaction at the fear in his enemy's eyes. Instead of meeting him as an equal, Drok ran for cover.

Don't let him escape, his father said.

Killing was wrong, but it was kill or be killed. Zeke pulled WIMPs from space and thought them inside the ship, feeling a boost of energy from the Tamans. The dark spark of Drok winked out as did those of his close associates. There were no humans on board, but there was a room full of dead bodies stacked in a bin. Zeke stopped his assault.

One down, two to go, his father prompted.

We could let them go, Zeke said. *Without Drok, these few wouldn't destroy anything.*

Without the Maleem, they will die a painful death. Plus, they are still within range of your planet. They could still cause trouble.

You're right. Disheartened by his task, Zeke made quick work of the other spaceships.

He encased each ship in a solid formation of space rock and shoved them as hard as he could until they left Earth's orbit.

You did it, his father crowed. *You beat the Maleem.*

We did it, Zeke answered. *All of us. We neutralized the threat to Earth.*

That was amazing, deep, cultured baritone voice said.

Zeke noticed a host of orbs surrounded him. More Tamans had arrived. *Nice of you to join us*, he said. *But you missed the main event.*

There will be great rejoicing throughout the Alliance, baritone continued. *We must return and join the celebration.*

One by one the orbs vanished, until only his father's light remained at his side. Zeke glanced down at Earth, trying to take it all in, wishing he could be with his friends. With Jessie.

You coming? his father asked.

I need to dismantle the wall, Zeke said, thinking of practicalities. *Earth can't survive without access to the sun. If I leave the wall up, it will be trading one death for another.*

Didn't think of that. I'll help.

Together, they thought the WIMPs apart and eased them back into invisibility. Zeke glanced around the vast reaches of space. It seemed infinite. Surely, Earth would return to her former anonymity. Surely, she wasn't on the superhighway of interstellar travel. *Will they send more ships, Dad?*

Perhaps. They're explorers. But who knows how many millennia will pass before they come this way again. Your people should be safe for generations to come.

My people. How I wish I was one of them. I had so much ahead of me. My life was so rich, so full. And Jessie. I should've had a lifetime with her. I feel cheated.

You gave Jessie the ultimate gift. You died to save her.

Zeke's orb dimmed. His awareness contracted, and his senses seized. The endless nature of space fogged, and with it, his perceptions. Instead of feeling invincible, he felt nauseous and frail. He glanced over at his dad. *What's happening?*

His dad laughed. *It appears your mate isn't done with you yet.*

Chapter 66

Zeke's body convulsed. His arms and legs weighed a ton. His fingers ached with cold. Where was he? He gasped in a ragged breath and tried to think.

The ocean. He felt the power of ocean waves breaking on shore. Wet sand cradled his body. He was at the beach. Wind blew across his skin and damp clothes.

He shuddered and coughed again. Everything hurt. His lungs. His heart. His gut. His head. Especially, his head. It throbbed.

Voices tickled the edge of his hearing. Was he in Tween? No. He didn't feel sandy or cold in Tween. And the ocean. He never heard its mighty roar while communicating with his Taman ancestors.

If only he could see.

He concentrated on moving his eyelids. They resisted his efforts. It was easier moving WIMPs, he thought. He tried harder, managing a small slit of an opening. Dark shapes and shadows out there. Something moved, coming closer to him. Fear licked at his gut.

A pale globe appeared.

A face.

A human face.

Jessie's lips grazed his.

"Welcome back," Jessie said.

His arms and legs tingled. His skin felt too tight and hot. His lungs burned. But he was alive. Gloriously alive.

Jessie.

She'd done this.

She'd brought him back.

"Jess," he managed, his voice sounding like crushed glass.

Memories surged. He'd died. To save the world. To save Jessie, and she'd saved him. Emotion welled up from a place so deep he barely recognized it. He reached for her, for life.

"Easy," she murmured, covering his hand with her warm palm. "You've been through a lot."

"Kiss me," he whispered. "Please."

Her fingers intertwined with his, and he tugged her close, his gaze intent on her sweet face. Her lips touched his, and he knew the truth. He was home. She was home.

Cheers erupted beside them. With reluctance, he ended the kiss. Words couldn't express the depth of his feelings, but he had to try. "Thank you for saving my life."

Her slow smile tugged at his heart. "It seemed only fair, since I was the one who killed you. Are you all there? Sidra worried you'd have brain damage."

"I seem as good as new." He levered up on the sandy beach. As friends he'd known his entire life clapped him on the back and welcomed him to the land of the living, the pink-tinged sky promised a new day. Dawn. A new beginning. Just like his second chance at life. He'd better not screw this one up. Few people got a do-over.

"Let me get you something to eat," Jessie said. "I'll be right back."

Sidra hugged the breath out of him. "You saved us. You vanquished the Maleem and saved us. You're awesome."

"We all played a part in saving the planet," he replied neutrally. Being a hero didn't fit his low profile status.

"You can tell yourself that, if you like," she said, "but every person on this beach knows the truth. We wouldn't have a home if it weren't for you. Your name will go down in history, dude."

Zeke grimaced. "No, it won't. Officially, this never happened. We can't tell anyone what went on here on this beach or with the WIMPs. That information has to be kept a secret. Top secret."

"We agree with you," Baggy said, glancing at the islanders behind him and turning back to Zeke. "We don't want hordes of people coming down to our island and studying us like bugs. We like things the way they are. We want to keep our homes off the radar. It's enough to have the Institute folks in and out of Tama Island. We don't need anyone else down here making waves."

Zeke nodded and absently fingered the bit of stone at his throat. This Taman artifact had seen tough times. But his father's keystone necklace was part of him, part of the island and his life. He understood so much more of what a Guardian knew and did.

Sidra frowned. "You're saying the government will make up some kind of Area-51 story to go with all the strangeness in the sky? Even if they do that, they can't erase the Maleem from people's memories. We all saw the green people. Entire sections of Beijing, London, and Manhattan burned to the ground. They can't mass hypnotize the entire populace."

"No need," Zeke said with quiet confidence. "World governments know how to spin these kinds of events. They've had lots of practice. They write the history books."

"This has happened before?"

He thought about the Tamans, about his father and grandfather. "Not this exact scenario, but other things have happened. No way is this our first contact with extraterrestrials."

"You're creeping me out," Sidra said.

"What about the dolphins?" Zeke pitched his voice for Sidra's ears only. "How did they come through the ordeal?"

"They were quite upset when Jessie held you under. Boz rammed her in the legs and knocked her under. But I explained it to them so they understood we were following your instructions. Nicola wouldn't leave your side afterward, wouldn't let us take you out of the water. Once the fire stopped flashing across the sky, and it was pitch dark here, the dolphins said it was time to revive you. I couldn't do it. I thought sure you'd have brain damage."

He'd have written a person off as well. It was logical. But little about this evening could be explained logically. It seemed fitting that another illogical event had happened to round out the evening. He rejoiced that his Taman heritage allowed him to return from the dead. "How long was I out?"

"It seemed like forever. But maybe it was only a few minutes," Sidra said. "Jessie is amazing. She's so strong. She took command when I couldn't. Oh. Here she comes now with one of the islanders."

Jessie strolled down to the water's edge and handed him an energy bar and water. Naomi wrapped him in a warm blanket. The heat felt good, but truthfully he was spent. Too tired to stand up. Too tired to go home.

The unmistakable sound of chopper blades caught his attention. A single helicopter approached from the west and swept the length of the beach. As the transpo neared, islanders melted away two by two, so that only Jessie, Sidra, Zeke and Forman remained to greet the visitors.

Forman rolled up beside Zeke. "Sorry about the chopper. I contacted your uncle when the firestorm stopped. I notified him of your death. I thought he'd want to see you before the coroner arrived."

"It's okay, buddy. Please help me up. Uncle John has our best interests at heart. You were looking out for me, and I would've done the same thing in your shoes. I was gone. I died, but now I'm alive. It's a bit much to absorb, even for me."

Forman lifted Zeke to his feet. "I heard you telling the others that your role in vanquishing the Maleem can't be known. Will my memory of the battle be erased?"

Zeke shrugged, amazed at how much energy that took. He braced his legs, locking his knees. "I don't know what your future holds. All I know is that I must keep a low profile."

"No one could be lower profile than me," Forman grumbled. "No one sees a Jethro."

That sounded like the Forman he knew. The corners of his lips kicked up. "We'll see about getting you a better shell now that the world is safe from alien invasion. I'll speak to Uncle John about an upgrade as soon as I get some rest."

The chopper landed a ways down the beach. His uncle stepped out of the transpo, his bushy white hair, blowing in the onshore breeze. Waves lapped at Zeke's feet.

"You're a sight for sore eyes," Uncle John said. A cheesy grin stretched from ear to ear.

"I'm happy to say that reports of my demise are greatly exaggerated."

"I bet you have quite a story to tell."

"We did it."

"That you did, my boy. The Maleem ships are no longer visible by telescope. They've vanished. The remaining necklaces went dark, and the friendlies are rounded up and in detox. The threat to our planet appears to be gone."

Zeke nodded.

"How did you do it?" his uncle asked.

Self-preservation had Zeke carefully choosing his words. "Nothing that translates to a written report or a logical summation of facts. Trust me, the Maleem are gone and won't be back in our lifetime. This mind over matter stuff is nonlinear and not something I want recorded in any way." He regarded his uncle steadily. "No publicity, Uncle John. I want my quiet, island life back."

"Any chance you can deliver the ships for us to study?"

"Those ships were destroyed."

"Pity. One of these days we'll have a long talk about this."

"Perhaps."

"Now who's being cryptic?"

Zeke didn't have to think it through. He couldn't tell all. He didn't want to end up being a lab rat locked away somewhere. "I'm a survivor, Uncle John. I have few needs but anonymity is chief among them. The Guardian of Earth must be anonymous if he is to be successful."

Uncle John regarded him steadily. "That's something I can deliver."

Chapter 67

The party started that evening when Sidra and her quiet companion Ronni arrived on Zeke's porch with a pot of Spanish rice. Jessie opened the door and let them in. "This smells amazing. I didn't know you cooked."

Sidra bounced inside, blue hair springing with every stride of her platform heels. "I don't. I know someone who knows Cherry Supreme in Savannah."

"The granddaughter of world famous cooking sensation? No wonder my mouth is watering. I can't wait to taste it."

"Is Zeke up?"

Jessie stifled a yawn. "He slept through the afternoon. We all did. Even Forman recharged. I was looking around the kitchen and wondering what we'd do about dinner. Somehow an energy bar didn't seem enough to feed the man who singlehandedly saved the world."

Sidra deposited her steaming dish on the stovetop. "I can't believe it's over. I tried my best to sleep today, but all I could think about were the times I couldn't do what he asked. If the fate of the free world rested entirely on my shoulders, we'd be dead or enslaved by now. I can't thank you enough for rising to the challenge."

In many ways, Sidra reminded Jessie of her sister. Ultra talented in one area but sorely lacking in others. She'd worried that Sidra aspired to be Zeke's girlfriend, but her worries were groundless. Zeke loved her, not Sidra.

"People underestimate me," Jessie said. "But I've been in training for this role for a very long time. I know what adversity is like, and I trust myself to make good decisions. Managing my sister's singing career brought new crises every day. Vendors tried to stiff us, musicians quit if they had the wrong type of drumstick. I've mastered international travel snafus, stalker fans, and crooked producers. You name it in the music industry, I've seen it."

"Sounds like a chaotic life."

"It was."

"You're done with it?"

"I am. I've needed a change for a while now."

"I see." Sidra circled around to the window. "What about your sister?"

"Bea will rebound from this. She always does. If she still wants to tour, fine. I'm out of the game. She's old enough to stand on her own two feet. I'm ready to live my life now. A life with Zeke."

"He's special."

Jessie's jealousy flared. Was Sidra thinking to worm her way into Zeke's affections? Keeping her eyes locked on the younger woman, she said, "Yes. He is."

Sidra burst out laughing. "Relax. I think of the man as a brother. And his eyes have never gone supernova when he looks at me. I want to be part of this. I want to live here."

"I don't have any say about that. Zeke's uncle, John Demery, is the one you should talk to about relocating. The Institute governs most of the island."

"I will, but first I needed to make sure you were okay with that. If I stay, Zeke and I will work closely together."

"Another thing I've learned along life's rocky path. To speak only for myself. Zeke's choices are his own, as my choices are my own. I love Zeke and want a future with him. I won't get in the way of his work, but I will ease him out of the lab at the end of each day. It won't work if you and I are in conflict."

"I have no intent of causing conflict, but I feel a connection to him. I've never met anyone as smart as he is, anyone who could grasp the finer points of different disciplines in a matter of moments. His mind is special, and I want to be a part of that greatness."

"He keeps a low profile."

"He does. I'd never heard of him before Demery asked me to come here. I almost didn't come. Funny how that one choice completely changed my life's path. Coming here was the best thing I ever did."

"I felt the same way. There's something about the island that feels like home to me." Jessie turned at another knock on the door. She hurried to greet the familiar figure holding a plate of something dark orange. "Baggy! Is that for Zeke?"

"Pumpkin bread. My granny's recipe."

"Zeke will love it, I'm sure." She accepted the dish and waved him forward. "Come on in."

"Is he awake?"

"I'll check. Please make yourself at home. You know Sidra, right?"

They exchanged nods. While they greeted each other, Jessie padded back to Zeke's sleeping quarters. He lay abed, the covers rumpled around him. She smoothed the covers up, intending to tiptoe out, but he caught her hand.

"You're awake," she managed.

Heat filled his eyes. "I am. I've been waiting for you."

"You have? I kept the house quiet so you could rest."

"I have a better plan." He tugged her close and kissed her. "I want to sleep with you."

She chewed her lip, needing to be certain she was reading between the lines correctly. "I'm not sleepy."

His eyes glittered. "Neither am I."

"Oh." As he removed her blouse, she remembered his guests. "People are here. They came to see you."

When he hesitated, doubts invaded her thoughts. Was he creating a decision matrix? She didn't want him to choose between her and his friends.

She reached for her shirt. "I should go."

"You should stay." He held onto her, lightly stroking her shoulders. "We need to get this right. You said you loved me. I said I loved you. I've never said that to anyone before, but it's important."

"As important as saving the world?"

"Yes. I hadn't intended to make such a public declaration, Jess. I'm a private man. I'm wired a little different, and I'll be up front with you. I'm a terrible catch because I live for my work. But I'd like to live for you as well."

It wasn't the marriage proposal she'd hoped for, but it was something more. Something very Zeke-like. A commitment that went bone deep. She would never doubt this man's fidelity.

She owed him an explanation. "I'm flattered and honored. I tried to make you act a certain way, and that was wrong of me. I'm new to being in love, too. I made another mistake and put my sister ahead of us. There are so many things I'm not, Zeke. I'm not as smart as you. I don't even have a job anymore. I've lived in hotels and convention centers for years. I don't know how to make a home. But that's what I want. A home. With you. On this island."

"I accept," he said.

She blinked in confusion. It was hard to think straight around him. "You accept what?"

"If nothing else, I've learned important lessons today. Life is short. It can zoom by in the blink of an eye. You and I don't have all the answers. We may never have them, but we both feel a strong need to take this journey together. We care for each other."

She pushed against his chest to create breathing room. He let her go. "What if this is the heat of the moment? What if you only feel this way because of the danger? What then?"

"I love you, Jess."

"You sure?"

"As sure as I am of the sun rising each morning. I can get Forman in here to quote you the probabilities if you like, but I guarantee you they are greater than ninety-nine percent."

She snuggled next to him. "I love you, too."

He laughed low and husky. "Let's get the rest of these clothes off."

Chapter 68

People spilled in and out of Zeke's house. *I should have moved this to the beach,* Zeke thought as Naomi handed him another beer. He hadn't finished the last one, but he accepted it because tonight of all nights he didn't want to feel like an outsider.

His father's talisman showed through the open collar of his shirt. He wore his heritage proudly. Every native son of the island had been over tonight, and then some. The Institute people had heard about the impromptu party and flitted over, but they'd passed on through. Only Forman, Sidra, Jessie, and the islanders remained.

He'd never hosted a party before, but it felt nice. He caught Jessie's eye across the room. It felt very nice. The Tamans were sure Jessie was his mate. He was as sure as a person could be. He loved her, and she was committed to him. They were a couple.

His cousin Angie appeared in his doorway. She wore the traditional island garb of orange robes, looking nothing like a superspy who'd traveled the world. And the stars. He couldn't forget that.

"Angie!"

Her crushing embrace darn near killed him again. "I didn't know you were home."

"Got a new assignment." She thumped his shoulder. "Looks like you'll be seeing more of me."

"You'll be staying on the island?"

"Yep. No more jet-setting for me."

"Will you miss traveling?"

"The action will be right here, trust me."

"How so?"

She gestured toward the doorway. "I'm the frontrunner of a host of VIPs. They'll be walking through your door any minute now."

"What? How? Why? Who?" he sputtered.

"You didn't think you could save the world and pretend like it never happened?"

"How do you know I did it?"

"I know. So do others. Here they come."

A parade walked of world leaders strolled through his front door. Uncle John. The president. The German chancellor. The English monarch. The Chinese general. The head of the United Nations. And four men and women he didn't recognize.

"May I have your attention?" Uncle John said.

The room fell silent. Jessie moved to Zeke's side and took his hand. Angie and Forman jostled to see which of them would occupy his other side. Angie won. Forman rolled in beside her.

The president cleared her throat. "Friends, today marked a special day in history. An alien force attacked our planet. They came here to harm us. We were outgunned and outmaneuvered. Just when things were at their darkest, when three major world cities had been leveled and energy pulses rained down across our planet, help appeared.

"John Demery says this man, Dr. Zeke Landry, saved our world. I don't understand how he did it, but my best people tell me the Maleem ships are gone, and that's good enough for me. Dr. Landry, would you please step forward?"

The islanders, Jessie and Sidra clapped and cheered. Zeke felt heat rise to his cheeks. "I don't want any kind of fuss."

Jessie gave him a not-so-gentle shove. "Get over there."

As Zeke moved to join the president, the woman continued speaking. "Dr. Landry, I speak for the assembled leaders and those who couldn't be here today. We're in your debt. We'd like you to accept these tokens of our appreciation."

Zeke accepted the plaques, trophies, and medals with a quivering heart. He'd nearly lost everything. This morning he'd been dead. Now he had his life back and a bright future.

He cleared his throat twice before he found his voice. "I didn't do anything that any person in this room wouldn't do. And I didn't do it alone. Every islander in this room helped. The idea of how to defeat the Maleem originated with Dr. Sidra McIntyre, but there's a lot about mind over matter that we don't know. I'm thankful our fledgling effort paid off. Truthfully, I don't want any fuss."

The head of NATO stepped forward. "Which is why we're here in the dead of night. We have pledged to keep the details of this heroic effort a secret, but we couldn't let such valor, courage, and bravery go unrewarded. Please accept this as a humble token of our gratitude."

Zeke untied the red ribbon and opened the box. The large

lettering on the paper inside said "Deed." He blinked back tears. "I don't understand."

"This island is now entirely owned by you. We moved mountains to accomplish this in such a short time. The transaction was recorded in your local courthouse and is fully legal. A fund has been set up to pay all taxes and levies for the next one hundred years."

"The island? I own it?" he managed to say.

"Tama Island is yours, lad," his uncle said. "I'm hoping you'll keep things the way they are, with the Institute renting space as before."

He owned it. The idea wouldn't sink in, but it pleased him beyond belief. His lighthouse would be secure. His dolphins would be safe. His family and friends could do as they pleased.

"I didn't expect this."

"That's what makes it so right." Angie crossed the room to hug him. "We didn't know what to get for the man who can fight off spaceships with his mind. But the island seemed like a great start."

"I get to keep my job?" Zeke asked, feeling his way through this new wrinkle.

"I'm counting on it," Uncle John said.

Zeke glanced around the room. Everyone beamed with happiness and good will, except for his rust bucket of a robot. "What about Forman?"

"We'll get him fixed up again, lad. Engineers are working on a new prototype shell for him as we speak. The council of nations issued a worldwide pardon to Forman for opening our eyes to the perfidy of the Maleem. He'll be free to use the same name or select a new one. Completely your choice."

"Thank you," Zeke said simply, shaking hands with each dignitary. "I'm honored by your presence and your tribute."

"The feeling's mutual, old chap," the English monarch said.

After a few more minutes, the VIPs departed, and Zeke heaved a sigh of relief. He turned to Forman. "I'm not cut out for diplomacy."

"I've always said there's more to you than meets the eye," the robot said. "Thanks for sticking up for me."

"We're pals, first and last. That won't change."

"I take it Jessie's moving in."

"Yeah. She is."

"About time."

Zeke glanced around the room, reflecting the happiness he felt. Going up against the Maleem changed who he was. It changed how he thought, how he ranked his priorities. Work was important. So was family, leisure time, and love.

No longer would he live in the shadows of loneliness. He had good friends and family who cared for him, who loved him. In Jessie he had a mate who believed in him. She didn't think he was weird.

She loved him.

He didn't understand the logic of love, but he accepted it at face value. He cared about others. He cared about this place, about Earth. He was Taman, but he was human, too.

The Maleem had made a big mistake when they targeted his planet. He'd risen to the challenge and kicked them to the curb.

He guarded this planet with his life because that's who he was.

The Guardian of Earth.

ABOUT THE AUTHOR

Formerly a contract scientist for the U.S. Army and a freelance reporter, Southern author Rigel Carson, the pen name of Maggie Toussaint, is a multi-published, award-winning author in suspense and mystery fiction. Her background in environmental science and toxicology, as well as years spent doing water research, provided the impetus for this new dystopian thriller series set in a futuristic Earth. Book 1 of this series, G-1, is a Kindle Scout winner. Look for G-3 to release soon.

Maggie lives in coastal Georgia, where secrets, heritage, and ancient oaks cast long shadows. Yoga, beachcombing, and music are a few of her favorite things.

Visit her online at:
http://www.maggietoussaint.com
http://www.RigelCarson.com
http://mudpiesandmagnolias.blogspot.com
http://www.facebook.com/MaggieToussaintAuthor
http://www.twitter.com/MaggieToussaint
http://www.twitter.com/RigelCarson
http://www.BookloversBench.com

BONUS EXCERPT G-3

Zeke jogged to the beach, shed his clothes, and waded into the midnight-black surf. He dove through the breakers, enjoying the cool wash of water against his heated skin. Several meteors streaked across the dark sky. He opened his thoughts, summoning the dolphins.

A nudge to his side came almost immediately. Little Boz. And Nicola, Klickie, and Tunis. The pod dove and splashed Zeke for a moment, rejoicing in the contact, then Zeke settled into a back float, his hands on the heads of Nicola and Tunis. His thoughts linked with theirs, but instead of vectoring out to connect to the Tamans as he expected, the dolphins commandeered the link.

The water, Nicola said. *It's bad.*

Her mindlink words intrigued him. *Bad? How?*

She showed him a picture of sediment-filled water.

I don't understand.

Dirty. The water feels wrong.

Something was wrong with the water? His interest heightened, and he ventured deeper into the mindlink. *I can analyze the chemical and biological composition of the water. Anything else?*

The ocean feels bad, she repeated.

Does it hurt? Does your skin burn?

No burn. Hard to swim. Thicker.

The specific gravity of water didn't change. But the dolphins were reporting a problem. *I'll look into the matter.*

Boz butted into Zeke's hand. *I'm tired.*

What did dolphins do when they tired? *How can I help?* Zeke asked.

Fix the ocean. Boz said. *You are the Waterman.*

While Zeke's expertise was in hydrology, he had also studied oceanography. However, Boz's new moniker pleased him. He'd never had a nickname before he became the Guardian of Earth. The Waterman. He liked it. *I'll do what I can. Do you require medicine?*

No! All the dolphins echoed in his head at once. *No medicine. No Browning Charles.*

Dr. Charles had captured Boz once before in the name of science and nearly drowned him. Zeke wouldn't hear of his dolphins being anyone's research subjects ever again. *There are other, nicer people than Browning Charles who can help dolphins.*

The water, the dolphins reiterated. *Fix the water, not the dolphins.*

Message received, Zeke said. The link quieted, so Zeke moved into the vacated space and quested out. His thoughts arrowed through the galaxy to Tween, the place where the spirits of his people resided.

His late father entered the transmission first.

Son, everything all right?

Yes. The dolphins summoned me. They're disturbed by the ocean. They say it's too thick.

Odd. Anything unusual happening?

Baggy reported he can't catch a bottom feeder to save his soul.

Was he serious, or just shooting the breeze?

Sure sounded serious to me. I've heard other rumblings about missing catfish and toadfish. But there have been no reported sightings of sharks or gators, which would have eaten them, and there hasn't been a deluge of recreational fishermen in the area. Perhaps it's a normal population dip.

Not like you to speculate. Have you studied the matter?

Zeke blushed. *I'm learning to be a husband.*

Ahhh, his dad replied. *Say no more.*

A deeper voice boomed through the link. *Is there a problem with the ocean on Earth?*

I'll look into it, Zeke promised.

Anything else to report? Deep Voice asked in a harried tone.

Let's see. Thanks to global warming, the Earth's getting hotter every year. Our economy always seems poised on the brink of collapse. International powers can't agree on how to disperse the hoarded drinking water. And our planet is receiving a once-in-a-lifetime meteor storm. Big chunks of meteorite are whistling through our skies.

The link quieted from gentle murmurs at the other end and then without warning burst into a frenzied uproar. Zeke cringed as the shouting filled his head. In the din, he couldn't hear his dad's voice at all. He didn't know how many Tamans listened to his transmissions, but at times like this the number seemed quite large.

Deep Voice quieted the noise. *Tell us about the meteors.*

They're calling it the Great Meteor Storm. Unlike our routine meteors, this crop is from deep space. Astronomers have been aware of its approach for decades. Some of the material is entering our atmosphere now and putting on quite a flash-bang show.

These meteors – they're different?

Only in point of origin. No one seems alarmed about them. We get tens of thousands of meteor strikes each year.

The noise on the link increased again.

What? Zeke asked, impatient to learn what they knew. *What do you suspect? Are we in danger?*

His dad spoke above the roar. *Easy, Son. As you say, space is full of debris. You plan to check the water and the fish?*

Yes.

Use stainless steel sampling containers. No glass. And weigh your containers before and after sampling. Check for rare trace minerals, along with your standard tests.

What aren't you telling me?

No need to get alarmed. Meteors are commonplace. But worlds between the Taman home world and Earth experience unusual distress following a certain type of meteor.

Zeke felt the chill and the seriousness of the matter invade his thoughts. *We just repelled an alien invasion a few weeks ago. Can't we catch a break?*

Being Earth's Guardian requires vigilance. Your job doesn't have regular hours. You have to be prepared to respond when threats arise.

Is this what it was like for you, Dad? Were you constantly being pulled into intergalactic skirmishes?

I had periods of busyness. Sometimes it seemed we careened from one disaster right into the next, other times I did a lot of fishing.

I had no idea.

I didn't do it alone, Son. Remember that. Use your support system. We're here, and you have a network of helpers through the Institute. And your mate will ease the way for you.

His mate… His wife. *Something I should mention. Jessie's pregnant with our son.*

The link burst into cheers, claps, and whistles.

Good job. Keep a close eye on her. Some Earth women have a difficult time in the first trimester with our progeny. You must make sure the embryo is seated correctly.

Why?

Gestational differences. Use the robot to provide the initial prenatal care for your wife and child. They must be protected at all costs during this vulnerable period. What about your cousin?

Angie? She's off doing something for Uncle John. I haven't seen much of her lately.

Don't worry. That will change soon.

The link faded. As usual, Zeke resisted letting go until the last possible second. Questions pulsed through his mind about the unusual water sampling stipulations, about extra safety measures for his family, and about his cousin. One thing he knew about his ancestors. They would be great at writing books. They parsed out barely enough information to keep him coming back for more.

BOOKS BY MAGGIE TOUSSAINT

Science Fiction, writing as Rigel Carson
G-1 (book 1 The Guardian of Earth series)
G-2 (book 2 The Guardian of Earth series)
G-3 (book 3 The Guardian of Earth series)

Mystery
In for a Penny (book 1 Cleopatra Jones series)
On the Nickel (book 2 Cleopatra Jones series)
Dime If I Know (book 3 Cleopatra Jones series)

Death, Island Style
Murder in the Buff

Gone and Done It (book 1 Dreamwalker series)
Bubba Done It (book 2 Dreamwalker series)
Doggone It (coming soon, book 3 Dreamwalker series)

Romantic Suspense
House of Lies
No Second Chance

Muddy Waters (book 1 Mossy Bog trilogy)
Hot Water (book 2 Mossy Bog trilogy)
Rough Waters (book 3 Mossy Bog trilogy)

Sweet Romance
Seeing Red

Reviews are welcomed and encouraged!